To Barb enjoy!

SWEET DREAMS

Jennifer Button

Jennifer Button

Sweet Dreams

Published by New Generation Publishing in 2012

Copyright © Jennifer Button 2012

First Edition

The author asserts the moral right under the Copyright, Designs and Patents Act 1988 to be identified as the author of this work.

All Rights reserved. No part of this publication may be reproduced, stored in a retrieval system or transmitted, in any form or by any means without the prior consent of the author, nor be otherwise circulated in any form of binding or cover other than that which it is published and without a similar condition being imposed on the subsequent purchaser.

www.newgeneration-publishing.com

New Generation **Publishing**

Jennifer Button

To my husband Alan

SWEET DREAMS

JENNIFER BUTTON

Jennifer Button was brought up in Brighton and studied fine art at the Brighton College of Art. Although she still paints, writing now takes up most of her time.

Multi-talented, Jenny has explored three areas of the arts; fine art, drama and writing. She worked at Oxfam for twelve years in their education department, where she wrote several books and articles about Development Education. After Oxfam, she set up a drama group for children, and wrote many children's plays which were performed in village halls and primary schools across the UK. After becoming involved in her local Am Dram group in Kent she then wrote, produced and directed five plays for them too.

Jenny now lives with her husband Alan and two miniature dachshunds, in a beautiful 16th century house in Kent. Her writing career is developing apace: "Sweet Dreams" is her second novel and she is about to publish a book of short stories.

CHAPTER 1

Stella sat bolt upright. There was no need to look at the alarm clock: she knew exactly what time it was. A sulphurous glow seeped into her small room, polluting everything it touched. The world was eerily silent for a mid-March dawn. Where was the chattering clamour of the sparrows? Surely they were home from Africa by now? Had something frightened them off? Drips of cold, salty sweat trickled into her puffy eyes. The dam that had been constructed over the past forty years was cracking. Fighting back unwanted tears she dragged herself out of bed.

Stella trampled over the single duvet which lay crumpled on the floor where it had fallen during the night and her thin figure made its way, mumbling and muttering, along the landing to the bathroom where she turned on the cold tap. As the water ran, the face of her father stared back from the mirror: hooded, sunken eyes, a narrow slightly overlong nose pinch-marked on either side from the constant wearing of glasses. Turning her face to the sink she cupped the icy water in her hands and threw it hard. It worked: shocked her into a waking reality. There was no point going back to bed. Grabbing 'Old Faithful' from the hook on the back of the bathroom door she drew the belt of its comforting fleece tightly around the bony protrusion of her hips. Her cheek rubbed against the upturned collar, but today 'Old Faithful' failed to comfort her. Her size eight feet slid without guidance into fluffy slippers which waited obediently beside her bed to lead her downstairs to the kitchen. Not bothering to switch on the light, Stella lifted the kettle, automatically gave it a quick shake, and flicked it into life. While the water boiled she allowed herself time to revisit the dream that had woken her yet again at precisely 4.44am.

*

The gates were quite rusted through. The fact that they still hung there was testament to their iron will, and the dense, fibrous plaits of black ivy that secured them to the sentinel pillars. She slipped through the gates with ease before starting her journey down the avenue. This was Stella in her prime: young, unrestrained by convention, undeterred by danger. Maybe just her soul - some detached free agent - ventured through the unfamiliar gates in the dark night. It was very dark: a cold, heavy dark, made darker by thick clouds that competed to block out the watery moon's light. Giant trees flanked the path. Their branches swept upwards, to meet stars at an unseen vanishing point. A sinister orchestra tuned up: the leaves brushing against each other, whispering venom and hatred.

The same wind that agitated the leaves tugged at her thin nightdress, while her thin arms wrapped closely around her thin body, and her thin hair wrapped around her thin face. The path scrunched beneath her feet, and the sharp edges of the gravel pierced her skin making her progress slow and painful. Behind the enormous trees she glimpsed shadowy wraiths, visible for a second as they darted between the guardian trunks. The gradient grew steeper, the avenue climbing onwards to its crest where the trees stood silhouetted against the sky. It would be light soon. She had to get there before the sun rose. Nothing else mattered. It would be over soon enough. She cursed the trees. Why were they ganging up on her: taunting; calling out cruel, unwarranted names?

Her arms ached from the weight of her suitcase. It was too large and heavy. It was slowing her down. She had forgotten why she had brought it; she could no longer remember what was in it. She stopped, resting just long enough to catch her breath. The trees scolded her for being so pathetic. Over and over they chanted her name "Stella. Stella. Stella"; sharp fingers prodding, willing her to fail.

"Too late...too late...always too late... Stella, Stella, Stella...stupid silly Stella."

She was wet with rain and tears; wet with fear and sweat which ran from every pore. Her thin, cotton nightdress clung tenaciously, strangling her. Her mouth snatched at the air in short hard gulps, not staying long enough to relieve her empty lungs. Nothing was as it should be. Nothing was where it should be. '

"Why am I here?" She shouted her question to the wind. Fragments of memory fluttered through

her mind, vanishing before they could form into thoughts. Looking up at the trees she screamed, but her voice was drowned out by the clamour of leaves in the wind.

"Shut up! Shut up... I want to think... please... let me think."

The ground began to dip. It was still too dark to see, but her journey was easier. She began to go faster: her feet hovered inches above the ground, her body propelled by an external energy far more powerful than her own. Her legs, her feet, her arms, all were weightless, redundant. She was carried by the air, out of control.

"Too late... too late! Do you give up, stupid Stella?" The poplars muttered their disapproval.

Stella had no breath to answer.

"You've lost!" They spat out the words, then their nagging ceased with a hiss. The wind dropped as abruptly as the slamming of a door. The roar of accusation vanished, leaving a heavy stagnant silence. The lack of sound was stifling. Stella could not breathe. For the first time in her life, she wished she was dead. Just then the moon pushed through the clouds, her feet hit the safety of the ground, and she saw it.

It stood alone, unlit - a large detached Victorian house. She climbed the front steps, counting them carefully, avoiding the crack on the fourth. Ten steps led to a tiled porch. Heavily patterned: brown, yellow, blue and white Victorian tiles. Very busy, very cracked and very familiar. Most of the dark paint had peeled off the imposing front door, leaving bare, blistered wood. A brass door knocker, shaped like an oak leaf, hung in line with her eyes. She grasped the leaf with both hands and struck it forcefully three times against its iron base.

*

The thud of the post hitting the mat shocked Stella back to reality. She was staring into a cup of cold tea. It was 6am now and light outside. The birds were mumbling an apology for their belated dawn chorus in competition with the traffic rat-running up and down Maple Street. Forced to leave her comfort zone she crossed the hall to retrieve her letters. The postman's shadow was still visible through the frosted glass of the front door. Stella watched as it retreated down the short path to the road. Her hand went up to touch the glass, but she checked herself in time. There were six letters which she carried back into the kitchen. With no more than a cursory glance she dismissively tossed five bills onto the table then examined the remaining letter in detail. Deftly she slit the envelope with a knife. It was her appointment with Dr P. L. Devant, MRCPsych. Stella let go of the letter and watched it flutter down to join the others. Yawning and stretching she padded and counted her way back up the thirteen stairs. By 7am she was washed, dressed and waiting on the corner of Maple Street. It was just another day.

*

Stella stood patiently in line as the 94 bus pulled

up. She shuffled on board, showed the driver her pass, and took her usual seat, near the rear. Removing her glasses she dried them on her hanky, replacing them automatically. Her mind wandered back to her dream. She had dreamt of that same avenue, which led to the big house with the oak-leaf knocker, at least once a week for twenty five years. Yet each time it was as though she was dreaming it for the first time. Unlike Maple Street (where every nook, every cranny, each paving slab and crack reeked of familiarity) the Avenue house, was different: it never failed to intrigue her.

The house always maintained its mystery. It had never been boring or threatening, but recently it had mutated to exude different atmospheres: always intriguing, sometimes exciting and now disturbing. Last night's version had left her confused; afraid she was responsible for some awful happening, yet unable to remember what that 'something' was.

Stella smiled at the woman with the straight mousey hair pulled back into a neat pony tail. She wore plain silver-framed specs and a bright peacock scarf. The woman was smiling back. Through habit Stella removed her glasses once more to wipe them on her hanky. The woman in the glass did the same before disappearing in the mist.

Stella often felt her life lacked substance. In actual fact her daily life was probably no worse than that of all the others who had climbed aboard the number 94. The bus was always empty when it arrived at Maple Street (except for the woman in the woolly hat) its passengers having got off at Asda. Stella had only been to Asda once. That was enough. She preferred M & S on the High Street; you got fewer Darrens, Sharrons, and buggies. At Maple Street the bus filled up, everyone (except the woman in the woolly hat) heading for the industrial estate at the edge of town.

Stella had been catching the same bus for 30 years, so had 'The Woolly Hat'. Her hat had changed over the decades but, like Stella, her route never varied. She was always there. Stella liked to think she got on at the depot and stayed on, riding round and round on a continuous loop. One day Stella would ask her, but not today.

Along with the other passengers, Stella got off at Carlisle Road. They turned right from the bus stop, and made their way down Carlisle Row to enter the gateway to hell that was the chicken-processing factory. Once inside they either turned left to reach the desks of Purgatory, or right where they donned white aprons and matching gauze hats (the uniform of the women Stella called 'The White Devils') who worked in the very belly of Hell. Stella turned left; she operated a computer in the office section. But in Purgatory one could not escape the sickly stench of dead chickens. It hung in the air, all invasive, seeping through the air-vents, rising from the drains, polluting the atmosphere for miles around. After a while it permeated one's clothes, one's hair, one's skin and one's soul. Once it got into your nose it was with you for life. Having worked here for a quarter of a century, Stella felt she stank of dead meat.

At the tender age of sixteen she had begun her working life, first as a gofer, the lowest of the low then gradually she had climbed the greasy pole. Now she had reached the giddy heights of stock controller. She had no more love for the place now than she had when she nervously made her first round with a squeaky tea trolley. She saw the factory as a concentration camp: an Auschwitz for poultry, and not much better for the human inmates, although she never shared this thought with anyone else. In fact she tried hard not to talk to anyone, unless it was a matter of urgency. Fortunately her exalted position as stock controller tied her to her computer, which allowed little contact with the other workers.

It was different in Hell. No men worked in Hell. Only the male supervisors, who passed through, forced to run the gauntlet of 'The White Devils' rude signs and obscene outbursts prompted by any alien presence. Left alone again the daily banter, which got them through their disgusting tasks, continued until clocking off. Stella found it strange that these women could tolerate, seemingly enjoy, such an existence. She tried not to take offence at their crude jokes and gallows humour, but although sorry for their lot, her real sympathy lay with the millions of dead chickens - the continuous conveyer belt of innocent victims that passed through the camp in various stages of disembodiment.

Over the years Stella had tried not to feel superior to 'The White Devils'. Mostly she had failed. She was different; she knew that. It was not her age - some Devils were even older than her. True, her conventional suit and fake pearls separated her from the lip-gloss and earrings brigade, but it was more than that: it was an attitude. Their willingness, their very eagerness, to share every trivial detail of their personal lives over giblets and gore astonished and appalled her.

When she had first arrived all those years ago, she had stuck out like a sore thumb, her reserve marking her out as a snob. 'Who did she think she was, little Miss Hoity Toity, with her unfashionable clothes and middle-class attitudes?' She was referred to as Miss Lardy Da Sankey, accompanied by a finger pushing the tip of the nose sharply upwards. At other times, they went cross eyed, twirling a finger at the temple to imply insanity.

That was then. By now, Stella had become part of the factory. Her reputation had been handed down, and watered down, from one generation of conveyer belt to the next; the factory had a rapid turnover of Devils. With time she had merged into the background: easily looked through, like the transparent film that wrapped the processed birds. 'The White Devils' might have taken more interest in Stella, had they known what really set her apart: Stella was a creature of the night.

CHAPTER 2

On her homeward journey that evening Stella's thoughts returned to last night's dream. She had never felt threatened by the trees before. She wondered if the shift related to the strange happenings over the past week. The thought made her shudder and, from the security of her usual seat, she reached in her bag to retrieve the letter. She wiped her glasses and read the contents again. One week 'til the appointment. She gazed out of the window at the outskirts of the town. At that exact moment Stella saw Martina.

The girl was leaning against the wall of the old school. It was the coat that first caught Stella's attention. Long, black, made of unyielding leather, it covered the long figure from head to foot. A thick leather belt pulled it in tightly around a narrow frame, and the hem missed the ground by less than an inch. A stout black boot anchored one of the long legs to the pavement while the other leg stuck out, bent at the knee; its foot pressed flat against the wall. Just then the bus lurched and Stella dropped her letter. The driver cursed a van which had pulled up and blocked the road.

This temporary halt gave Stella a chance to study the girl. A wedge of jet black hair concealed half of the narrow face, while contrasting dramatically with the whiteness of the skin. The effect was exacerbated by heavily painted, downcast eyes and dark almost black lips. Neither the eyes nor the lips smiled. She exuded coiled anger, straight out of one of those unfathomable art films: black and white and reeking of revolution; a Kalashnikov slung over the square shoulder would not have been out of place. As the bus pulled away, the girl spat out her cigarette and slowly slid her foot down the wall so its boot could grind the butt into the granite slab.

The bus lurched and continued on its way leaving the strange girl staring at the pavement. Stella bent forward and retrieved her letter. How on earth had she let things get so out of hand? She prided herself on her strength of character, her control. When had it all begun to slip away? 'The Tie' had told her to sort herself out. Maybe he was right? He was her boss after all. But his conditions seemed rather extreme. Really all she needed was a holiday, time to reflect, time to give herself a good talking to. Not psychiatric therapy!

Stella shuddered at the thought of seeing a psychiatrist. Logic told her that it must be possible, in the twenty-first century, to prescribe some pills to make one dream nice things. Happy, exciting things - like she used to when she was young. She did not want to stop dreaming. God no! Unthinkable.

Stella had always dreamed a lot. Not ordinary, quickly forgotten dreams; never a regurgitated mishmash of mundane daily events. Oh no, her dreams were so much more vivid than the world she experienced when awake; more engaging, more thrilling, certainly more sexy, and altogether more fun.

Sweet Dreams

In her dreams Stella could be any age, assume any guise. She could be cunning or vulnerable, predator or prey. Her dreams were tangible and solid; she could function without all the irrelevance that surrounded her when she was awake. Being awake was to live in the shadows: a weak insipid existence without purpose or challenge. Normal dreams were available to everyone: something each human being experienced, like eating or drinking. Stella's dreams had been part of her for as long as she could remember and were far more real than her mundane waking life. They gave her access to a parallel universe that was hers and hers alone. It was this that made her special. Keeping it secret made her safe.

*

From birth Stella had slept right through the night. She also slept for long periods during the day. Later, at the age when most toddlers were fighting off the desire for sleep, little Stella gave in contentedly long before the first yawn. She loved sleep. It took her to Wonderland, where she was allowed to be different; special. Her mother never worried that her child was sleeping too much, nor did she consider it odd. There was nothing to hint at abnormal behaviour. No specialists monitored rapid eye movement or fitted electrodes to baby Stella. They all just let her sleep and, as she seldom uttered so much as a whimper, she was mostly left quite alone.

Her mother considered herself an extremely

fortunate woman to have given birth to a docile, contented baby. Friends endorsed this having suffered long sleepless nights. While other parents were developing ploys to persuade, coax, even bully, their little darlings to go to bed, dear little Stella was imploring her mummy to dispatch her at some ridiculously early hour. Had it been left up to the child, her entire life would have been spent fast asleep.

By the time she could talk Stella tried to tell her parents about her dreams, but they did not listen. They preferred the incessant TV. A lukewarm, 'That's nice, dear' was not what the child wanted, but it was what she got. When her vocabulary increased, she attempted vivid descriptions of her dreams, mostly to her doll; at times resorting to acting out the most exciting parts in a vain attempt to arouse interest, rather than gain attention. It failed. Such behaviour was dismissed as the product of an overactive imagination: childish fantasy, not something to be encouraged or worried about. They continued to concentrate on football, soap operas, and knitting.

They were right about one thing. Although she never displayed it while awake, young Stella had a very vivid and inventive imagination. The child felt hurt that such an intrinsic part of her life should be dismissed as mere fancy. Her dreams were as real to her as daily life, not linked in any way to fantasy or fairy tales. Dreaming was an integral part of her being. That her mother did not realise this confused her - this same woman who insisted on being told of anything unusual that may have happened on the way to or from school; the same woman who drummed into little Stella the need to speak up if anyone tried to bully her or if a teacher treated her unfairly or if, God forbid, anyone tried to 'interfere' with her. Stella knew that should her bedroom catch fire she should alert her mum. By the same logic, when a Lakota chief, sporting full tribal regalia, eagle-feathered headdress and war paint, visited her and made her a present of a paint pony, taught her to hunt tatanka and make a medicine wheel, surely her mother should be told?

With such lack of parental interest it was hardly surprising that young Stella learned to keep her dreams to herself. To turn all this creative energy inward and let it flourish in the dark recesses of an agile, receptively malleable mind was asking for trouble. Stella was laying the foundations for an unhealthily reclusive attitude towards life; a life where to share and display emotions, whether from a waking or dreaming state, was no longer normal.

Meanwhile, Stella gave the appearance of a bright, if introverted, child. Her school-work got done without fuss, and she managed to slip through the whole of the education process hardly being noticed. At home, by keeping her head down, never making a fuss or demanding attention or doing anything to upset the repetitive routine of family life at number 9, she blended into the appalling wallpaper and appeared content. Her parents were happy as long as her reports were good and she ate everything they put in front of her. Apart from the occasional outing to the countryside for an uninspiring family picnic, they spent very little time with their daughter, leaving Stella alone with her dreams.

Mr and Mrs Sankey were ordinary, hard working people. Mrs Sankey eked out a living, cleaning. Occasionally she served behind the checkout in a minimarket in the busy suburban high street behind their two-up-two-down. Her husband was a sales rep for a soft drinks company. She seldom saw him during the week. He earned a fair wage and kept his family well provided with ample supplies of 'Seven Up' and 'Coca Cola'. Affection came in less abundance, but little Stella was loved.

Throughout this 'happy' childhood Stella's dreams never came as fragments. They were not half-remembered titbits disappearing before she could grasp them, they were whole, fully rounded stories. They were made of a strong substance, intact and tangible: strong enough to survive the journey from the dream-world to this one without the need for reconstruction. They were stored in her mind's eye, ready to be downloaded and viewed again at will. Some were a click away on the desktop of her mind; the rest formed a vast and valuable folder, zipped up and filed away.

*

The first dreams Stella could remember had been colourful adventures, all bearing U certificates. This was not surprising as Stella loved old movies, particularly films about 'Cowboys and Indians'. Her dreams replayed these films over and over again, expanding the plot to include her. They came in wide screen Technicolor: three dimensional and action packed. Sometimes she found herself locked into the slowest of slow motion, out of sync with the world around her. She loved this sense of floating, of being outside her physical body. It gave her distance to absorb everything in her own good time. Alone and on foot, surrounded by tribes of savage Sioux, their nippy paint ponies whooping and hollering around her, she watched on: grounded, yet so alive and vibrant.

Of course there were times when she was frightened, even terrified, but these were wild adventures, never nightmares. The red-skins that chased her were those heroic creatures of the wild, Wild West; friends or foes that she respected, honoured, loved, and feared. Fear played a major role in these early dreams. It was one element that was totally missing from her waking life. Fear became a stimulant for inventiveness. She developed coping tactics to get her out of any really tight spots. She learned to fly, to overcome the slow motion and soar effortlessly without wings. At times she hovered above a situation that did not suit her. At others she would sweep out over cliff tops and mountains like a hawk. It was liberating, exhilarating and breathtakingly beautiful.

This freedom to explore was one of the most vital aspects of her dreams; it let her loose in a world where beauty and courage were paramount. It challenged her to test the limits of her own endurance. No more grey streets with sad little drab two-up-two-downs. Welcome to high snow-clad vistas, dense jungles teeming with wild creatures, vast oceans as deep as they were wide, prairie lands of scented grasses making a giant Mexican wave as they danced in the moving air. And those smells: Frangipani and cloves, wild thyme and wet straw, baby monkeys and jungle grasses, steaming paint ponies and dead bodies: countless marvels filling her nostrils. Flavours peppered her dreams too: buffalo with wild rice, the dry heat of tobacco on the tongue, water taken from the Oregon, the Nile and the Amazon; as different as wines from Gaul, Olympus or Tesco's. Stella tasted all these wonders and more.

*

Stella's growing lack of respect for her parents did not sit easily with her intrinsic kindness. But she was afraid of ending up like her mother: she learned to pity this empty woman who seemed content to lead a life of drudgery alleviated only by tedium. Stella's pragmatic side told her that, in all probability, her own life would appear boring to an outsider. But her secret life provided more than enough excitement to compensate for a few waking hours of nondescript monotony. She could immerse herself totally in her delicious life on the other side of waking. How could life in Maple Street begin to compete?

*

Sweet Dreams

There must have been a thousand of them. The dust churned up by their un-shod hooves filled her eyes making them run with tears of red liquid prairie. The powdered mist collected in her throat, drying and cloying, until her voice was buried in fertile earth. She wanted to cry out, but there was no-one to hear her. She stood alone, apart from the frenzied horde galloping. They had long since ceased whooping and hollering. Only the drone of the horses' feet pounding the sun-baked earth rose above the silence.

Round and round they swarmed until the earth sank down, milled by the incessant pummelling, carving a high plateau from which Stella watched the circle of dust as it screwed deeper and deeper into the red rock.

Night fell like a blanket, blocking out the light. In the distance she could hear a lone wolf howl. The earth changed from black to umber to madder to crimson to gold as the waking sun rose higher and higher from the great hole in the ground where the riders had gone. Fingers of rock stepped out of the shadows, pointing with wonder up to the sky, in awe of this daily miracle.

Runs-With-The-Buffalo stood beside her, chants emanating from somewhere deep inside his head. His headdress of eagle feathers framed a face streaked with bright paint which caught the light of the growing sun. The vibrations from his stamping feet passed up through her own, through her body, filling her head, leaving no space for fear. He did not look at her, but bent down to scoop the red dust in his strong scrawny fingers. Lifting them high above his head, he baptised himself in the powdered earth. Stella did the same. Raising her arms above her head she felt the earth purify her as it bathed her hair in blood-red ash.

The old chief continued to ignore her as he lifted each foot in turn: replacing it with ceremonious precision on the exact same spot. Stella's feet took up the rhythm. The speed increased. They were dancing together on the promontory, the whole world at their stomping feet.

*

When she reached puberty Stella's dreams became more personal; alarming rather than frightening, but always emotionally charged. Stella had no knowledge of boys, other than the annoying yobs that hung around in gangs at school, jeering or calling out obscenities, wolf whistling at the prettier girls. Stella never joined the other girls in any of the responses - the giggles or expletive retorts. They seemed an unnecessary waste of effort. She preferred to keep her head down, ignoring what she considered to be an unknown, somewhat baffling species. In her dreams the opposite sex was dashing, daring and not interested in anything other than kissing.

School had covered the whole topic of sex one wet Friday afternoon. Unfortunately for Stella, she was home in bed with a bad head cold. Her parents never talked about, or thought about, sex. God forbid they should discuss it with their daughter. So Stella remained innocent, ignorant and vulnerable. When she reached puberty her body underwent physical changes that embarrassed her. To survive she created a logic all her own - based largely on her dreams. This private pattern of thinking provided a coping mechanism. More importantly it allowed her to avoid the intervention of others.

The teenage Stella loved the Stella of her dreams: bold and uninhibited. It became her aim to achieve a similar degree of self reliance in her waking life. Inwardly her self confidence grew, while her private, withdrawn nature deceived those around her into thinking she was repressed, almost timid. Her peers labelled her an outsider, a bit of an oddball, quirky and just a bit scary. Her parents continued to assume she was a normal, at times unlikable, teenager.

*

At the tender age of sixteen, Stella left school and applied for a job in a local chicken processing factory. She was accepted without an interview and told to report for work on the first day of August. The long blissful stretch of freedom, the summer holiday, suddenly shrunk to a few meagre weeks. From now on she would get just three weeks' paid holiday a year, with bank holidays or days in lieu. The prospect of work did not frighten her, it depressed her. This would be her life for the next forty years. The thought was soul-destroying.

Her working hours would be longer than school hours and the journey to and from work added another forty minutes to each working day. She consoled herself with the fact that there would be no homework and she was only required to work one Saturday in four. Stella calculated that with careful management her dreamtime would in fact increase by about six hours a week. A lot could be achieved in six hours. Her adult life was mapped out before her. Meanwhile all she had left of her childhood was one short Bank Holiday, which her father insisted they spent on a 'nice treat for the family'.

*

Father parked the Fiesta in a layby off the A40, and Mother immediately set to plating up the inevitable tinned-salmon sandwiches and crisps. Stella sipped her 'Coke' from an orange plastic cup and listened half-heartedly to the same old conversation, wishing she was at home. The Magnificent Seven was on Channel Four - wonderful food for dreams. Instead, here she was in the middle of nowhere, the sun was weak, a chilly wind was blowing from the east, and there was not a cowboy or a six-gun to be seen.

Stella wobbled uncomfortably on the fold up chair. She had wanted to sit on the ground; to curl up and snooze, but Mum hated slouches. On command she sat upright, wearing the mask of a smile. It was too much effort to complain. Behind the mask she was snuggled under her duvet, watching long-legged heroes strut their stuff among scurrying white pyjama-clad peasants. They flickered on the screen before melting into her private world.

In her dreams her ability to rise to any situation was never doubted. She was encouraged to be more than herself, to feel more, to be flamboyant, to hurt, to love, to hate and to thrill. She entered their world and took her chance along with the others. In her dreams she was never called names or mocked. She never felt ashamed or inadequate. Her looks fitted: she could be stunningly beautiful or fiercely ugly. She could be young or old, love without cringing, without fear of rejection. She could be vulnerable or heroic, male or female, happy or sad. Every choice was hers - physical and emotional alike: Stella was in charge, Stella called the tune. All in all, frame for frame, file for file, dreams won over life every time.

Finishing her sandwich, Stella mumbled something about going for a walk. Her mother told her not to go far or talk to any strangers; her father grunted from beneath his newspaper. Cutting through a little copse she found a foot path. She hitched her skirt and climbed the stile, then set off into the unknown led along by curiosity and the path. She crossed through to some trees, counting as she went. The scenery was nice, a bit samey, but a vast improvement on her father's gaping mouth emitting loud erratic snores to compete with the regular click, click of her mother's knitting. Two hundred and five steps later the path took a swing to the right. She began her count again from number one. Twenty paces and she reached a fork which she followed to the right. After another forty paces she stopped. To her left she could see two stone pillars supporting a pair of impressive black, iron gates.

They were imposing, not ornate. These gates were strong, fit for purpose. They were made to keep people out – or to keep someone in. Either way they impressed Stella with their stately presence. On closer inspection she noticed that they stood ajar. There was nothing to say it was private property or that trespassers should keep out. Anyway, they were open. Beyond them stretched a wide avenue of old poplar trees. It was enchanting, inviting almost hypnotic. Stella glanced at her watch. Not wanting the inevitable argument if she was late back, she dutifully, reluctantly, turned around.

"WAIT!"

Stella turned back. The tall trees astride the broad avenue whispered to one another then in perfect unison they stopped and called again.

"WAIT!"

Instinct was compelling her: stay and explore. That was what Stella the dreamer would do. But this Stella felt wide awake, governed by a different logic. She turned and headed back to the layby.

*

The picnic was already packed away by the time Stella reached the car. Her parents were sitting in the front seat with their seat belts secured and the ignition key poised to turn. Her mumbled apology was lost in the stream of Mrs Sankey's anger and, as she climbed in the back next to the picnic basket with its stinking fishy smell, Stella she knew she had made the wrong decision. After her mother's initial blast, no one asked why she was late, or if she had enjoyed her walk. They did not ask if she had seen anything interesting or met anybody. They conveyed their annoyance silently.

Father turned the key, listened to the repetitive choking, emitted a similar sound from somewhere deep in his upper body, then switched the engine off. He repeated this unsuccessful manoeuvre until the car reeked with the nauseating combination of tinned salmon and petrol fumes. Stella felt sick. Mr Sankey tut-tutted as he climbed out of his beloved car and disappeared beneath the bonnet. Eventually he emerged, wiped his hands on the cloth his wife produced from her copious hand bag, and announced that the engine was flooded. They would have to wait at least twenty minutes before it would start.

Stella left the nauseating stench of the car behind, ignored her mother's protests and set off back to her avenue. Such defiance did not come easily. As she retraced her footprints, she justified her actions, telling herself she had rebelled partly to distance herself from the awful smell and partly to be out of earshot of her mother's grumbling.

When she reached the stile she stopped and sat down, resting her back against the trunk of the nearest tree. The afternoon sun was warm on her face: it was going to be a beautiful day after all.

The short rest was enough to dispel any nausea. The Stella that opened her eyes felt pleasantly refreshed and ready to pursue any adventure come what may. She glanced at her watch and was delighted to see it was a minute before a quarter to five. She still had plenty of time.

The avenue was much closer than she had remembered. This time she did not hesitate. Being on the skinny side, she slipped through the gap without disturbing the gates. Her whole being entered a heightened state, like the start of a dream. Such wonderful alertness, combined with the knowledge that she was awake, brought a unique thrill. Stella was alive.

Loose gravel crunched beneath her sandals. She strode off down the avenue marching in time to a beat only she could hear. The avenue was lined on either side with tall grey-green poplars. Stepping off the path, she stood under the nearest tree. Its branches swayed in synchronised formation, but the rebellious leaves jiggled and wriggled to their own liberated improvisations. Each branch swept upwards from a single main trunk, composed in turn from hundreds of smaller threads all knotted and twined together for strength and unity. They were so beautiful, so very beautiful: symmetrical perfection.

Stella put her ear against the tree; the bark was rough against her cheek. She allowed her eyes to follow the upward sweep, lifting her gaze, staring vertically upwards. The swaying tower rose sixty feet above. Her head began to swim. She closed her eyes, steadied herself and listened. The strengthening easterly breeze caught each of the oval leaves in turn. They brushed against each other whispering as they moved. As the air gathered force they became a frenzied mass, their moaning building to a solid wall of noise. Stella clasped her hands over her ears to block the crescendo. As she staggered back into the middle of the path, the song of the leaves dampened to a muttering. The tiny voices still mumbled and grumbled, refusing to let the eaves-dropper catch one word of what they were saying. But Stella knew. They were talking about her. They knew she had come back.

The wide avenue stretched as far as the eye could see. It did not deviate from its path, but led on straight and true. Stella walked down its centre, counting her steps as she went. By the time she reached four hundred and forty she lost count. At least ten foot of path spread out on either side of her before the gravel met a wide grass verge which fell away into a shallow drainage ditch. A solitary blackbird lay in the gulley. Decayed it gave off the putrid smell of death. Stella didn't like dead things. Averting her eyes to the grass on the verge, she wondered who kept it so well cut. She tried to picture the men who had planted these magnificent trees with such precision, but it was impossible to imagine a time when they had not been here. They belonged exactly where they were. Everything did. Even she belonged. Even the dead blackbird belonged. She had found her home. She wanted to stay forever.

Stella paused to check the time. It was 4.44pm,

but her watch had stopped. Judging by the low angle of the sun twinkling through the poplars, she guessed it to be about five. Reluctantly she turned to retrace her steps. As she did she heard the trees calling to her.

*

"WAKE UP, STELLA, look lively. You start work in the morning. Then you'll know what life is really all about. None of this airy fairy nonsense, my girl. You won't be able to drop off as and when you like then, young lady. You can make a start now … make yourself useful… get in and put the kettle on… And bring that hamper in with you - it's been stinking the car out all the way home."

CHAPTER 3

The stairs leading to the surgery were steep. They spiralled back on themselves in a claustrophobic curve, finally arriving at a small landing. It was barely big enough for the three chairs and 1950's coffee table. The table's legs groaned beneath a confusion of well thumbed magazines and untouched leaflets containing information on every possible phobia and addiction.

"Take a seat, Miss Sankey. Doctor Devant will be with you shortly."

Stella spent a long time deciding which chair to sit on. She had resolved to stand when a figure pushed passed, propelling her to sit in the nearest one. She only caught a glimpse of the long leather coat. That was enough. There was no mistaking it. It was 'The Girl without the Kalashnikov'. The disembodied voice spoke again and Stella turned to face it.

"Would you like to come this way?"

The voice wormed around the door accompanied by a large moon-shaped smile. Stella, still thinking of the girl, had imagined a long, lean, person, not the 'Humpty Dumpty' woman that now ushered her into the surgery. This small, light room was filled with a large desk. Like every other flat surface it was piled high with books. The wall between the two windows was occupied by an open, overstuffed filing cabinet on which a

Christmas cactus was dying. A skeleton hung in the far corner, partially obscuring a poster which displayed an intriguing cross-section of the human brain. Stella would have liked to study this fascinating diagram, but a woman disconcertingly younger than Stella and nearly as untidy as the office arose from behind a pile of papers and thrust an outstretched hand towards her.

Doctor Devant, smiling and still proffering her hand, deftly caught her glasses which were sliding off her head. She shoved them back through the tangle of brown hair, where they sat poised to slide down again. Her right hand remained outstretched throughout.

Stella noticed that the doctor's cardigan was buttoned wrongly. She refrained from commenting and politely offered her hand. The ensuing handshake was of such ferocity that she wished she had merely said "Hello". She snatched her hand away to examine it for breakages.

"Hi Stella, take a pew. Please try to relax there is absolutely nothing to worry about... Oh and by the way that isn't my last patient!" The doctor laughed at her perennial joke and moved the skeleton out of harm's way. Stella cringed: an hour of this and she really would need a psychiatrist. The doctor spoke with a soft colonial accent. Her hair was a mess, her dress casual; not what Stella expected of a consultant with so many letters after her name. There was no sign of a white coat, not even one hanging on the door. Instead of a stethoscope, a long rope of irregular glass beads dangled around an overlong neck.

"Now then, let's find out what's bothering you, shall we? I promise there is nothing to worry about."

That was the second time the doctor had said that. Stella noted the second reassurance and continued to examine her right hand for damage. She used the time to think.

The thought of leaving crossed her mind. This analysis business was a stupid idea. She had only agreed to it because of her boss's ridiculous ultimatum. He had threatened to fire her. His last words had been 'get your act together'. Stella had found them most offensive, having always considered she was a very 'together' sort of person. In all her forty years she had never once fallen apart. Who else was going to offer? But, she needed her job, so here she was.

Stella smoothed her mousey hair. It was tightly pulled into its usual low ponytail, never stylish but always neat. She wriggled and tugged at her skirt until it was straight. Then, satisfied that she appeared calmly in control, she settled back and looked at the doctor: not directly between the eyes, but slightly higher and to the left. She found this a good way to unnerve one's opponent. Directing one's gaze on their forehead made them feel under scrutiny while rendering them incapable of staring back. It worked. The Doctor averted her eyes. Stella smiled.

Next there came an endless barrage of questions. Fact gathering: date of birth, address, name of parents, that sort of thing; all the rubbish information that revealed more about the inquisitor than the subject. Stella assumed that all these facts were already in the folder on the desk in front of her, also backed up on the computer, along with countless other files relating to Miss S. Sankey. None of it would explain who she really was or why she was here.

Why was she here? This was the only question the idiot doctor should be asking. Stella continued to trot out all the right answers, until she realised this was a ploy to discover whether or not she could answer them correctly. She needed to decide, and quickly, whether to answer by the book or fabricate a wonderful string of nonsensical replies that would make the experience so much more interesting. She decided to play it straight. The sooner she was out of here the better. Meanwhile the doctor prattled on, while fidgeting with the cluttered array of papers covering her desk.

The status of Stella's sanity had only once been in question before, but that was a long time ago. This time, she realised, was different. Her job and her life as she knew it were under threat. The suggestion that she should see a shrink had come after a particularly embarrassing incident late one Friday afternoon about a month ago. Stella had been entering a string of figures into her computer; a task she could perform perfectly well in her sleep. That was the problem; she must have drifted off into one of her dreams. As always, she could recall every detail.

*

The protagonist - a tall, handsome man with a neat beard - held the beautiful Stella transfixed. His penetrating eyes were steel blue: cold and fascinating. She had no option but to stare back and drown in their metallic liquid. She was drifting under his spell until she could no longer resist him. Wearing exotic underwear like the concoctions they sold in the naughty shop along the High Street, she knew she looked sensational. She felt it. Her bra was black and scarlet. It forced her pert breasts upwards until the nipples spilled over the top of the sexy black lace: a pair of succulent, ripe peaches waiting to be drooled over. A red, satin heart - barely large enough to cover her pubic hair - was held in place by a thong which cut between the firm clenched cheeks of her bottom. Her lips glistened as her tongue caressed them keeping them moist and soft.

The man was stark naked - apart from his tie which was a vivid blue with diagonal stripes of a darker shade. He was obviously aroused. They both were. A mutual sexual excitement buzzed between them - sharp electric convulsions – bringing simultaneous pain and pleasure. Unable to disguise her body's eagerness to be taken, she stood with legs spread wide, her hands fondling her breasts, her lips red with the heat of her own blood. Her skin was tingling, breaking out into tiny goose pimples, and she felt the hair on the back of her neck prickle as his steely eyes bore deep into her soul. He had a look of evil about him which made him all the more attractive. Stella braced herself and gave herself up.

Suddenly loud, blood-curdling screams filled the room. They appeared to come from the floor directly above. Were there more rooms like this, occupied by other couples behaving just as flagrantly? The room had no doors or windows and the walls moved in and out, continually altering its shape and size. At times it was a vast empty space, the size of an aircraft hangar; then, before she had time to explore it with her eyes, it shrunk to no more than a broom cupboard. Emptied of any contents, it had been swept, scrubbed and left clinically clean, apart from the unmistakable smell of sex. Imminent danger caused her heart to pound against her ribs. Her instinct was to flee, but she knew she would stay. It thrilled her. Had it not been for the child she would have surrendered to him without a second thought.

She could sense, rather than hear, the child. It was somewhere in this sealed room, not upstairs where, mercifully, the screaming had stopped. She found it crouched in the corner, sobbing its heart out. The child's distress, its presence, the very idea of it witnessing such an ugly, depraved event made Stella shudder. It was time to wake up.

This presented a serious dilemma. The child's safety was of paramount importance. What if Stella woke up and left the dream, only to leave the child behind, all alone and even more vulnerable? Would the dream end for the child too? Was this the child's only life-form: a life into which Stella had jumped, fallen or been pushed? As owner of the dream, she knew she must assume total responsibility for the welfare of this poor little innocent. She had to act selflessly and at once. Damn the consequences.

Stella lashed out, striking the stranger on his face with her clenched fist. She watched him reel off balance, then, before he had time to react she threw a right hook. She hit him as hard as she could...

*

The rest was history. It was a clean knock-out. When Stella woke up her boss was out for the count. He woke up in hospital with a broken nose, four loose crowns and a gash above his left eye requiring five stitches. On returning from the hospital he presented Stella with his ultimatum: "See a psychiatrist or collect your cards. You need to get your act together."

Stella had willingly told the doctor some of this, but certainly not all. Not her dream; that was private. Having said as much as she deemed fitting, she lapsed into silence. After an excruciatingly long pause, the doctor asked her next question.

"So, Stella, why do you think you're here?"

The question, once so obviously logical, sounded ridiculous to Stella. They both knew perfectly well why she was here. Nagging doubts began to wash over her. She was sweating and shivering. Maybe she had got it all horribly wrong? Had she dreamed the incident at the factory and lived the encounter with the naked sadist? Had she actually done something really bad? Killed her boss? Massacred the chicken pickers? (Visions of a host of white bodies turning crimson as their entrails merged with the chickens' gizzards flashed on her inner eye; a sticky red river.) And what had happened to the abandoned child?

Where were the boundaries between her dreams and her reality? Was she going mad? Had she already gone mad? Realising that she was stammering and stuttering like an idiot, she swallowed hard and looked the doctor straight between the eyes as she threw the challenge back.

"You tell me."

The doctor moved her head, rather sneakily Stella thought, so that her eyes caught her patient's angry glare. Stella immediately averted her eyes and stared down at her handbag.

She became fascinated by the large metal rings that held the straps in place. She had never noticed how they fell flat when the bag was laid down. She continued to stare at her bag, examining the mechanism of these intriguing rings. Her interest diverted to the carpet tiles and how they were laid in a brick pattern. She found herself willing them to open up and swallow her. How would it sound if she explained to this probing busybody that she had knocked her boss out cold, mistaking him for a naked sadist? Now that was certifiable: the ramblings of a mad woman.

When eventually Stella raised her eyes from the carpet, the doctor's face was very close to hers.

There was no escape. Stella took a deep breath and opened her mouth, listening, with mounting curiosity, to what she was about to say.

"I hit my boss. I was under a lot of pressure and I lashed out. I am really sorry. He was very nice about it. It was such a freak happening. I promise nothing like it will ever happen again." Stella tried her best to sound both convincing and contrite. She felt her face distorting into a grin; it took all her concentration to keep it straight and serious. Her future was dangling on a thread. Never before had she needed so desperately to stay in control.

"He didn't actually tell me to come and see you there and then. It was the next day, I mean on the Monday - there was a weekend in between. I assume you know the rest, Doctor."

Surely that was enough to satisfy her inquisitor? Stella smiled: her well practised smile. There was no warmth in it, no kindness. Neither was it sinister or malicious. It just lacked any depth. Behind her mask she recalled every single detail of that miserable Monday.

*

Stella had hardly had time to clock in and hang her coat up before 'The Tie' summoned her to his office. It had been a relief to discover he was alive and well. His nose looked a bit crooked and the bruising around his eyes had become an amazing rainbow of colours. His left eye was still not fully open, but he was alive. 'The Tie' (Mr Andrews) had his office on the mezzanine floor which was separated from the secretaries work station by a set of five metal steps. This was his eyrie from where he looked down on 'the girls'. Stella was one of five who manned the computers and the copying machines. She had a desk in the corner. It was the best desk, in her opinion, being next to the only window in the lower room.

'The Tie' rarely came down to their level unless on a matter of paramount importance. On this particular Monday, he came in person to summon Stella. Stella counted the five stairs as she climbed.

"You know we really value your input here, Stella, but your behaviour last week…"

She recalled how he had paused and touched his left eye, wincing as he had done so,

"… it was so out of character."

Stella remembered seeing the large gap in his front teeth: four little pegs in place of his immaculate white crowns. She shuddered to think of it.

"I've been thinking", he had said, "you haven't taken a holiday for a long time, have you? Well, perhaps you should. You've had such a stressful time, what with both your parents passing in the space of a year. You didn't miss a day's work – which is to your credit. But you are obviously under a great deal of stress. So I am granting you a month's leave – fully paid - to get yourself sorted out. No, don't thank me. It is the least I can do. I don't bare any grudges - my eye is healing quite well, thank you. The surgeon is pleased with my nose and says it will look almost normal in a few months… or so."

Stella had tried to apologise, to decline his generous offer, but he had held his hand up before she could get a word out.

"I won't take no for an answer. It is not negotiable. Think of it as compulsory gardening leave." He had tried to smile, but it obviously hurt. "Collect your things on the way through and we'll see you in a month's time – that is supposing the doctor gives you the all clear. Alright, my dear? Good. Now don't worry, I'm sure we shall manage to scrape by without you."

"I'd rather stay, Mr Andrews. I promise nothing like this will ever happen again…"

'The Tie' stood up, "This is not negotiable, Miss Sankey. See a psychiatrist or collect your cards. Get your act together." With that he led her to the stairs.

Her head was still spinning when she stood outside the factory clutching her bag. Had she just been dismissed? How dare he? She had given him, not to mention his stinking chickens, the best years of her life and this was all the thanks she got! She wished she had killed him when she had the chance: the self righteous prig.

*

Of course Stella could not relay any of this to the doctor. According to her watch their time was almost up. In her estimation the hour had gone quite well. Presumably the doctor would tell her to take it easy for a few weeks. In fact, a month off work sounded quite nice, even if it included a few more sessions of therapy. Stella felt she had the hang of it. If she could prepare herself, work out her answers beforehand, it might actually be fun. She felt her face lift into a smile.

"Why are you so angry, Stella?"

'Another stupid question.' Stella bristled at this woman's habit of leaning forwards as if she was really concerned. Stella was convinced it was all false. To her the doctor always seemed preoccupied: searching in her drawer, rifling her handbag, shuffling around that stupid mountain of papers. Stella had even caught her gazing out of the window. This was not what she expected from a doctor. The doctor opened another drawer and began to search through the contents, and Stella assumed she was no longer aware of her presence. *'How could someone with so many letters after her name be so crass?'*

In fact Dr Devant was quite on the ball: very little escaped her notice. She had noted her patient's reluctance to answer questions. She watched with interest as Stella toyed with the nameplate in front of her, picking it up and turning it around absent-mindedly. She saw Stella's half-smile, the sidewise glance she threw her way.

As the nameplate hit the desk the doctor hit the panic button.

'Humpty Dumpty' burst into the room looking flustered and decidedly out of breath. Stella's immediate reaction was to offer her a chair, fearful that the woman might suffer some sort of seizure. The doctor remained unruffled as she coughed, nodded her dismissal and returned her gaze towards her confused patient. Without offering an explanation the doctor rose and extended her hand to Stella, stating that she would like to see her again in a couple of weeks. Her suggestion that they might talk about – she actually used the word 'explore' – the death of Stella's parents was not at all what Stella had been expecting. She nodded acquiescently while making a mental note that she would need a coping strategy in order to remain in control.

*

'The Girl without the Kalashnikov' was crashing onto the landing as Stella left the surgery. She pushed passed Stella and barged straight into the doctor's room. Stella stood transfixed listening to the muffled sound of angry swearing, loud banging and general kerfuffle. 'Humpty Dumpty' jostled passed her and joined the fray, only to emerge after what sounded like a brief scuffle. Her strong portly arms gripped the angry young woman.

Stella realised she was staring. Pulling herself together she made her way down the spiral stairs and back into the street. A voice called "Hang on – I want to talk to you."

She turned, to see who was being addressed and by whom.

"Yes you. I want to talk to you."

It was the leather-coated girl. Fear and curiosity made Stella stop.

"Are you talking to me?" she asked, looking around again to see if it was aimed elsewhere.

"Yeah. Like, I really need to talk. Okay? Have you got a minute?"

That was how it began. A brief encounter. A chat on a street corner. The girl simply talked at Stella for five or ten minutes before announcing,

"Right, I've gotta go now. See you." As an after thought she added, "Thanks."

With that she strode off down the road with no backward glance. Stella continued to stare until the tall black figure had disappeared round the corner. The girl's anger had touched her. Was that because she too was angry? The doctor thought she was. Stella wanted to cry; to let go; to finally lose control.

CHAPTER 4

When Stella got home she slammed the front door behind her, nearly shattering the frosted glass. The curtains at number 7 went into spasm. Uncharacteristically slinging her coat and bag on the sofa, she marched into the kitchen and violently shook the kettle. Her first thought was to call the factory and report in sick. A cold wave of relief reminded her that she had been suspended so, nursing a mug of tea, she curled up on the sofa. Reaching behind her to grab her coat she pulled it over her head. Stella needed to get away.

It did not matter what form her dream took, so long as it took her somewhere else; somewhere other than this nightmarish reality. This had been a difficult day, and the next week and the next and the next held the promise of action replays. The doctor's suggestion that they should 'explore' her parents' deaths filled her with dread.

*

Emotionally Stella was inept; she only just managed those everyday encounters that most people take for granted. The strange episode with the Kalashnikov girl had unnerved her; astounded her. That a total stranger could unburden her innermost emotional dilemmas to another was a revelation. Stella knew that she would never be able to do that. The prospect of externalising traumatic, distressing episodes of her own life - to pick at them, to squeeze them like so many spots - was abhorrent, undignified and mortifying. She had deleted them, banishing them to the recycle bin, where they would remain until they were no longer retrievable. To an outsider they might well appear innocuous, harmless events - memories that might evoke sympathy, even pity, but to Stella they were monumental testaments to her inadequacy, worthy only of shame and derision. Certainly not the sort of thing one paraded in public.

In order to convince this interfering doctor that she was sane she would have to act fast. It occurred to her that having taught herself to wake at will, she could surely learn to dream to order. If she reset her worst memories as dreams, she could control them by stopping, rewinding or deleting where or whenever she chose. If replay got too painful, she could simply wake up and wait until she felt ready to face the challenge again. Once this was mastered, it would be possible to train her waking self to relay a practised account of her past with the assurance of a competent actor - faultlessly word perfect, displaying all the right emotion without actually feeling a thing. It would be exactly like recalling a dream: a dream she had written herself. All she needed to do was switch her memories to her dream files. If she was going to have to parade her dirty laundry in public, it would first be subjected to a thorough pre-wash.

Stella was confident that there was nothing in her life that was so bad that she would be unable to face it in a dream. Certain that this was the perfect way out of her dilemma, Stella made herself a cup of tea with the added treat of a sweet tea biscuit. She hung up her coat and bag and went off to bed with a spring in her step and a feeling bordering on euphoria. This strategy would enable her to familiarise herself with every nasty, traumatising detail of her past without having to confront any unwanted memories which smouldered just beneath the surface. That doctor had got one thing right. Stella was angry. She thought about the girl, but dismissed these thoughts. What she must do now was concentrate on her parents – on her past.

*

Stella squirmed over boxes of old photos, listened with distain to old records of Mantovani and Frankie Vaughan, until finally she managed to dream about her parents. It was uncanny: their voices were unaltered; their mannerisms clear in every detail. What part of her brain had stored the image of her mother pushing the last morsel of food into her mouth with her index finger, her lips distorting into an ugly, protruding 'O'? Her father never sat still. In her dream she saw him raise his heels and jiggle his legs in a constant, unconscious spasm; drumming his bony fingers on the table in time to his private thoughts. He would wink at her, jerking his head quickly to the side and back again, his right eye closing slowly and meaningfully, accompanied by a click of the tongue. A secret sign that he was on her side; they always ganged up against mother. It all came back in her dream -

a bearable, informative dream - but of little use. She would have to try again.

In her next dream her mother had completely lost it. The woman was swearing and hurling bowls of semolina at the walls. Stella remembered that semolina – it had the consistency of wallpaper paste. The swearing, however, was so far out of character, so ridiculous that it woke Stella immediately. She was supposed to be dreaming facts, not fantasies. Nights followed, filled with boring pointless dreams involving her parents, none of which had any grounding in actual historical fact. Sometimes reality and fiction combined. In one such dream she was about to sit her final exams when her mother appeared in the doorway of the great hall waving a sanitary pad and demanding it be taken to her daughter in the third row. In real life the object in question had been wrapped. But Stella squirmed in her dream much as she had at the time, ashamed, knowing that all eyes were on her, all thinking that she was incapable of packing her own school bag. The machete with which she slashed her mother to pulp before turning it on the poor unsuspecting class and teacher was enjoyable, but pure fiction.

Not one to give up, Stella persevered, systematically recalling the death of her mother, carefully editing as she went. Its transference to a dream was slow and painful. But, little by little she was getting there. Then one night she managed to dream the whole incident without having to wake up at all. The dream appeared to be accurate enough, without including any of those horrendous feelings that had dominated the actual event. Four times she made herself dream it until she deemed it ready to be logged away and printed out at her next appointment. She practised her delivery, made sure that she was word perfect, finally congratulating herself on being able to recite it at will, whether she was awake or asleep.

*

I had been working at the factory for five years, but I was still living with Mum and Dad at Maple Street. It was not ideal but it was convenient. I remember it was a Friday, pay day. When the bus arrived at my stop I noticed a small crowd gathered outside number 9. An ambulance was waiting - its engine running - as the paramedics loaded a stretcher into the back. I ran the last few yards and peered at the woman in the oxygen mask. It was Mum. I told the crew who I was, climbed aboard, and we set off at breakneck speed. The siren was so loud it hurt my ears, but I must admit I enjoyed it, although of course I was very worried about Mum; it was exciting racing through the streets before coming to a dead halt directly in line with the accident and emergency unit. You have to admire those drivers, don't you?

Throughout the ride I kept out of the way. The medics were busy, and I didn't want to interfere. When the doors swung open, I was amazed how many people were there just to help my Mum. They rushed her along the corridor, the trolley crashing through doors, them all running alongside, holding up drips, shouting orders, being busy. One of the trolley wheels had an awful squeak and I remember thinking 'Dad would make them stop so that he could put a drop of oil on that'. He was like that, very pernickety. It was organised chaos. I just ran behind - playing follow-my-leader. I remember I was clutching Mum's bag. My own had slipped off my shoulder. It kept bashing my knee as I ran. It always does that. I don't know why. I must have sloping shoulders - not designed to hold a long strap. I look quite normal in the bathroom mirror... maybe a bit thin... but surely that's an advantage... isn't it? For keeping straps on, I mean. Anyway, the doctor said they were very sorry, but there was nothing they could do. It was a massive heart attack, it would have been very quick and she would not have suffered. He asked if I wanted to see my mother. I told him I preferred to remember her the way she was. I remember trying to hide my tears, but it was hard. He asked if I had someone I could phone... someone who could be there when I got home... someone who could stay with me. I remember thinking, 'Who are all these 'someones'? Now Mum is gone there is no one. Well, only Dad', so I mumbled "Thank you" and left.

*

Stella was pleased with the revised version. She had not included the perplexed looked on the doctor's face, the way his eyes had searched hers for an expression of grief, anger - anything. She had shown no emotional response. She had none. He had obviously expected an answer to at least one of his questions. When he asked if she would like to see her mother, Stella had answered abruptly with a sharp conclusive 'No'. In her dream she had responded with warmth, offered profuse thanks and even managed a few tears. In life she was not interested in her mother's pathetic body. The whole business of death was over dramatized, quite unnecessary. Death shouldn't be a soap opera. It was just a full stop. In life Mum had never kissed her to say goodbye. Nor had Stella ever grieved for her when they had been apart. When Stella's grandmother died and Mum had gone to stay with her, no one had cried then. Why should Stella start now?

Stella recalled how she had left the hospital feeling light, and unburdened she had decided to call in at the supermarket on the way home. It was en route and would save her a bus trip later in the week. She would be the one doing all the shopping from now on; and the laundry; and the cleaning. The relief washed her clean. She felt an overpowering sense of freedom. It was a feeling she wanted to hold on to, like one of her better dreams. Before calling at M & S, she turned left and entered Livingstone park where she made straight for the duck pond to let out a jubilant scream. It came from the depths of her soul and emerged from the top of her head, purging her, whilst scattering the poor ducks to the far corners of the park.

*

Her next task was to rewrite and dream the death of her father. This death had been so very different. It had come within a year of her mother's demise and she still recalled those months of hell: his gaunt face as it morphed into a skull, the sunken eyes beseeching her with each agonising attempt at breath, the stench of the sick-room and the endless bowls of unspeakable waste. The memories were etched deep into her soul. Both of them had wanted it to end, but the powers-that-be seemed determined to let it crawl on for as long as possible - prolonging the degrading journey to the inevitable. Many times Stella had been tempted to place a pillow over his hideous features - to let the hollow-filled fibres put an end to the painful wheezing and coughing. Had she actually done it? Could she remember his pathetic attempt to fight her off? Had she imagined the vomit-ridden pillow that she had burned in the fireplace? Could she have dreamed it? He had smoked his way into an early grave and Stella had found comfort in the fact that he would finally end as ashes in that great ashtray: the crematorium on Fowler Road.

Her father had always coughed. It was part of his character, along with his jiggling knees and rapping fingers. His breathless spluttering into his hanky was one of her earliest memories of him. He would light another fag as a remedy and it seemed to work. He never moaned about his chest and his coughing never kept him awake, although his wife hardly slept at all. Stella could sleep through anything, so the deterioration of his lungs went pretty much unnoticed by her.

After Stella's mum died, Stella and her father had a working arrangement that suited them. She did all the shopping, cooking and cleaning. He collected his pension and tipped over the money every Thursday without fail. They hardly spoke to each other. Not out of malice or dislike. It was just how it was. Number 9 was a quiet house. The telly rumbled away in the corner and the sofa squeaked when you sat in the centre. Apart from that, there was only the occasional whisper of a tap running or the jolt as the boiler kicked into life.

When his condition worsened, a Macmillan nurse appeared each morning to wash him and give him his medications. Stella did the rest, not reluctantly, but not willingly either. She just did it. When he died it was loud and unpleasant. It was not what one would call a peaceful passing. Stella was alone with him as he gasped and retched in his last throes of life. There was nothing she could do but watch. Finally his skeletal head fell back and his sad eyes stared unseeing at the ceiling. His skinny yellow body lurched into an arch letting loose a long rattling sigh from his lipless mouth. He was gone. Death had not galloped in on a pale horse to snatch his quarry; he had sneaked in through a drain and left a nasty smell.

Stella did not hate her father or her mother, but they had never given her cause to rejoice in their lives. The process of living had all been a bit of an effort - something one did until one didn't do it anymore. Well the end had come and Stella could see no point in feeling sad or happy, downcast or elated. Apart from a slight easing nothing much changed with their departure. Stella was in sole control of her life now, waking and sleeping. She still had the house to run and her job to go to. Life went on.

*

Transposing her father's death into a dream was hard. Stella struggled to recall such hideous memories without reliving the pain. Death was no stranger to her dreams, but it was always romantic, dramatic or powerful. It could be terrifying - but never small and pathetic. The deaths of her parents had been insignificant, more like apostrophes than full stops. Her father's passing haunted her having been unnecessarily nasty, while her mother's race for life had seemed as consequential as missing a bus.

To prepare a convincing account for the doctor Stella knew that she had to inject some emotion. To turn the mundane into a tragedy, with her - suffering and bereaved - at the centre. She practised crying at will. She wrote the conversations she should have had with her dying father. She included her wishes that the 'nightmare' would end quickly. Not too many - just enough to add a touch of pathos. It was hard to rekindle these suppressed memories and she cursed her boss for making her go through this unnecessary ordeal.

Stella transferred her vexation with her

employer onto the doctor and the fat receptionist. As professionals they should have seen the whole thing for what it was - nonsense - and dismissed it as such thereby calling a halt to the whole stupid business. But Stella knew this would not happen. So she crafted her dream until she had a plausible, if sanitised script; well rehearsed and ready for her to deliver at her next visit. She was all set to let battle commence once more. Round four was going to be hers. Then the night before her appointment the unexpected happened.

*

She had gone up to bed even earlier than usual. She was excited. These manufactured dreams were becom-ing quite enjoyable. They brought the same anticipated pleasure that came with watching familiar old films. Knowing what was coming next in no way detracted from her enjoyment. If anything it enhanced it. Each re-visit brought some new, tiny discovery - an emphasis or inflection that she had missed first time - adding an extra poignancy to the story. She had become expert at noting each nuance and including it in her presentation. Tonight was the dress rehearsal and she had to be word perfect. She drank her tea and put on a clean nightdress for the occasion. The moment her head hit the pillow she entered her dream, but it was not the one she had prepared for.

*

She had not noticed just how heavy the rain was that Friday evening, not until she left the 94 bus at the bottom of Maple Street. Her brolly was wedged in her handbag and, as she tried to fish it out, it got caught by the strap, sending the bag and its contents spilling into the gutter. Her life was splayed out in pathetic trivia, the dirty rain turning it soggy and black. She bent down to grab her belongings just as a little girl jumped off the bus landing heavily on Stella's hand. She recoiled in pain and wondered how such a tiny creature could emit such a loud laugh and inflict such intense pain. A toothless grin leered at her as the child proceeded to jump on her hand again. Desperately trying to stuff her exposed life back into her bag, she realised with horror that it would never fit. Her whole life was swelling as it greedily soaked up the foul black water. Forced to abandon her past, she watched with resignation as the dark smelly hole in the gutter gulped it down.

That was when she first noticed the crowd milling around her gate and peering into the square bay window. They were trampling on her mother's rose bush, not caring how violently the curtains twitched at number 7. Stella turned to climb back onto the bus and follow it to the depot, but it too had vanished down the storm drain. Her mother, wearing her wedding hat and coat, walked out of the house and threw a cursory glance at her desecrated shrub. Then she climbed into the ambulance, turned to face the crowd, waved regally and began to speak. Her mother was addressing the masses. There was no mistaking that shrill voice. Stella dropped onto all fours and, crawling from the rear, through the legs of her mother's followers, she reached the front.

The throng was cheering and waving, applauding the oration. All Stella could hear was gobbledygook; some foreign language - Russian or Finnish, nothing that she could identify. The orator gave a final wave, lay down on the stretcher and the ambulance took off. Stella ran full pelt to catch it, clinging onto it as it raced off into the dark rain. The siren spilt her eardrums and the wind blasted against her skin. If only she had her umbrella, but that was gone, washed away with her childhood. The horrid child was clinging on beside her, still grinning inanely. She kicked at it until it let go. It bounced off down the road, crashing and squashing and squealing as it ricocheted from bumper to bumper, caught in the glare of the oncoming traffic.

Her mother waved goodbye and said it had been nice knowing her then disappeared. Stella, back at her house, picked up her handbag and walked through the front door. The crowds had gone. It was deliciously silent. Her father was in the bath, his head thrown backwards as if he had been laughing. His lungs were on the chair beside the bath, folded neatly with his trousers and shirt. Stella gathered his things and took them down to the kitchen where she sorted them into coloured and whites before reloading the washing machine and turning it on only to find it was a car. The engine started slowly and there was a slight smell of fish, but when it had stopped she was pleased to find they had arrived at the layby.

The avenue seemed different - shorter and less inviting. Bringing the picnic basket with her was a big mistake and she decided to bury the whole thing in the ditch, alongside the dead bird. Unimpeded she continued on her journey, gliding noiselessly between the rows of Poplars. Tonight even the sentinels were silent; their leaves hung limply, incapable of dance or speech in spite of the wind that stirred the air. A baby cried in the distance. It sounded hungry. Stella told herself it was her own hunger calling her. Reaching in her pocket she took a handful of crisps, crammed them into her mouth and immediately spat them out. Her mother knew she hated cheese and onion even more than she hated salt and vinegar. She had packed them out of spite. Stella spat again. Washing the taste away with a swig of 'Coke' she hurried on towards her destination.

The house lay straight ahead. The ground moved beneath her feet - a conveyer belt propelling her towards the front door. She counted the steps, careful to avoid the crack on the fourth. Her hands reached up automatically to grab the door knocker and strike it hard against the base. One, two, three...

*

Stella sat bolt upright. Her alarm clock confirmed that it was four forty four.

CHAPTER 5

"Let's explore violence today, shall we? Have there been any other incidents of violence in the past?" The doctor retrieved her glasses from the top of her head and looked down through them at her notebook.

Stella stared at her bag. 'What was all this talk about violence?' She had been told they would be talking about the death of her mother and father. She had prepared exactly what she was going to say. Suddenly the rules had changed. They were going to talk about violence. What violence? That unfortunate incident at work was certainly not typical behaviour, surely the doctor realised that? There had been no violence in her life, other than in her dreams. Was that what the doctor wanted to explore - her dreams? Stella was scared. If she said nothing her silence might be construed as guilt: if she related one of her dreams it could open up a whole field which she had resolved to keep private. Stella's brain went into overdrive, scrolling down her stored memories. There had been an incidence on the bus that would do. It involved violence, with her an innocent bystander, a victim not a perpetrator. Perfect. She clicked the file open then prepared herself with a deep breath, ready to edit or delete with a click of her mouse.

*

"There was one time, on the bus. I take the number 94 to work. Well I do when I'm working." She paused and threw what she hoped was a meaningful glance at the doctor. "It leaves from the bottom of my road which is handy. I'd only just started work so I was about 16 years old. I'd had cereal for breakfast, Rice Crispies, I always eat Rice Crispies, I have ever since I was a child. I still love the popping sound they make when the milk hits them. Anyway, I left the house as usual and waited for the bus. It's always on time, but this morning - it was a Monday - it was four minutes late. When I got on, there was a man sitting in my seat (well it's not actually my seat, but I always sit there. I still do). Anyway, this man - I recognised him. He usually sat at the back of the bus - at the back on the long seat, slouched over, listening to his Walkman. He winked at me once. Anyway, I always called him 'The Slouch'. Not to his face, you understand. I never spoke to him, nothing like that. Anyway, I don't like change and I remember on this particular day - it was a Monday - sorry had I already told you that? I felt annoyed - a bit put out. He must have sensed this because he got up and gave me the seat.

"He was quite tall, quite dark and quite spotty. He called me 'darling' which would have been romantic if he hadn't spoken so badly. His accent was rough - Estuary. He had an amazing hairdo. It was black and purple and stuck up in a great spiky crest like a cock-a-too. His jeans were skin tight, and there was a tear across the left - no it was the right - knee. And there was a logo on his T-shirt that I didn't understand. He smelled lovely. It was the first time I had been that close to a man's aftershave, Dad never wore it. I expect 'The Tie' does, but I never get close to him. He's my boss, Mr Andrews. I like to give people nicknames, it makes them less forbidding - silly but I've always done it. Mr Andrews must have dozens of ties, he wears a different one every day, but always the same dark blue suit; although I suppose he could have several the same - or similar I should say, suits that is. I've got two identical skirts for work; it saves having to decide what to wear. 'The Tie' probably does the same. It was really nice, intimate, smelling a stranger... like sharing bathrooms. Later I found out the smell came from his hair gel which put me off a bit."

*

The doctor was sitting watching Stella as she spoke, nodding occasionally to show she was listening, which she was. But mostly she was watching every movement her patient made. By now Stella was in full flow, her body language was relaxed and she told her story in a fluid, natural manner. To her surprise, Stella had indeed relaxed into it, finding, she was actually enjoying the process. Her determination to edit and select dissolved as her voice switched to autopilot, and she sat back to listen to herself.

"He stood up to let me sit down which was odd because the bus wasn't full... there were plenty of seats. It never fills up until it reaches the Livingstone Estate. I felt all peculiar and I know my face went bright red as everyone was looking at me. Kevin (I didn't know his name then, I only knew him as 'The Slouch'), well he stood up and brushed passed me holding onto the pole. I had to brush against him to squeeze into my seat. It's the window seat in the fourth row, just before the raised bit where they all sit and face each other. I hate that. I'd never sit there. He stayed there holding on to the pole and I could feel him press against me when the bus turned left. Do you know the 94 takes twelve left turns and only three right turns between Maple Street and Carlisle Road? You'd think it was going round in one gigantic circle! Then more people got on and he took the seat behind me, the end of the long one. But I could still feel him staring at me and I think he touched my hair; it must have been on purpose.

"There are nine stops before Carlisle Road, and at the fourth a gang of yobs got on. They were a rowdy lot and by now the bus was pretty full, so they hovered in the aisle, swinging like monkeys on the poles between the seats. They used words I'd never heard before, but I think they were offensive. They knew 'The Slouch', they called him Kev, but he just told them to F-off. Their behaviour was extremely uncouth and I guessed they must be one of those gangs they are always going on about on the news. The driver had no control over them in fact he was worse than useless.

"Then they picked on 'The Woolly Hat' and she's an old woman. Well, that's not on, is it? Anyway, they reduced her to tears; snatching her bag and throwing her stuff around the bus. Do you know that stupid conductor did nothing, even when they emptied her purse and scattered the pathetic contents all over the floor, all of ten pounds, fifty-nine pence. One woman - I recognised from the factory - one of 'The White Devils' – well she tried to snatch the purse back, but the yob pushed her back into her seat. He took out a knife, which he began brandishing around, much to delight of his mates and the horror of the other passengers. I remember thinking, 'Silly move - she could gut you, that's what she does all day.' But he had the knife."

Stella's body language changed. She began jiggling her legs and using her hands in expansive, exaggerated gestures. Her body was animated; her introverted demeanour forgotten as she got more and more involved in her story.

"A glint of steel flashed past me which I took as my cue. In one swift move, I sprang up and lunged forward, whacking the nearest yob sharply around the head with my handbag. He slumped to the ground, clutching his head. Blood began pouring from his nose and spread out over his horrible pale grey hoody. I remember thinking it was the exact same colour as cranberry juice, which was funny because it matched his face. He was covered in acne - horrible red spots, oozing pus. I decided to call him 'The Berry'. If I had skin like that I'd

stay in, or keep my hood pulled down really low. It was then that I…"

*

All the time Stella was relating her tale the doctor was listening attentively, observing her patient. What started as a calm recollection of an incident on a bus was fast turning into a fantastic account of a film, or a dream – totally out of keeping with this quiet, unprepossessing woman sitting in front of her. When Stella's voice faltered, Dr Devant smiled and with a sight nod of her head indicated she should continue.

*

"I leapt over the seat in front and grabbed 'The Berry' by his hood. Whooping and hollering at him, I watched him cower; he couldn't believe his eyes. He was being attacked by this skinny, half crazed girl! So, now I had the knife and I slashed out, cutting him across his hands which he waved pathetically in front of his poxy face. I tossed the knife from left to right just as I had been taught – the Sioux are really good with knives. I knew how proud Runs–With–The-Buffalo would be; I could hear him urging me on. If the bus hadn't screeched to a halt and the automatic doors sprung open, I might well have killed 'The Berry'. I was debating whether to scalp him when I saw the look on the face of 'The Woolly Hat' and decided that this would be inappropriate behaviour; certainly not

befitting a passenger on the number 94. Anyway, the next stop was mine so I got off."

*

Dr Devant was still smiling benignly, when Stella stopped talking. It was time to end their session, but she needed to make sure Stella was in control before she dismissed her. The case fascinated her. If the facilities had been available she would certainly have sectioned Stella, for a brief period, to get a detailed assessment, but the system was stretched to capacity and a place at Priority House was out of the question. She also needed to establish how much of the incident Stella realised was fact and how much was fiction. Her informed opinion was that Stella's grasp on reality was diminishing. But, as so often happened, the clock decided for her. She continued to smile at Stella, telling her that she would like to see her again in two weeks, when they could continue their discussion. Stella baffled her. She displayed no obvious signs of being anything other than neurotic, so she either had such a strong, amazing imagination that she sucked herself into the story - believing it to be true; or she suffered from bouts of disassociated personality disorder which bordered on the psychotic.

*

Stella left the surgery feeling drained. She walked home, hoping the fresh air would do her good and give her space to think through the past hour. Her first reaction was positive; she had answered the doctor's request convincingly without revealing too much of her private life. Stella was sure the doctor would soon declare she was fit enough to return to work, presenting no further danger to her boss. As she turned the corner into Maple Street she stopped. Doubt had replaced her confidence. It occurred to her that she may have misread the purpose behind the doctor's question: that she may have been inquiring about violence directed at her, possible childhood abuse. Why had she assumed otherwise? Was it possible she had misread the whole situation?

She adjusted her shoulder bag and continued on down the street, trying desperately to recall exactly what she had said. But the more she thought about it the fuzzier her memory became. She knew she had talked about the incident on the bus when those awful louts had harassed 'The Woolly Hat', but the image of herself brandishing a knife - where had that come from? Had she imagined it? Had she dreamed it? And, more importantly had she mentioned it to the doctor? These questions spun round and round in her brain. By the time she arrived home she was totally confused and scared. She removed her coat and hung it on the rack in the hall before going into the kitchen and making a mug of strong tea. Sitting in the corner of the sofa to avoid the squeak, she made her mind focus on the episode on the bus.

*

There had been a scuffle on the bus, of that much Stella was sure. Whether or not a knife had been used was debateable. She remembered the assault on 'The Woolly Hat', and she remembered going to her aid, that had all been real. How much more had she fabricated? Memories began to surface, memories she had buried with the past, but whose consequences now filled her with horror.

*

The rest of the day was predictably boring. At 5.30 pm Stella clocked off. 'The Slouch' was leaning against the factory wall. There was no way of avoiding him so Stella continued walking until she drew level with him. She didn't dare to look at him, but she could feel his eyes boring into her. From the corner of her downcast eye she saw him slink forward like a snake - straightening his body slowly and deliberately as he rose. He was taller than she remembered and even now her skin pricked at the memory of him. He said he wanted to buy her a drink and that he'd never met a girl with balls before. Stella had no idea what he meant, but it had sounded like a compliment rather than an anatomical observation so she accepted his offer; it was easier than saying no. She remembered looking down at his hand as he took hold of hers and she remembered not daring to look up.

This was Stella's first visit to a pub - a new experience, almost an adventure. Casual conversation was not possible between two such socially inept people and when, after a long, painful silence, they had both asked the same question at the same moment, the shock of hearing their voices left them reluctant to try again. Silence lapped round them like a pool of gradually stagnating water. They had little in common other than their age and their shared journey on the 94 bus. Kevin drank a single pint of lager and introduced Stella to the delights of a Cinzano. She paid for the drinks which made her feel embarrassed in case anyone else noticed, although they were the only two in the bar. Her self consciousness was exacerbated by the fact that every time she allowed herself to snatch a glance at him she caught him looking right back. Determined not to peep again Stella turned her attention to her surroundings.

There were framed photographs of the town, ancient sepia postcards with white writing at the bottom which she couldn't read because she hadn't worn her glasses. The ring-marked table was made out of the base of an old sewing machine - exactly the same as her mother's. Remembering her mother brought a heavy cloud of guilt which sat visibly on her sloping shoulders, hunching them into an arc, accentuating her thinness. She had not told her parents she would be late back. Would they be worried? Would they be angry? Would they notice? These thoughts only compounded her guilt. Her body was rocking back and forth. To stop it she coughed loudly and made herself sit upright. She stopped looking around - staring at the table top ahead instead. Her hands gripped her empty glass, turning it round and round. She wasn't hinting that she wanted a refill. It was simply something to do. When the bell rang for last orders, they left the little table in the window with mutual relief. As they got up to leave, Stella took the empty finger-marked glasses and placed them on the bar. It seemed the polite thing to do.

The car park was dark and deserted. It was, after all, Monday night. When 'The Slouch' took her arm and led her to the wall beneath an elder tree she followed obediently. The evening air was full of the smell of hair gel and wheelie bins.

This was her first kiss. It was much wetter and noisier than she expected. Stella had seen loads of people kiss on screen and it had always seemed to be a rather dry, tasteful, certainly rapturous event, which, apart from a soft sigh of pleasure, was silent. By sharp contrast, this was repulsive and noisy. Trying to mimic the movie stars, she closed her eyes, hoping this would do the trick. She was desperate to find something romantic to savour and replace the taste of stale lager and spit.

Her disappointed eyes opened wide and abruptly, as slobber and suction flooded her senses. Nauseous and disgusted, she was afraid that she might throw up. Meanwhile Kevin was fumbling with her dress, pulling it up until she felt his hand reach up under the elastic of her knickers. His other hand was busy unzipping his tight, ripped jeans. Stella stared up into the elder tree as she felt his hand brush against her pubic hair until his fingers found her tightly clenched vagina. His knee pressed against her thighs forcing her legs apart and the probing fingers reached their target. Unfiled and rather grubby fingernails scratched and forced their way inside her. She squirmed, held her breath, feeling them pushing and screwing deeper and deeper into her body. Then he removed his fingers and forced his penis into their place. She thought he was going to tear her apart. Each thrust was harder and more penetrating than the last and each was accompanied by an animal grunt which offended her ears and filled her nostrils with the stench of his breath. There were six; she counted each agonising push. Then it stopped and she breathed out.

Kevin stuffed his penis back in his jeans. He was mumbling something about how great it had been, and that they should do it again sometime. Stella, who had been clutching her handbag throughout the ordeal, thanked him and turned away to throw up. He was still trying to zip up his flies as he scurried off.

Stella was left feeling dirty and sore, standing alone beneath the elder tree in the pub car-park. She struggled to pull her skirt down and hoped the two other revellers could not see what she was doing as they straggled by. One even called 'goodnight' to her. Once she was sure she was alone, she removed her knickers and used them to wipe the blood and semen from her crotch and down between her legs. She tossed her soiled pants into the large blue wheelie bin and walked home slowly and painfully. Real sex was such a noisy, painful and smelly business Stella decided in future to only experience it in her dreams.

CHAPTER 6

Seven months later, in the cold December bathroom of number 9 Maple Street, Stella gave birth to a skinny, baby girl. There had been no outward signs of pregnancy. Her periods had always been erratic, unpredictable things so the whole event came as a total shock.

Her mother had proved surprisingly stoical. She had come upstairs bursting to use the lavatory only to find her daughter standing in a pool of blood. Mrs Sankey had snipped the cord and dealt with the after birth, finally taking the tiny bundle away saying she would take care of everything. It had not cried or whimpered. It had entered the world silently, early, unannounced and unexpected. As her mother swaddled the baby in a towel, Stella saw a mop of thick black hair, shining and wet, as though it had been smothered in hair gel. The hair sprouted out above a purple face of screwed up features lost in a sea of wrinkles, blood and slime.

Her mother returned and told Stella the child was fine. She then told her daughter to have a bath and go back to bed.

Mrs Sankey rummaged in her knitting basket for some suitable wool and knitted a pink blanket and a tiny teddy bear. Then she found some pink emulsion paint and gently pressed the tiny, shrivelled hands and feet in the mixture before blotting them onto a sheet of Basildon Bond. She wrapped the baby in the blanket with the teddy and before it was light she slipped out of the house. She returned later, empty handed and spent the rest of the night knitting another blanket and another teddy bear. These she wrapped in a large sheet of tissue paper and finally wrapped the whole thing in a larger sheet of brown paper. The package was placed, carefully and respectfully, in the bottom drawer of the tallboy in Stella's room, alongside an envelope containing the tiny hand and foot prints. This was Mrs Sankey's laundry drawer. They would be safe there, with the lavender sachets and the moth balls.

The next morning she told her daughter all she needed to know. She explained how she had wrapped the precious bundle in a blanket and left it, with a teddy, outside the local hospital. She described how she had waited out of sight in the cold night air until she saw someone pick the bundle up and take it in to the warm safety of Milburn General. She did not mention the bottom drawer. That was for her sins not for her daughter's. She then told Stella to get a move on or she would be late for work.

That brief glimpse of matted wet black hair above a changeling's face was the only time Stella saw her child. The image was locked into her memory and the connection was stored in her heart. To the outside world, the miracle of life passed unnoticed. Kevin never took the 94 bus again which denied him the joys and responsibilities of absentee fatherhood. The subject was never mentioned in the Sankey household.

Sweet Dreams

*

Stella's mind kept going back to her last session with Dr Devant. The wretched woman had just sat there - almost as if she wanted Stella to trip herself up - to let slip some guilty secret that should remain buried and forgotten. What possible good could it do to drag it all back out into the light now? The baby was history. She tried not to think about it. It was so long ago – twenty-five years; twenty-five years, five months and six days to be precise, and Stella liked to be precise. Now after all this time it was once again foremost in her thoughts: its presence gate-crashed her conscious mind with such atomic force she felt she would explode.

*

The next few sessions were easier; Stella's confidence growing with each performance. Massaging the facts was becoming an enjoyable game. She no longer dreaded sitting opposite the po-faced woman, although she had not yet come up with a really satisfactory nickname for her, which was annoying. Dismissal was easier when someone's name was in your control. On her fifth visit the doctor had written out a prescription for some pills which she said would allay some of Stella's anxieties. Unaware of any such anxieties, Stella looked at her reflection in the bathroom mirror. As she turned her head from side to side, she scrutinised what she saw. Her mousey hair was tinged with grey and her face had a few fine lines sketched on it, mostly around her mouth and eyes. Her teeth were good, she was glad she had treated them to such a strict hygiene routine. She did look alarmingly like her father though.

Life still promised her a good few years. She was receiving sick pay, while she was off work, so she had no financial worries. She had plenty in her savings account and she lived frugally. Besides she would soon be back at the factory once what's-her-name had finished with her. Stella took one of the little white pills out of its foil casing and flushed it down the lavatory, watching it disappear in a whirlpool of blue foaming loo-freshener, then she went off to bed with her cup of tea. Tonight her dreams could take her anywhere they wanted. No more calculated fiction. Tonight she wanted excitement and a rest from 'The Inquisitor' – yes that was a good name for that nosey cow. Stella was still smiling when her eyes closed and she entered her private world.

*

Stella had been waiting at the bus stop for eleven and a half minutes and was trying to decide if she should walk on to the next stop or not. It would make no difference to the fare, as she had a season ticket, but standing around doing nothing was such a waste of time. Then again, the chances were that as soon as she had turned the corner the bus would come along and she would have to wait ages for the next one. Just as she had opted to stay, her transport pulled up in front of her.

Sweet Dreams

The great beast moved slowly and deliberately. Swaying precariously, he lurched like a galleon in full sail until, with a final heavy thud, he was kneeling on all fours. Strangely, although lumbering and awkward, he maintained an air of majesty which complemented his age and size. As his bulk lowered, so his great oval eye drew level with hers. She peered through the black hole in its centre and saw deep into his pumping heart. The huge yellow iris rolled, blood red tributaries crisscrossed the white ocean as Stella watched a large teardrop break free from the reservoir, hover on the brink, before cascading down in a cataract of pain.

The elephant was crying; sobbing out his humiliation and agony; his loud trumpeting proclaiming that it was demeaning for such a splendid creature to carry a howdah on his strong sloping back. Stella watched the tear roll down the scaly face and felt tears of her own welling up. Then suddenly, a mischiev-ous twinkle appeared. The great leathery lid, fringed with eyelashes to die for, swept across the shining pool like a powerful windscreen wiper. When the eye opened, it gleamed with approval at the array of brightly coloured silks and sparkling profusion of jewels that surrounded him.

The canopied seat of the howdah was resplendent with silken cushions; silver trays overflowed with sweetmeats and bonbons. Weighty tassels of purple and saffron silk swung beneath the elephant's belly responding to every majestic movement. Another of vivid pink hung from the triangular cap that covered his forehead, held in place by a single ruby, which vied for brilliance with his topaz eyes. He smiled, and his great eye winked again as he spoke.

"Funny old thing life! One minute you're down the next you're up. It's hard adjusting to captivity, but you have to resign yourself or you'd go crazy. I've learned to love all the pomp and ceremony; being the centre of attention suits my personality. You have to admit I look magnificent. Mind you, it's not all buns and treats. The whip hurts and the food isn't always up to much. But, it could have been worse. I could have been shipped off to a zoo or to a circus, God forbid. So yes, I lost my freedom - the right to roam at liberty, to inhabit my beloved jungle as the proud head of an esteemed family: but being the lead elephant in the mighty Nawab's fleet comes a close second. Just look at my nails."

He wiggled his great toes and a string of jingling silver bells rang out. Each nail was painted and polished until they too vied with the ruby; each ivory unguis was studded with diamonds as big as ostrich eggs. His broad face was painted with the blues and greens of the peacock and his haunting eyes were outlined in red madder and jet black kohl. Garlands of saffron marigolds wrapped around his throat and his harness jingled with a thousand more silver bells. He was scrubbed, decorated and perfumed with rare pungent spices and unguents. No wonder he held his head high.

His eyes turned sad again for a moment as he

continued,

"The cutting of my mighty tusks was the cruellest act. It rendered me subservient, wounding not just my body but my proud elephantine soul. Elephants do have souls you know. What is a bull elephant if he has no tusks? He is impotent and ready for the sacred grave yard. Not even poachers put any value on a Tusker without tusks. But after the pain died down, more men came and capped my stumps with burnished silver - beaten and fashioned with such skill one had to admire the result.

"So you see, even that indignity grew bearable with time. I began to forget my past, to look forward to years of regular food and endless adulation. My mahout is a kind enough man and, here in the compound, I lack for none of those bodily comforts that I often went without in the wild. Now I count my blessings, do as I'm told, and have become a loyal servant of the young prince. I lead the processions and the other elephants look up to me. I tell myself that I am happy - much like you do, my dear."

The young prince was unnervingly handsome. The inner rims of his molten eyes were brushed with kohl just like the elephant's, and the black cream bounced from rim to rim accentuating the whites of these dark weapons as he flashed them at Stella. She was enchanted, made to feel beautiful and special. She, like the elephant, enjoyed being the centre of attention. She, like the elephant, believed she was happy. Maybe she was.

The prince took her hand and guided her up the

ladder into the howdah. Then he climbed in and sat beside her. The rain fell in heavy drops that bounced and echoed off the jewelled canopy. They were going to hunt tigers and Stella was glad she had worn her hair-slide. As the procession set off, crowds of people lined the streets, waving flags and shouting blessings to the Nehwab. Stella searched in her handbag for her season ticket.

"Take care, Stella," the young prince said. "The elephant is not used to carrying such a cargo as you. But he is kind and he likes you."

The howdah lurched forward as the elephant rose. Then it pitched backwards before settling into a rhythmic sway as they entered the dense jungle. The prince peered deep into Stella's eyes. He laughed.

"You may feel a bit sick, but you will not fall. You are safe with me. However, remember that the tiger is clever. He is fierce and cunning. Never trust him. No matter what he tells you, you must not trust him. He will eat you given half the chance. I have shot many tigers in my life. Tigers contain great power. It is an honour to kill a tiger."

Stella had no wish to see a tiger shot, and asked the prince if she could get off at Carlisle Road. The young prince made her a solemn promise that no tigers would be killed today, in honour of the beautiful English girl. Stella's hand rose to touch her hair- slide.

In front of them the jungle became denser, making it difficult for the elephant to lift his lumbering feet. He reared up wildly and began to stamp on the vegetation. With each hefty stomp, the howdah tilted from side to side until it began to lean dangerously to the left. Stella screamed, but the young prince held out his slender brown arm and swept it in a great arc across the impenetrable tangle of jungle that lay before them. His many bracelets jangled, then settled in silence as one graceful arm returned to fold across the other. Stella was about to witness the power of the boy's command.

The congested roots and tangled vegetation, which barred their progress, fell away. Knotted roots lifted to extricate themselves from dense undergrowth, then bowed in retreat as the royal procession passed by. Hefty trees drew effortlessly back, knotted grasses parted to the tumultuous sound of clapping hands, and whispering voices as a great wind swept in front of them to provide a wide clear avenue. Palm trees taller than the far pavilions sat on either side of their path, swaying in time to the jingling bells of the dancing elephant. His great feet, free of all impediments, thundered over the baked earth, gathering speed with every step. Soon he had cleared the runway and soared high above the tumult, flying with ever increasing speed over the green chaos far below. The elephant jet carried them upwards.

The water was deceptive, its cold appearance belying its temperature. It was like taking a warm bath - a pleasant welcome surprise. Stella dived in head-first, cleanly cutting the green-glass surface. Her naked body took on the colour of the water, rendering her barely visible. She had become a nymph, a water sprite. Not swimming, but being carried along by a powerful current, she thought she was all alone, until she saw him swimming alongside her. She assumed it was the prince, then her eyes adjusted to the water and she saw him clearly.

The great cat moved effortlessly and she watched with wonder at the span of his giant limbs; each massive sweep of his paw propelling him along. She noticed that his feet were webbed: green scaled membranes stretched between each toe. Like her, the tiger was totally submerged - a feline torpedo, racing through the water with such ease and beauty that Stella wanted to cry. His slipstream carried her along, until his amber eye drew parallel to her own. Unlike the elephant's, this eye had never been lowered in submission. This eye surveyed a realm that it ruled. The tiger's beauty outshone anything she had ever dreamed of. Her hand reached out to touch his fabulous stripes, and she heard the prince's warning ringing in her ears: "He will eat you given half the chance." *Stella withdrew her hand.*

"We are not yet out of danger. Hold on to my back we must dive again. Hold tight." *His voice was deep and there was the hint of a purr in his throat.*

He was seducing her, rendering her powerless to resist. Paralysed by fear and awe she tried not to listen to the tiger's lies. He sighed. The force of his breath whipped the water into a whirlpool of foaming bubbles.

"You have a choice. Stay here and be shot. Of

course you might drown first. Or you can trust me and do as I tell you. Life is hard. Death is easy. Life or death: it's always your choice."

Stella gripped his fur and once again felt power surge through her fingers. The tiger was fully charged; an electric-blue flame flickered around the two of them, co-joining them with an azure aura, as they cut through the green water. They swam deep, way below the surface, almost skimming the bed of the river. They travelled for days, not speaking, but each aware of the other's presence. Stella felt she had become part of this fabulous creature. Sometimes a fear as deep as the water would grip her, turning her blood to ice. Her hands would begin to slip from the thick wet fur and she would see him for the wild killing machine he was. Then he would look straight into her eyes and she would feel safer than she had ever felt before.

"Remember that feeling, you must learn to recognise it," he said. "It's called Trust."

Now they were out of the water and she was astride the tiger as he charged through thick choking undergrowth. His body moved with such ease that there was no sensation of motion: so different from the swaying lurch of the elephant's great lumbering progress. The vegetation parted willingly before this king without the need for spoken command. He had ruled this domain long before man had threatened to destroy it. He feared nothing and everything bowed down to his strength. All other creatures moved aside to let him pass, with a tangible reverence.

From the sky, which hung somewhere beyond the congregating tree tops, came the unmistakable crack of a rifle. The tiger was gone. Stella stood alone; he had betrayed her. The young prince had told the truth. What if the tiger came back for her? This time he would eat her. He had been playing with her, lulling her into a false sense of security. Calling to the hunting party was futile; no sound came out of her mouth. She looked up into the thick canopy. Even if the plane flew directly overhead they would never see her down here, hidden by a thousand years of trees. Her head tilted up to where she supposed the sky to be.

A feeling of nausea engulfed her. When she tried to look down, her head would not obey. Then a sudden up-draught snatched her feet from under her, lifting her high off the ground, turning her until she was spinning, rotating faster and faster, caught in the eye of a tornado. The vortex was sucking her up into its funnel, where the sudden drop in pressure squeezed her breath from her as the wind continued to spin her round and round, pulling at her from the inside of her body, tearing her inside out.

It was time to wake up. What was the key word? She had forgotten it. Who had forgotten it? Forgotten what? Was she still dreaming or was this real? Suddenly it no longer mattered. All she could feel was pain: excruciating agony as her head was wrenched from her shoulders. A loud crack, her neck snapped like a wish bone and her head spun out of sight.

Far below lay the avenue of trees. The poplars

waved to her. This was her avenue. These were her trees. This was her home where she was safe. Far below, on the gravel, she could see her mother and father. They were standing beside the iron gates. But they were not looking up at her. They were staring at the headless body of a tiger, watching as the hunters divided up their booty. They were tearing off his genitals and cheering with triumphant delight as they waved their horrible, bloody trophy above their heads.

The young prince helped her down from the bus and handed his rifle to the driver. He brought his hands together and pressed his thumbs to his chest in Anjali mudra the prayer position. Slowly he lowered his head to his hands and bowed. Stella noticed he was wearing her hair-slide in his black greasy hair. Angrily she reached out to snatch it back, only to see that her own hands glistened with hot, wet blood. Was it the blood of the tiger? She planted a rose bush in his memory, but it died as soon as the last spade full of earth touched its roots.

CHAPTER 7

Stella spent the next few days in bed, enjoying the indulgent fantasy of her dreams. In her waking hours she found herself thinking of 'The Girl without the Kalashnikov'. There was something haunting about the solitary figure. Not romantic, or mysterious, just intriguing. Stella began to make up stories about her: speculating as to who she was, where she had come from - her background. These fantasies went on for several days. Stella became quite inventive, yet curiously each invention would lead back home: to Stella. However tenuous, there was always a connection. Maybe the girl was a Russian or Polish refugee; perhaps they shared a long lost distant great-grandfather. Or could the girl be a secret agent. At times Stella even thought of visiting the old school where she had first seen the girl. Her head filled with imagined meetings, conversations, a relationship. She frightened herself with her own whimsy. It was getting ridiculous.

Eventually hunger prompted her to get up, restock her grocery cupboard and attend to her neglected fridge. After an extravagant trip to M&S, she sat down that evening to a delicious meal of fresh lamb chops with mint and new potatoes. Eating her silent supper it occurred to Stella that she had too much time on her hands.

Being off work provided a wonderful opportunity to do all those things she never had time to do - like spring clean the house. Maybe even do a little decorating? In all the time she had lived at number 9 she could not recall any decorating - let alone re-decorating - being done. For that matter, her mother's old willow pattern china and pastel pink bed linen was still in use. The carpets were worn through in places, and she had hated the flowery 60s wallpaper for a whole lifetime. The perpetual sales were still offering bargains. She might even indulge in some new curtains.

The prospect of change excited Stella. There was all that clutter in the attic: her parent's lives stuffed into so many tea chests. If she moved the wheelie bin out onto the pavement, there was just about room to get a skip in the front garden, between Mum's rose bush and the wall. The neighbours might object, but it would only be for a week or two. She might even put some gravel down and replace the old rose bush with something new - or maybe not. It hardly ever flowered now and had vicious evil thorns, but it was a survivor, after all it was at least twenty-five years old.

Fired with enthusiasm, Stella washed her knife, fork and plate, resetting her spoon and dish ready for tomorrow's breakfast. Meanwhile her brain went running on ahead. She would start bright and early at the top, working her way logically through the whole house. Her mother had been an inveterate hoarder, accumulating a wealth of junk. The prospect of rummaging through the past was both exciting and depressing, but her resolve was firm. It was time to jettison the lot.

That night Stella's dreams were of houses. They were vast, rambling, some familiar, and some totally unknown, often, paradoxically, at the same time. She had been visiting such houses ever since puberty. She relished the stimulation of surprise arising from the familiar. Always her dream would begin in well-known surroundings - the front room of number 9 - or her bedroom. Then a door would appear - one she had never noticed before. It would lead to an attic or cellar, which would inevitably lead to a vast new area, a magical construct, paying scant regard to architectural logic.

This night her dream had one notable difference. In each house, each room, whether familiar or strange, she caught a fleeting glimpse of a young girl in a long leather coat, a Kalashnikov slung casually over her shoulder.

*

Stella woke up to find it was nearly nine o'clock, unusually late for her. She felt pleasantly refreshed. A bowl of Rice Crispies later and her mind had finished its review of that night's events. No more fantasy; a day of practical tasks was just what she needed. Stella had not felt this vigorous since... well she did not choose to remember when. It was imperative not to waste such new-found energy.

Access to the loft was simple, but not easy. Her father had used a pole with a hook on the end to release the catch and the ladder simply slid down onto the landing, always with alarming speed and force. The pole lived under the stairs. It was surprisingly heavy and this combined with its length made it difficult to manoeuvre. Eventually the hatch was opened, but the wretched ladder refused to descend. A battle of wills ensued. Stella won. She leapt for safety, but it came down so slowly, it posed no threat whatsoever. Stella was glad there was no one to witness her ridiculous, unnecessary gymnastics.

It was with trepidation that she climbed up through the narrow opening. The past hit her unsuspecting nose with a nostalgic punch so powerful that it brought tears to her eyes and a lump to her throat. Recognising it for what it was - dust and debris - she dismissed it with a loud, uncontrolled sneeze. Having cleared the air, her fingers located the light switch and turned off the dark.

It was a relief to find that, with careful positioning, she could stand upright. She took stock. The glass-fibre lagging made it difficult to tell where it was safe to tread. The memory of her father scratching for months after laying the unwieldy, itchy stuff filled her head. To be on the safe side Stella stood in the middle, surrounded by a collection of boxes, crates and old suitcases. A dolls' house without its front faced a high-chair lovingly decorated with faded cut-out paper roses and daubs of rusk. Her mother's dressmaker's dummy blinked at her through thick layers of grey dust, and the matching grey squirrel coat that draped over its shoulders had clearly been infested and digested by several generations of mice. The old Singer sewing machine lay silently alongside; for a brief moment Stella heard the soft comforting whir, her mother's foot sending the wheel spinning round. An old blackboard still stood aslant on its wobbly easel - a stick of white chalk lying in the groove exactly where little Stella had left it. Here was her childhood, buried in dust, ready to reach out and snatch her back.

Boring holidays filled with the drumming of rain on caravan roofs, over-thumbed comics and the inevitable tinned- salmon sandwiches crowded on her mind's eye: memories of a time when she had been unaware that happiness and sadness existed as opposite sides of the same coin.

Stella struggled to shift the first of the suitcases: a faded green and brown canvass monster with leather belts and a smell of the 60s. Holiday camps marshalled by fierce redcoats doling out humiliation reached out to her; but she blocked them with a determined grinding of her teeth. Her father had loved Butlins. For him it was one of life's great treats. Mum accepted it; it catered to their every whim and came wrapped in similar packaging to the rest of their lives. Mrs Sankey did not expect holidays to be different or special and, as such, the holiday camp never disappointed. As for Stella, she simply thanked her lucky stars that Dad's salary only afforded them one week away a year.

As a child Stella had never tried to work out what it was about Butlins that she hated so vehemently. With hindsight, she realised it was the embarrassing lack of privacy. Number 9 was small, but the chalets at Bognor Regis were miniscule. This meagre space was shared with her parents. The fear, that they would know when - or worse still - what she was dreaming, alarmed her. So from a very early age, Stella had taught herself to behave discreetly when asleep. She was pretty sure she did not cry out or talk in her sleep and, although she had no way of knowing for certain, she was pretty sure she had never walked in her sleep. But, being observed was only one half of the problem. Close proximity made her a voyeur, an unwilling intruder on her parents' privacy.

Once, as a small child, an abscess on her tooth had kept her awake and she had gone into her parents' room hoping for some comfort and Aspirin. Unfortunately she had caught them 'at it'. Although she had no idea what 'it' was, the horror of witnessing such an act had never left her. Butlins came with the remembered strain of having to keep her eyes screwed shut, her face buried in the pillow, her poor ears painfully stuffed with cotton wool in case it happened again. It never did, not so far as she knew, but the fear was ever present.

Returning to the task in hand, Stella checked the rest of the cases, tipping the contents into the empty largest one. A pair of swimming trunks, a Hawaiian shirt and an evening dress of her mother's, none of which would have been considered high, or even low, fashion. The suitcase was filling rapidly. The grey fur coat, some ice skates, tarnished tinsel and broken baubles all mixed together. In no time it was full. Getting it through the hatch was no mean feat. After much pushing and panting, the case finally popped through the hole and out of sight. Stella listened with horror as it crashed against the bannisters, plummeted down the stairs and landed heavily in the hall.

An unscholarly collection of books, foxed and mouse-chewed, the dreaded Mantovani and Frankie Vaughan boxed-sets; all followed the holiday relics into the waiting cases and boxes. Crates of china and glass had to be re-boxed into manageable loads then manhandled through the hatch until they too stood on the cluttered landing. Stella wished she had never started this ridiculous exercise as, with considerable difficulty, she navigated her way downstairs, to make a sustaining cup of tea.

Lost in the task of stirring her drink, the young girl popped into her mind again. Stella stared into her tea, watching the brown liquid swirl around. She wondered if they would meet again. Was fate pulling them together? She noted her regret at not having suggested that they meet up, and, with a swift sharp tap on the side of the mug, she cast the spoon and her idle speculations into the sink. Day dreaming was not Stella's bag. It led to too many 'what ifs' and 'if onlys'. Life was hard enough without allowing irrelevances to invade one's thoughts. She remembered the tiger's words, 'Life is hard. Death is easy.' Well, he had certainly got the first bit right.

Stella ground her teeth, admonished herself for doing so and re-applied herself to the task in hand.

The Yellow Pages provided the number of a skip-hire firm and she ordered their smallest to be delivered that afternoon. A bigger one would not fit on the tiny patch outside the front, not without destroying her mother's roses. The small one would have to do. It was certainly big enough to set the lace curtains twitching at number 7. Laboriously she dragged the remaining contents of the loft down the ladder, down each of the carefully counted stairs where they sat, banished from her life for ever.

Next she turned her attention to her parent's bedroom. It had been a good seven years since Mum had died, with Dad following close behind her, just as he always had. It had not occurred to her to clear their room before now. She had dusted it and pushed the carpet sweeper around once in a while, but for the most part it had remained exactly as they had left it. The guilt of trespass hung over her as she entered their private space. There, on the dressing table, the little shepherdess and her shepherd still faced each other, still in love after all these years. Next to the lovers was a frilly tissue box case, that had come all the way from the Austrian Tyrol; a gift from an adventurous friend. It had never held so much as a single tissue, and now it never would. A stale bottle of Eau de Cologne sat in the centre of a white ring, the thin veneer of walnut eaten away to expose cheap, anonymous wood beneath.

The top drawer still held her mother's nylon slips, bras and knickers. Those below were crammed to the gunnels with hand- knitted sweaters and cardigans. Skirts and dresses filled one half of the wardrobe. The other half sat empty, except for her father's one good suit and four pairs of rather shiny trousers and their matching jackets, less worn, but equally tired. Six shirts, some underpants, some vests and a tasteless selection of ties lay on the shelves, leaving floor space for two pairs of over-polished shoes and a pair of carpet slippers. Stella raised a slipper to her cheek, checked herself just in time, and bundled it unceremoniously into the bin-liner.

The empty room was twice as big as hers and at the back of the house. No toxic yellow light got in here. Stella decided to paint it pale blue and to treat herself to new velvet curtains and a blue satin duvet with flowers and sequins on it. Her old room could be left empty or even let out if, God forbid, she lost her job at the chicken factory. An involuntary shudder rippled through her at the thought of a lodger. What was she thinking, letting her mind wander on that far into the unknown world of the future? "Stupid woman," she thought. "It will never come to that. Just count your bridges when you get to them. And don't mix your metaphors."

*

By the end of the week the house, apart from Stella's own room, was purged of all unwanted memories. The skip had gone and, miraculously, the rose had survived, in spite of being crushed during the duration. One of its three main stems was snapped off; the other two had veered to the right in an attempt to find some light leaving it lopsided and looking sad. Stella felt a pang of remorse at its suffering. Her mother had planted it, tended it with loving care and it had repaid her every year since, by providing a bit of summer colour. Its sorry state left the front patch looking even more untended than before. Using her kitchen scissors, Stella reshaped it, turned the earth around the roots and watered it thoroughly.

The interior of the house was indeed shaping up. Three large tins of magnolia emulsion were applied, on top of the worn out old wallpaper, and the floors were scrubbed bare ready to be varnished. Stella congratulated herself, estimating the total job would be completed by the end of the second week. The physical process of clearing out was proving to be extremely therapeutic. But the emotional rubbish that clung to in the farthest corners of her mind was harder to jettison than old shorts, books or cobwebs. Her next visit to the doctor was looming. She wondered how she would cope if the subject of the baby came up. This would be far more of a challenge than having to think about her parents and their deaths. She would have to revisit all the associated memories and sort them into digestible portions, then regurgitate them for that damn doctor's collection. How humiliating.

To her horror Stella realised she had left just two nights to apply herself to this daunting task. It would mean having to abandon her decorating and concentrate exclusively on getting her story straight. Then, like a sharp slap on the forehead, it dawned on her. 'The Inquisitor' could not possibly know about the baby. There was nothing in any medical records. The birth had never been registered and, as even she had not known about her pregnancy until the baby popped out, there had been no ante-natal procedure to record. Stella wondered why it was so hard to forget something you had never really seen, apart from a fleeting glimpse.

In the main, Stella tried not to think about her baby but, caught off guard, she would find herself speculating as to what had become of her. God willing it - she - had gone to a nice home, somewhere more exciting than number 9. Hopefully it - she - had not been dumped in an institution, to be abused and mistreated. Hiding beneath her own pink blanket of guilt, she would hear her mother say, "There's no use crying over spilled milk". So Stella didn't cry. Stella tried never to cry.

For some reason, possibly the preservation of Stella's sanity, her baby never appeared in her dreams. At least, not until the night before her appointment with Dr Devant - the first night she slept in the newly decorated room that had once been her parents' bedroom.

*

The curtains were open but the yellow toxic light from outside was noticeable by its absence. All the lights in the world had been switched off; even the wide crack beneath the bedroom door was dark. And yet the room was awash with an unnatural light. It appeared to come from the bottom drawer of the tallboy. Stella was back in her old room - the front room - the room she had occupied since childhood. Climbing out of bed, she moved over and pulled the heavy drawer out by its round wooden handles. It was stiff and she had to kneel down, pulling each side in turn, easing it out inch by painful inch. The light hit her full in the face with a megawatt blast, knocking her backwards, until she was sitting on her heels, with her hands shielding her eyes.

Parting her fingers she saw the baby: a papoose, swaddled tightly in an Indian blanket. It was wide awake; totally content in its cocoon. Black penetrating eyes stared back at her. There was no fear in its face. She knew it could see her, recognise her, but it did not smile or cry. It lay very still examining her with fixed, intelligent eyes. She picked it up and the light rose with it, lighting their way like a beacon, as they crossed the landing and climbed into a waiting boat. No one steered the little craft, it drifted into open water where it made steady for the distant shore. Stella waded ashore leaving the little boat and her baby to sail away. Alone, she stood staring at the vanishing light until the darkness consumed it, like the dot that disappears when the television is turned off. Stella smiled, climbed back into bed, and went to sleep - a sleep which carried her away to another time, another place.

*

Stella held the baby close to her chest. It was raining and it upset her to know that a knitted blanket was sadly inadequate to protect such a newly born creature. The baby was blue with cold. So was Stella. Her veins were filled with ice, emitting a chill which flowed from her into the baby. The umbilical cord had wrapped itself around Stella's throat, but not before it had encircled the tiny throat beneath hers. Stella choked as she felt the cord tighten. Grey blood hammered against her skull - cold and thin, bereft of oxygen.

A woman appeared from nowhere and proceeded to cut the cord with the proficiency of a trained nurse. Silently, she unwound it from the mother and the child, severing the only link between the two. Stella felt her blood run warm and red, and as she placed the bundle on the bench she turned to thank the lady. There was no one. And when she turned back again the pink bundle had also gone. It was as if it had never existed. It was just another dream.

*

Stella woke up in her parents' room feeling thoroughly depressed and confused. Her dream hovered about her, keeping a sinister hold on her conscious thoughts. Had she dreamed a memory? This was the day she was to see the doctor again and she had no story prepared; no alibi to offer in her defence. Did she need an alibi? What had happened to her baby? Had there actually been a birth? The logical thing to do was look in the bottom drawer, the only place to have survived the blitzing, but she was not brave enough. The tiger's words came, nagging away at her daring her to choose life with all its difficulties. It took three cups of tea before the words stopped playing on her mind.

CHAPTER 8

Climbing the stairs to the doctor's surgery felt particularly portentous on this first Friday in May, although Stella was not sure why. Each step needed to be counted with extra care. Of course, Stella knew there were exactly thirteen. As she climbed her resolve deepened. She had to gain the high ground - take control and maintain it. Each step assured her that the doctor had no facts. She could not possibly know anything, certainly not more than she, Stella, knew. All Stella had to do was to keep calm - to keep telling herself that there was no need to feel threatened or anxious. What was the worst that could happen? She might get embarrassed. She might lose her temper, or she might clam up and go into a catatonic trance. So what? Nothing could be that bad. "Remember the tiger", Stella thought: "Death is easy."

By the time she reached the thirteenth step, Stella found she was not alone. 'The Girl without the Kalashnikov' was occupying one of the three chairs. She was not seated so much as draped, and she gave no appearance of waiting. She was just there. Her presence was palpable. Stella's heart missed a beat. Observed at such close proximity, without the web of anger encircling them, the girl was considerably younger than Stella, probably just in her early twenties, certainly no more than twenty-five. Her tight jeans had faded patches down the fronts and she wore the same clumpy leather boots as before (which Stella later discovered were Doc Martin's). Layers of thick knitted scarf dangled down her flat front and wound around the long neck. A thick leather belt, with an over-sized silver buckle, secured the worn black leather coat which looked to Stella as though it had survived the last war. Stella was debating whether to ask the girl if she was armed, when 'Humpty Dumpty' appeared on the scene, handed the girl an appointment card, verbally confirmed the appointment time and showed her out. There was no nod of recognition - nothing to hint at their previous encounter. "But", Stella thought, "Why should she remember me?"

Meanwhile, Stella had committed what, in her book, was a cardinal sin. She had allowed herself to become distracted. Thoughts had entered her head that had no business being there. Before she knew it she found herself standing in the surgery, facing 'The Inquisitor' with an unprepared mind. As it happened, nothing could have prepared her for what came next.

"I've been giving your case a lot of thought, Stella. I don't think we have been pursuing the right tack. With your permission, I should like to try some hypno-therapy on you. I don't want you to get alarmed. It is quite a routine procedure which, I believe, will help us cut to the quick with far less pain than having to dredge up a lot of unnecessary and, if I might say, rather confused memories."

The doctor peered at Stella over her half moon glasses. Outwardly Stella showed no signs of her internal turmoil. She had been hypnotised in her dreams - several times - and it had never been that bad. At times, it had been quite exciting, but then she could always escape by waking up. This session was real. In her dreams the objective was usually erotic, or at least a means to exert dominance. This, she assumed, would be different. She presumed the purpose was to get her to talk. 'The Inquisitor' was still rabbiting on, but Stella had not been listening. She was trying to find a reply – while struggling to appear calm, rational and sane. At last she managed a question.

"Will I remember what I say or do?"

"Absolutely! We won't go too deep. Not the first time. Just deep enough to relax you. I shall be watching very carefully. You can come out of it at anytime. There really is nothing to worry about." The doctor was reassuring, almost too reassuring. Stella felt beaten.

*

One hour later, Stella was standing in the street, the hypnosis over. Another half an hour and she was home pressing her back to the door which separated her from the outside, waking world. Sleep was what she wanted now. She closed her eyes, only to be met with the image of the angry young woman. Her mind began to wonder off, confusing what had happened in the session with dreams she had dreamed and some she had yet to dream. Her mind travelled along lines she would never normally explore, and always the angry girl was there. She found herself speculating as to who the girl was, where she lived and how old she was? It occurred to Stella that she must be about the same age as her daughter - if she had a daughter. *"What if they have found her? What if they are planning to present me with my long lost child?"* Then her rational self would interrupt. *"This is becoming far too complicated and stupid to be real."* "Ha!" Stella let out a loud guffaw, "What onlys and what ifs! I knew it!" Her own voice caught her by surprise.

She was still standing in the hall, her back pressed hard against the door. Slowly, imperceptibly Stella continued to sink into that confused state between dreams and waking. The hypnosis had left her suspended somewhere she did not want to be. Her rational self told her that the session had gone well, but the back of her mind was shadowed by fear. How could she be sure she had not revealed things she did not want the doctor to know? Insecurities crowded around her bringing with them her childhood fears and doubts. She needed reassurance that her world was familiar and safe.

*

As a child Stella would let her finger trace the pattern of snowflakes on the frosted glass panel of the front door. The pattern came from just one little motif, repeated over and over and over, busily connecting up until the whole pane was covered in snow. She liked to count each flake in turn. When she reached three hundred, she'd give up and switch her attention to the swirls of banana leaves that made up the pattern on the hall carpet. Each leaf twisted, first to the left, then to the right, depending on which way she was facing. Starting with her back against the front door Stella's only concern was with leaves which turned left. She would count them, stepping on each one in turn. Four steps and she reached the stairs.

Young Stella had always liked to think of the carpet up the stairs as a banana tree, with only the left-hand leaves providing safe branches to stand on. The third step did not have a left-facing leaf. Stella would always avoid it, stepping over it onto the safety of the stair above. Half way up, she had to miss the seventh and eighth tread before she felt safe. As a small child this had meant a perilous climb, clinging on to the bannisters while she swung her body across the divide.

The banana carpet still dominated the hallway at number 9 and Stella still avoided the same three steps, although now it was easy. She had long since counted all the snowflakes on the window, but every now and then she would recount them just to check that the number hadn't changed. Now, as her finger traced the familiar pattern once more, she let her mind wonder free.

*

The great tree rose above her, towering up to the magnolia sky, its branches sweeping out before her, giant umbrellas masking their danger with twisted contorted lies. Stella had climbed this monster many times; it held few fears for her, yet she still respected its authority. It had led many, equally capable explorers to their deaths. They had not heeded the basic rules.

Far below lay the snowy window, snow thick enough to bury one for ever beneath its crystal flakes. From her exalted position – half way up the perilous Musa – Stella paused for breath. The next manoeuvre was the most difficult, requiring all her concentration and skill. The chasm spread before her, a wide yawning mouth. No one had survived a fall from this point. Stella checked her ropes, looked up at her destination and swung out over the gorge. For a moment her life was held by a single thread. Her breath was suspended, her thoughts were focussed. Then her feet reached safety. She had done it, she had reached the landing outside her bedroom.

At this point the landscape changed. This was the high country. From here on the carpet was plain, with nothing to guide her. Kneeling down Stella examined the floor for clues. There were always clues if you looked hard enough.

That was when she noticed the hoof prints: small unshod ponies, Lakota paint ponies; a good sign. The Sioux would not mislead her: she was 'Woman who Dreams'. They were her friends. The hoof prints led to a small gap just below the window, just big enough for her to squeeze through. Standing up, she found she was on a round veranda, surrounded by bannisters in the shape of wrought iron railings, just like those on the front at Bognor. These were painted black and white, she presumed to match the chequered floor tiles. Stella crossed the circle, stepping only on the black squares, until she reached a flight of steep steps, which led down to a long gangway. There were five hundred and fifteen steps. Stella hoped there was another way back, as the thought of climbing them was daunting. The railings continued on either side of the gangway which led to a tunnel.

The entrance was obscured by a large mahogany roll-top desk, where a man in a top hat sat writing in a great book. The man was dark skinned, inscrutable, with features that had dried and shrivelled with too much sun. His eyes were no more than pinpricks, yet they discharged shards of light, thin as lasers and penetrating as steel. Feathers hung from his hat and he wrote with a long feather quill, dipping it, without stopping to look, into an inkwell of heavy, frosted glass.

"Hello, Stella." He did not look up but continued to scratch at his book with his pen.

"Hello," said Stella. She took the ticket he offered her, thanked him politely and stepped into the tunnel. It was light inside. One side opened on the promenade, which was lit up by ornate lamp posts. The rain darkened the flagstones, and the lights drew squiggles on them.

Her mother stood at the end of the tunnel, holding a bundle of clothes in her arms. She appeared to be waiting for someone. Stella walked straight past her, neither woman stopping to speak. The bundle of clothes frowned at Stella as she passed. It was a baby.

The man with the feathers was signalling for her to get a move on, so Stella stepped out into the fresh air and walked on down the road. Soon she found herself in front of her own house and noticed that somewhere along the journey it had stopped raining. She was older now; she did not want to count the snowflakes. But, she did, just in case, although she knew perfectly well that there were five hundred and fifteen.

The man with the feathers was still writing, sitting at his desk next to the rose bush. He took the ticket Stella offered him and the door opened. In the hall, directly in front of her, was a set of scales. The ones her mother used when she baked cakes or made jam. Stella climbed into one of the bowls, her weight sending it crashing to the ground. The man placed the feathers from his hat - slowly, deliberately, one at a time - in the bowl alongside Stella. The bar lifted. It wavered. The man placed the last of the feathers on the scales. They balanced.

"Is that good?" Stella asked.

"Oh, yes, you are quite dead," the man replied. Then he continued writing in his great book.

*

Loud rumblings in her stomach told Stella she was hungry; she had not eaten since breakfast the previous morning. There was no cereal in the box and just one egg in the fridge. Carefully, she placed the egg in the pan of boiling water, remembering to turn the egg timer before going to check if there was any post. The mat was visible from the kitchen, but she went and checked the letter box, just in case. There was no post.

Stella's fingers rose up to touch the frosted glass. It was all she could do to stop herself from counting the individual flakes one more time. She did, however, trace the banana leaves to the bottom of the stairs. There were still four. Feeling suitably exonerated, Stella returned to her boiled egg, catching it just as the sand ran out. Such a satisfying occurrence deserved a reward; she placed an extra slice of bread in the toaster she prepared herself to recall yesterday's hypnotherapy session.

It had, as she had thought, been akin to dreaming and, once the business of 'going under' was over and done with, it had not been an unpleasant experience. However, the content, substance, memory or recollection - whatever one chose to call it - that it caused her to relate, had to be coming from somewhere, presumably her subconscious, which made it tantamount to dredging up the past. The worst aspect had been letting go: losing control. The one good thing was that, as she had hoped, it had been far easier than just trying to remember. Time had existed exactly as it did in dreamtime: following a form of logic of its own, obeying no external rules. It hurried over irrelevances, only lingering when necessary. The past came back in flashes; manageable bite-sized pieces. At no point had she felt threatened, although some of the memories were not how she thought she remembered them, which was odd.

It occurred to Stella that the truth, if such a thing existed, must lie somewhere between dreams and reality, between memory and fact. This premise began to fascinate her. Being hypnotised had cast a new slant on her past which, although she claimed a disinterest in the subject, began to appear as another country; one that might be an interesting place to visit.

In the light of this reflection Stella actually began to look forward to her next session, although she would never admit this - not in a million years - not even to herself.

*

The next few weeks bled into months which, in turn, became blurred inconsequential measurements of time. Stella's appointments came fast and furious. 'The Inquisitor' was hitting her hard with a relentless barrage of different techniques. Somehow Stella managed to get up each morning and function, albeit at a limited level. The doctor experimented with various pills, finally settling for some bright pink ones - Stella's least favourite colour - with an unpronounceable name, to be taken three times a day, with food. Stella's regular eating pattern was no longer consistent, but this was of little consequence, as she seldom took her medication. She now ate when she was hungry, which was seldom, and slept when she was tired, which was always.

Not going to work had sent Stella into the

timeless zone inhabited by many of the unemployed. Life spread out thinly like a mean covering of jam: flavourless and pointless, especially as the hypnosis was blocking her dreams. It was only because the sessions had become a habit that she continued to attend, always religiously on time. In rare moments of clarity, she could detect a little progress. At others she felt she was regressing. Always she felt that without her dreams it hardly mattered whether she made progress or not.

Such was Stella's state of limbo - she was neither happy, nor was she unhappy, neither was she a zombie. She was coping, whatever that meant. To her slowed down brain this was commendable. Her anger had abated and she showed no sign of aggressive or violent behaviour. Calm was the word she had used to describe her state of mind when the doctor asked her to define how she felt. Stella liked that word. To her, it implied that she was in control, unflustered. Stella was confident that the doctor was satisfied her treatment had 'worked'. She would be able to stop pretending to take the pills; she could return to work; back to normal and back to her dreams. In her own mind, she was cured.

*

Stella had completed counting the black squares in 'The Telegraph' crossword by the time the door to the surgery opened. But it was not the receptionist who emerged. It was the mysterious 'Girl without

Sweet Dreams

the Kalashnikov' who, despite the warmth of a bright May morning, remained cocooned in her scarf and cracked leather coat, covering her from neck to floor. She wore the same faded jeans and silver buckled belt, but with one noticeable difference. Her flamboyant, devil-may-care attitude had gone. In its place was the angry defiance of a cornered animal. 'The Inquisitor' had obviously put her through the mill. Stella felt a surge of compassion: a desire to wrap her arms around the girl, to hold her, to comfort her.

Where had this rush of empathy come from? She could remember feeling a need to take sides during her battle on the number 94, but that had been motivated by the prospective thrill of confrontation. This was different. A connection had been made between this young woman and herself; a bond which she hoped was mutual. Still pondering on this unfamiliar feeling, Stella watched the girl storm down the stairs. Reluctantly she turned, to trail, obediently, behind the doctor into the surgery. Later she too was descending the stairs down to the high street, furiously convinced that the last hour had been a complete waste of time.

*

The young woman was outside, leaning against the wall, smoking a cigarette. As Stella walked passed she stood upright, threw her dog-end on to the pavement, and ground it to a pulp with the toe of her boot. She reached out and touched Stella lightly on the arm.

"Hi." She said. "Fancy a coffee?"

Within minutes they were facing each other in the local 'Costa Coffee', each with a ridiculously large frothy coffee in front of them. Coffee which Stella had paid for. This was her first cappuccino, and she felt daringly modern as she stirred the creamy foam, watching it merge into the dark bitter coffee below. She sensed that this was also a rare experience for the young woman sitting opposite. Neither spoke for a while, they just blew on their coffees. Stella took a spoon full of foam to her mouth. She sneaked a glance at the younger woman to see if her undignified behaviour had been spotted. Their eyes met and they laughed, at first just their eyes, then their mouths broke into broad grins and they each let out a coffee-filled giggle. The ice was broken, they were free to talk.

They exchanged names: Stella and Martina: forty-one and twenty-five. Jobs: stock controller and unemployed. Status: both unmarried. Children: they both laughed. Formalities over with, they began to chat just for the sake of it. In all her forty years Stella had never chatted to anyone. After her session with the doctor, it was refreshing not to have to feel guarded about each and every word, not to feel that she was being monitored or recorded. Freedom to enjoy communicating with another person was relaxing. What's more it was easy, which astonished Stella. In fairness the younger woman did most of the talking with the older one listening enthralled to the story of the young tragic life. To Stella it sounded like the stuff of films.

Abandoned at birth, Martina had been brought up in a home. She related stories that made Stella's hair want to curl. Her short life had been hard, bereft of emotional warmth. But, as she explained:

"Listen, Stel, when life throws that much crap at you, you either build strong muscles to catch it and chuck it back, or you become a sodding victim for the rest of your miserable sodding life."

This young woman was obviously one of life's survivors. She talked of the bleakness of institutional life, the lack of guidance, the abuse both physical and mental, the pain of abandonment; the loneliness of the orphan. Stella soaked it up, her eyes and ears wide open, her heart exposed to feelings she had never felt possible.

The two women talked for over an hour, without any of those embarrassing silences that usually filled Stella's attempts at socialising. Far from being lost for words, their conversation flowed easily, fluently even. Stella felt relaxed; at one with this most unlikely partner. It hardly occurred to her that yet again she had said very little. Martina had taken the lead and dominated the conversation from the start. They had barely scratched the surface which left the future open to further exciting meetings. Stella felt sure they would meet again: this was no chance happening: no brief encounter.

They sat talking, or listening, until lunchtime, by which time Stella had developed an enormous admiration for this young fighter, who, with, or without a gun, had won a long, hard battle; one that Stella had never witnessed – except perhaps from the other side. Stella wanted to see more of Martina, to get to know her, maybe even become a friend. Guilt was a strong component of her mixed feelings and although not yet ready to admit it, Stella was salving her troubled conscience by 'adopting' this lost child.

They agreed to meet up again in two weeks, after their sessions with 'The Inquisitor'.

As she made her way down the high street, Stella felt uncommonly light. Her mood seemed to match that of the people around her. All at once the miserable high street was buzzing with happy people, dashing about, trying to cram umpteen tasks into their all too short lunch breaks. They wore bright clothes and exuded a contagious energy of purpose in their rushing. Why hadn't she noticed this before? She looked down the street, but there was no sign of her friend. 'Her friend'! That had a nice ring to it, Stella thought. She had never had a friend before, unless she counted 'The Slouch'. This was a special day. And it was only the beginning.

*

Stella was high. She did not realise quite how manic she had become. This was more than the distant end of the spectrum from depression. Around her was a fresh, exposed plain where the wild wind blew the prairie grasses: where life was uncomplicatedly raw. Only in her dreams had she felt such a level of awareness. Only in her dreams had life felt so tangible: so worth living. Dreamtime had been everything to her since she had been born. Now, for the first time she caught the glimmer of a chance that her life was about to change. Did Martina share that sense that life had taken a new direction today? A road that might, just might, lead to something one could call a life? Could it be possible that they were entering a space where reality was charged with an equally strong but opposing polar energy to dreams: one in which dreams would eventually take second place to life?

*

While her mind had been racing on, Stella's feet had led her to the High Street where they stopped at Mark's and Spencer's. A new line of jumpers had just arrived and, as she debated whether to branch out from navy, a voice behind her said:

"The pink would look lovely on you."

The voice came from a stranger, a woman of a similar age to Stella, with curly brown hair and a pleasant open approach. Taking the navy sweater from Stella's hands she exchanged it for a pink one which she held up against Stella's astonished face.

"There. See. That lifts your whole face. Don't go for navy – spoil yourself."

Stella looked at her reflection. The pink was flattering against her skin, but she would never wear it. She hated pink. It would be a total waste of money. She smiled at the face behind hers, but reached out to hang the rejected item back on the rail. When she looked up again, hers was the only face in the mirror. She turned to find the woman standing behind her, sifting through the other colours.

"Pity! You'll regret it." The woman smiled at Stella, her hand held out to introduce herself.

"Hi, I'm Anita. Nice to meet you..." She paused and Stella knew she should reply.

Panic gripped her. She grabbed the two nearest jumpers and headed for the pay desk. She did not look back, but she did not run away. She couldn't; her legs would never have carried her that quickly. She continued in a dignified and controlled manner. Pleased with herself, having almost spoken to a total stranger – again, Stella left the store and walked on, still in a controlled dignified manner, until she reached Living-stone Park.

The sun was shining. The usually dark, murky water had taken on a whole new aspect. It was alive with the reflected blue sky and the white of the scurrying clouds. Fluorescent ducks were diving, heads down, waggling comical, green bottoms in the air. Orange flippers splashed and kicked, flipping the birds over with total ease – nature's design perfectly fit for purpose. Specks of dazzling light bounced across the surface, settling on a swan who was building a nest on the central island; its mate assisted - offering twigs and moss from the bank.

There was a couple sitting on her seat. At first she was unsure: should she leave or hover until they left? Embarrassed that they might think her odd, she squeezed herself into the corner, still clutching her new purchases. The lovers looked at her, for what seemed an age, before they got up to wander off, arm in arm allowing Stella to slide to the centre of the bench. She did not know which sweaters she had bought, but she dare not look in case someone was watching. She hoped she had bought the bright blue, even the pink, not yet another navy one. Imagining herself dressed in pink, animated and bright, sitting opposite Martina in the coffee shop, chatting away so easily and naturally, filled her thoughts until it was time to catch the bus home. She had grown quite cold, but calm. Her panic had subsided. The incident in M&S had been dismissed as unfortunate, leaving her free to concentrate on the novel sensation that was growing and glowing inside her. Stella did not recognise it. It was what most people call 'love'.

CHAPTER 9

When Anita got home she unpacked her shopping. She had left M&S the first time without making any purchases. She had gone back there with the express hope of finding Stella, but with no success. To compensate, she treated herself to two sweaters, one pink, the other bright blue. Holding them against her, in front of the mirror, she knew she had made the right decision, unlike the sad lady she had seen there.

Anita had interpreted the episode very differently from Stella. Stella's panic; her jerky movements, rash decisions and irrational choices, had certainly not indicated a woman in control of herself. Rather she sensed someone in need: a person on the edge. As a psychic Anita was sensitive. The feelings of stranger's touched her, entered her space, transmitting their presence to her psyche. All the more so if she sensed they needed help. Stella was crying out for such help. Her aura was drained of colour, she was obviously ill. Her spirit was starved of love and care. These were signs Anita was expert at recognising. But more than this, Anita recognised that Stella was in danger in physical peril.

*

Anita had been psychic since childhood. Her mother had found it alarming that her little daughter would point to some stranger on a bus and declare, "That man's head hurts. I can feel it.

Mummy, it really hurts." Or she would rush up to someone in a shop, or in the street and pat them on the arm saying, "Don't worry, your dog will be better soon. Its tummy is sore, but it's going to get better." If the news was bad the child would cry, and her mother would be left not knowing what to say to the poor unsuspecting recipient of Anita's attention.

At first Anita had physically experienced the emotions and ailments of those around her. Later this had modified into a sense of awareness. Her ability to communicate her experiences became more subtle as her understanding of tact grew. This gift was both a blessing and a curse, as it often prompted her to get involved where she wasn't wanted.

At school she had been considered a soft touch – always sharing the contents of her lunch box without a second thought. Sweets seldom stayed in her possession. Likewise her pocket money was doled out to friends and foes alike. Not that she had any foes. Everyone liked Anita, especially her best friend, a chubby girl called Rita. Rita longed to be popular and thin, like her friend. But Rita was greedy. Rita's mother claimed the child suffered from a glandular disorder: the truth was that she was fed too many sweets. What teeth survived into Rita's adulthood, were very sweet ones indeed.

The two girls remained friends long after they left school. In time Rita married Doug and moved to Brighton. That same year Anita married Mick and started a family. The ties between the two friends weakened until all that remained of their often declared 'everlasting love' was an exchange of cards at Christmas – which always, for some long forgotten reason, had to include pictures of robins. This year no robin had flown from Brighton. Anita assumed the ties had finally broken.

What had started as childhood awareness developed into telepathic empathy which developed into full blown medium-ship. By the age of forty, Anita was well known on the rostrum of Spiritualist churches throughout the South East. By the time she crossed paths with Stella, she was seldom wrong in her diagnosis.

Her husband, Mick was used to Anita's predilection for 'lost causes' – his name for the poor souls who called out to his wife for help. This was a large and motely crew, as it included anyone who fell under her watchful eye and triggered her uncanny sixth sense. Stella had done exactly that. In that brief moment when their lives touched, it was apparent to Anita that this woman was in need. When she told Mick, he did what he always did: he advised her to say a prayer and offer it up to God who, as he so eloquently put it, "Has a lot more bloody time than you, and is far better equipped."

Although this was his stock reply, Anita knew that her husband was a caring man. Over the years of living with a psychic he had developed several coping strategies to keep his wife's 'gift' under a modicum of control, while protecting his own sanity. Left to her own devices, Anita's thoughts, her home and her heart would be full of the many waifs and strays – often totally undeserving – that she picked up in the course of her everyday life. Mick could not stem this flow of compassion, even if he had wanted to, but he felt it was his job to make sure his wife did not drown in it. So he installed himself as a human overflow, and since he was a plumber by trade, the system worked pretty well.

Their marriage was strong. Where many couples might have floundered, they thrived. He was her rock and she was his energy. It was a good combination, in the main. Just occasionally Anita got carried away. Mick had a strong foreboding that this small - seemingly chance encounter - was just such a tidal pull.

Its draw brought Anita back to M&S several times, in the hope of meeting her latest cause for concern. Her wardrobe increased, but she never bumped into Stella. In the end, she had to admit a temporary defeat and resign herself to wait patiently, confident that their paths would cross again in time. This was a given inevitability in Anita's book, and she was seldom wrong. She did as her husband advised: she offered it up in the firm belief that when the time was right she would be called.

*

When Stella had arrived back at number 9 it was nearly dark. She was cold from her overlong stay on the park bench, but still high from her meeting with Martina. The curtains twitched at number 7, and for once she could not resist waving back. The twitching stopped immediately and the net dropped back into place. Once inside Stella made a cup of tea, finished off the remains of yesterday's tinned beans and got undressed. She thought about the woman in M&S – Anita – and tried to imagine having the nerve to speak to someone one didn't know.

Yawning and sleepy, Stella climbed the stairs. Undressed and ready for bed Stella padded along to the bathroom. She removed a pill from its foil casing and flushed it down the loo, watching it swirl round and round, in ever decreasing circles, before disappearing down the bowl. She brushed her teeth vigorously using small, similarly circular movements. 'Old Faithful' smelled stale: its once fluffy fleece was tired and flat. Stella found herself wishing she had treated herself to one of those pale blue velour ones she had seen in M&S. She regretted rushing out before she had finished shopping. Her purchases still sat unopened in the sitting room. Her feet almost barely touched the stairs in her excited dash to retrieve them. Hoping to find the pretty pink sweater – although she really did not like pink – she examined her buys.

There was nothing pink, but the bright blue was different: it suited her well and you could never have too many navy jumpers for work. A slightly disappointed Stella climbed into her parents' double bed, pulled the new blue duvet over her head and, with a sigh of resignation, fell asleep.

Sweet Dreams

*

The gates swung open of their own volition carrying Stella in a sweeping arc. Her feet were firmly planted on the bottom rail of the left hand gate, her hands holding on to the tridents that ran along the top. She bent back letting her hair swing free. The touch of the wind on her scalp was potent with memories of prairies, ponies and warm red earth. On the tenth swing she jumped clear and watched the gates close behind her. Apart from a very slight kiss as they met, they made no sound. Not a squeak or a creak. They had been well oiled; someone took good care of these gates.

Dappled sunlight filtered through tall poplars which flanked the long straight road on either side. The rubber soles of her sandals scrunched on the sharp gravel. Her stride, repetitive like a train passing over sleepers, released that same hypnotic rhythm. "Scrunchity scrunch. Scrunchity scrunch." The poplars' shadows cut across the path from east to west, plunging her into shadow then light, shadow then light. It followed the rhythm of her feet. This was early spring and warmer than usual with hardly a cloud in the sky; a soft westerly breeze teased the tops of the trees and moderated the effect of the sun.

Suddenly compelled to run, Stella took off. She felt free, at one with her body, at one with her surroundings. Faster and faster, further and further her feet sped over the gravel. At last she stopped, turning around to see how much ground she had covered. The iron gates faced her, confronting her. They were shut and bolted. She was right back where she had started: back at the beginning.

Undeterred, she left the path and stepped onto the grass verge, pleasantly springy and soft. The grass had been freshly mown and the clippings still lay where they had fallen, giving off the scent of new-mown hay; deliciously sweet.

"Good enough to eat," the trees whispered.

Towering above her, they poked their heads out to where the sun shone uninterrupted; their faces turned to the warmth. Stella watched them greedily soaking in the energy. The trees were breathing. Burgeoning with life, new growth appearing as she watched - each intake of sunshine nourishing them. Stella turned her own face to the sky. Solar power surged into her, compelling her to run again.

Taking the centre of the road, she raced along, driven exclusively by this natural power source, with a vitality that charged through every cell in her body. Alive and vibrant, she felt ready to take on the world and win. Faster and faster her legs carried her, working as springs - coiling and releasing, propelling her on down the path. No one had ever run this fast before. No body had ever been this primed. The wind was behind her, pushing her faster then the light which flickered between the trees. She was a blur as she raced passed the cheering leaves. Once more she stopped and turned.

The gates were directly in front of her. Defiantly she turned again,

'So? What do I care? I am already inside. You

can't stop me now,' she called.

Her voice reached the tops of the trees. The leaves cheered louder as she ran on ever faster. Without a hint of breathlessness, she was invincible, magnificent. In no time she reached the crest of the hill. From here the road dipped down to where she knew the house was waiting. She knew she was dreaming, but dismissed such thoughts from her mind. This had to be real. To feel so alive, so powerful, so in control was awesome. She closed her eyes to fix the feeling in her memory.

Some flowers grew beside the path: daffodils, trumpeting heralds. She picked three. Immediately their yellow heads drooped down. They belonged in the ground. They would die now, unloved, with no one to watch or care. Stella felt ashamed. She looked at the pathetic limp daffs. They were already dead. "Death is easy", said a voice she thought she recognised. She began pushing them back, crushing their broken hollow stems against the unaccommodating earth.

"Don't worry. No use crying over spilled milk."

Stella's hands were sticky, white with milky liquid that ran down in between her fingers. Sap mingled with shame. She felt dirty, sullied by her own cruelty. Rubbing her hands against the grass only added a layer of mud to the remorse. Her sleeve proved useless too. In desperation, she began to lick the offending hands. The bitter taste filled her mouth. She shook her head violently, like a dog trying to dry itself. The trees did not approve. They began to laugh at her distress, their leaves no longer applauding.

"*Lighten up, Stella. It's just a few daffs. No big deal!*"

Her laces had come undone and she bent down to tie them – tightly, with a double bow - just the way her father had taught her. Once again she felt compelled to run. She ran in earnest; this time she was running away.

Her power had gone, this was hard work. Each stride hurt her legs. Her hamstrings pulled as tight as her laces. Her calves contorted with cramp. Her chest contracted. Her breathing grew laboured. Pain-filled, hard earned gasps. That awful rasping noise her father had made now rattled in her own throat. Her energy sapped away from her, like the milk from the daffodils, like the life from her father. Doubled-over with exhaustion, she braced her tired body, resting her hands on her knees. Her head hung down to let the cramp recede. Her breath came more easily. Slowly she unfurled her body, lifting her heavy head last, not opening her eyes until she was upright. She sucked in the still sweet air. The gates were directly ahead.

Undeterred she strode out swinging her arms as she marched along. A tune came whistling from her lips and her spirits began to revive. Her step became jaunty and the tune became a hymn - that one about a body mouldering in a grave: John Brown's body. What was it called? The Battle Hymn of the Republic – yes that was it. 'Glory, glory hallelujah, his soul is marching on.' She was singing now, out loud, uninhibited, the battle cry spurring her onward to glory. Invincible again.

Alive and important again. She did not need an offering of flowers to present when she arrived. She was the offering. Stella's soul was marching on.

At last she reached the house. It stood before her, square and solid. Two ornate urns on either side of the porch had been recently planted with tall purple hyacinth. Trailing yellow ivy wrapped itself around their wide square bases. The gravel here was rounder, smaller shingle which, when she walked on it, made a sound like compacted snow - creaking as it compressed tighter and tighter. It was freshly raked. There were no signs of traffic; the only footprints were her own.

The front door sat in the centre of a symmetrical facade. Long casement windows, painted in bright white, contrasted with the dark maroon door. The door was large, divided into four long panels. It made you want to approach it, to touch it, especially as the brass had been polished to shine golden like the daffodils. An oak-leaf knocker sat in the middle, with a figure 1 positioned above it, obeying the perfect symmetry of the place.

Anxious to remove any trace of the dusty road, Stella brushed herself down. She rubbed her feet against the back of her trousers. Taking a deep breath she climbed the ten steps that led to the door, avoiding the crack on the fourth. She took a second deep breath, and patted her hair. Her hand shook as she took hold of the golden oak leaf. Poised, with the knocker suspended in her hand, she knew that she was dreaming. That was a good thing. If she knocked she might wake up. That was a bad thing. What if she did nothing? Would that be good or bad? Surely someone would come along in time? The sun had disappeared from sight and the air had grown cold rather than chilly. Stella couldn't wait any longer. She knocked loudly, three times.

*

It was 4.44am when she woke up.

CHAPTER 10

Stella's next session with 'The Inquisitor' was ringed on her wall calendar, once in black and again in red. The black circle was for her appointment with the psychiatrist. The red was to remind her of her date with Martina. Not that she needed reminding. Stella felt confident that 'The Inquisitor' would be pleased with her patient's progress, pleased enough to give her a bill of clean health and permission to return to work. Stella traced the red ring with her finger, picked up her cup of tea and went to bed, turning the light off as she left the kitchen.

The last two weeks had seemed interminable. Versions of her meeting with Martina had been rehearsed over and over in her head. They had laughed and giggled and shared stories as all girl friends do. They had confided their innermost secrets, cried in turn, cried together. They had even sat in silence. But one thing they had not done: they had not talked about their dreams. Each time Stella had imagined broaching the subject her controlling mind had taken over, reminding her with relentless vigilance that divulging secrets was dangerous. The meeting was tomorrow, so close. Stella reviewed the situation again. She resolved that should the moment feel right she would take a chance and tell Martina about her dreams in general – about her avenue in particular.

*

Day dawned and Stella woke up to find sunlight streaming through her window making her want to rise and shine. From the moment she opened her eyes things went her way, starting with the joy of opening a new tube of toothpaste. The rose bush had two perfect blooms and a kind old gentleman held the door of the doctor's surgery open for her. A pleasant feeling of well-being embraced her like a comfort blanket. For the first time since her dismissal from work she realised just how unwell she had been. This acceptance, she recognised, was the turning point. From now on she could begin to mend.

The prospect of meeting Martina for coffee was, of course, the main source of Stella's euphoria; the thrill of talking about her dreams adding an extra fillip. As a result of her altered state, her session with the doctor went well – not quite granting her the bill of clean health that she had hoped for, but she was told she was doing very well. Stella left the surgery with a broad smile on her face, which was still there when she entered the café.

There was no sign of Martina. Undeterred, Stella bought two cappuccinos, with extra sprinklings of chocolate. Her concentration, on transferring the steaming, brim-filled cups from the tray to the table, was broken when a tearful Martina landed heavily on the seat in front, jogging the table and spilling a considerable amount of coffee into one of the saucers. Tut-

tutting and fussing over the spillage, Stella found it hard to listen to her distraught companion; her mind was on the coffee. Once satisfied that all was clean and tidy, Stella smiled at Martina, willing and able, finally, to give her her full attention.

Martina's displeasure at being ignored was obvious by her expression. But, once Stella had apologised and stopped faffing, the pout vanished and the tears began anew. Speaking through her sobs, Martina began to relay the recent exchange that had taken place between the doctor and herself. Apparently it had gone very badly. Visibly agitated, she blurted out her sorry tale, between snuffles and sniffs. Inappropriately cast as agony aunt, Stella felt inadequate and uncomfortable. She opted to listen in silence and only offer a response if she deemed it really necessary. Quietly, if obsessively, stirring a fast cooling coffee, Stella listened to Martina who continued to babble and blub, venting her fury out on the innocent paper napkins which she compulsively wrenched from a rapidly emptying dispenser. By the end of the story, both coffees were stone cold and the table was knee-deep in shredded paper, Stella's head was spinning from the amount of conflicting information Martina had poured out. Her story lay in shreds, along with the napkins.

As Stella collected the paper, she tried to make sense of the outpouring, feeding it back to Martina for clarification. Eventually it appeared that the doctor had dismissed Martina, rather bluntly and unkindly, telling her to 'keep taking the pills' and 'get on with her life'. Stella was not sure that a doctor would say something quite a blunt as that, but something had happened to upset Martina; her distress was very real. It turned out that she had also just been told that she was not entitled to Jobseeker's Allowance and, as if that was not enough, her landlord had threatened to kick her out that very morning.

Never before had Stella bothered herself with other people's problems, not in real time. The dilemmas they got themselves into always seemed to be trivial - unnecessary and mind-blowingly boring. But today, she found herself being sucked in, fascinated by both the singer and the song. Although she did not feel as emotionally connected as she thought she should, she wanted to help. Some unseen magnet was drawing her towards this girl.

Stella listened, enrapt, for an hour or so, until the café manager asked them to leave. He needed the table. It was, by now, lunch time.

The two women decamped to the park where they found Stella's bench occupied by the young lovers. Martina let them know, in no uncertain terms, that they were not wanted and they scuttled off, taking comfort in each other's arms, whilst Martina continued hurling profanities at them. Stella, feeling a little shocked, but reassuringly protected, bought some ice-creams and Martina began, once again, to chatter about her problems. She had a lot of problems. There was no chance for Stella to mention her dreaming which, she concluded, was for the best, it was after all still early days. When it got too cold to sit by the lake,

Stella suggested that they go back to number 9 for a cup of tea.

Martina was still there at ten, having inspected the spare room - Stella's old room, and pronounced it perfect. Somehow they had agreed that she should move in on the Friday. Still digesting this fact, unsure if it had been her idea or not, Stella heard Martina announce she was going to have a bath. Apparently her previous landlord had always kept the hot water thermostat pathetically low; a hot soak before she left would be great. She said she knew Stella wouldn't mind, leaving Stella wondering whether she did or not. It seemed churlish to refuse, although the thought of a stranger – even Martina – using her bath was unnerving. By the time she had made her mind up, Martina was soaking in Stella's bath salts, lathering her hair with Stella's shampoo and listening to Stella's transistor, retuned to a loud, heavy rock station. Stella retreated downstairs where the noise was less ear-shattering, but still horribly present.

When Martina finally left number 9 it was a few minutes to midnight. She left a dirty ring around the bath, three soaking wet towels on an equally wet floor and an empty hot water tank. Six used mugs lay in the kitchen sink and every cushion in the place was crumpled and creased. Stella was left in a state of shock. As she tidied up she realised that some serious house-rules were needed if this co-habiting arrangement was going to work. Stella hated the word 'if' - it left everything so unfinished, so up in the air. She needed to take stock. More than that, she needed to regain control.

It had all happened so quickly. There was no doubt that the rent would be useful – but she could not recall if they had got round to discussing rent. It was also true that the room was going begging. Besides, Stella told herself, she had been entertaining the idea of finding a lodger. Now one had found her, which saved her the bother of advertising. She wrestled these points until the early hours of the morning, finally reaching the conclusion that to have a lodger would be no bad thing - probably. She had convinced herself that she was relaxed with the way things were going, and resigned to the fact that, in just two days time, she would no longer be living alone. Meanwhile she was exhausted: she needed sleep. Had Stella been familiar with the term, she would have realised that she had been bounced into the situation.

After an hour of tossing and turning, Stella stomped back downstairs and put the kettle on hoping a cup of tea would do the trick. Never before had she been unable to get to sleep, quite the opposite in fact. The last sixty minutes had crawled by – three thousand six hundred creeping seconds. Eventually she admitted that she was scared: fear was keeping her awake. Taking on a lodger was a big thing. She liked Martina, but she hardly knew her. What if they did not get on? The loudness of last night's music had come as a surprise to Stella. Supposing Martina filled the house with that noise all day and night! Stella had no experience of evicting a lodger - how did one perform such a difficult act without being rude or causing offence?

The kitchen matched her mood. A pale grey light shone on the grey steel of the sink. Cold shadows, far larger than the objects that cast them, gathered around her. Without finishing her tea, Stella placed her mug on the draining board and watched its shadow reach across the draining-board, up the wall and over the ceiling, her own vast shadow eclipsing all the others. She drew 'Old Faithful's' belt tight, crossed the hall - counting the leaves on the carpet for comfort. Then, as quickly as she could, she climbed up to the room she still called her parents' room.

Sleep still wouldn't come. Un-named doubts and fears that only come at night hit Stella, like drips from a faulty tap. Her private world was being flooded, making her more vulnerable than ever before. How would she cope without her sanctuary? What if her innermost secrets were discovered? With horror she realised that, in the course of her mammoth clear-out, she had neglected to tackle her old room – Martina's room. There were things stored in boxes and drawers, stashed away in the unused fireplace, beneath the floorboards - it would take hours to sort through them. Panic made her short journey across the landing seem like a voyage of epic proportion.

It actually took less than ten minutes to remove the boxes and empty the bottom drawer. The treasures in the chimney and beneath the floor did not exist: they must have been figments of her dreams, but she was glad she had checked. Careful not to touch anything, her hands made sooty from searching in the fireplace, Stella made her way to the bathroom. There was only cold water which could not touch the black grease, merely transferring it to the taps, the soap and the sides of the sink. She thought again of Martina and shuddered, convinced it was a natural reaction to the coldness of the water. As she made her way back downstairs to the kitchen, her hands held like a surgeon about to operate, she tried to focus her mind on present needs and not dwell on the future.

A few kettles of hot water, several sprays of Dettol and copious squirts of Fairy later, the greasy soot was gone. Armed with a pair of heavy duty rubber gloves, Stella returned to her old room. Her 'secrets' needed to be confined to a black bin bag. What did she need with the order of service for two funerals, a certificate to say she could swim twenty metres and a hair-slide in the shape of a Highland Terrier? With a sense of profound relief Stella secured the top of the bag with some wire ties, carried it downstairs, through the front door and dumped it in the wheelie bin that stood by the gate. Then with a sudden change of heart, she opened the bin, removed the bag and untied the wire tie. Retrieving the slide, she kissed it and slipped it into her dressing gown pocket. Then she retied the bag and replaced it in the wheelie bin. She peeled off the gloves and threw them in too, closing the bin with her elbow. As the lid crashed into place Stella brushed her hands dramatically, proud of herself for having been so practical. She poked her tongue out at number 7 and returned to the task of sorting out her bottom drawer.

The mahogany drawer weighed a ton. This combined with its bulk, made it awkward to manoeuvre. Inch by inch Stella coaxed it until it landed heavily on the floor, with her sitting in front of it. As she carried the drawer into her parents' room, she made a mental note to refer to this as her room from now on. The drawer slid very neatly and conveniently under the double bed; the hiding place might have been made for it. Martina would adjust to not having a complete tall boy. She might not even notice the drawer was missing and, anyway, the gap it left was ideal for shoes or books. Satisfied with her night's work Stella climbed back into 'her' bed and fell asleep.

*

It was dark in the forest, an unnatural sort of dark, the sort of dark that made it impossible to know if it was night or day, ground or sky, tree or space. Stella was familiar with the smells that surrounded her: pine needles, wet earth and wood bark. Anyway her guide was by her side. The old man bent down and placed his ear to the ground, he was listening to the sounds beneath the earth. As he bent, the beads which hung from his wrinkled neck dropped forward, reaching the earth long before his tired old bones bent his body to join them. The earth was talking to him: something was approaching - something slow, something deliberate, something large. Stella kept very still just as the old man had taught her. She felt his smile in the darkness, marking his approval.

Stella had loved Runs-With-The-Buffalo since before she had been born. He was the one that had given her the paint pony, Arrow Foot. And he was the one who had taught her to ride bareback. He showed her how to feel the movement of the horse, to understand how the pony could feel her too, so that they could work together, not as a team, but as one.

The glow of distant fire penetrated the darkness. Runs-With-The-Buffalo was signalling, patting the air with his hand; telling her to stay still. In his other hand he held his knife, high above his head as if hunting bear. Her heart pounding with fear, she waited; body frozen, ears straining, nostrils twitching to catch the acrid breath of a grizzly. Her muscles tensed ready to react when it burst out from the undergrowth. The only sound came from deep inside her own chest, like drums around a fire at night.

He appeared from nowhere, his head surrounded by a halo of fire, illuminating the clearing where the two silent figures stood: 'Tyger, Tyger burning bright in the forests of the night.' The great cat lifted his head and his eyes shot deep into Stella's soul. The fire of his aura blazed, the great flames rising high into the night sky, yet nothing was singed, nothing burned: this fire was sacred. Stella remembered the story of the burning bush and, believing the place to be holy, removed her shoes. Runs-With-The-Buffalo was barefoot beside her.

Stella did not recognise the language that the

tiger spoke. He talked for a long, long time. His breath came out in tongues of flame and light. His eyes burned and every stripe of his fearful symmetry bore witness to his immortality. When he finished, he smiled at Stella. Then he was gone. There were no foot prints, no scorch marks, nothing to prove that he had been there, except that the once dark forest was bathed in moonlight, and the heavens were stuffed full of stars - so low one could reach up and grab them.

Runs-With-The-Buffalo began to sing: a slow rhythmic chant that started somewhere deep in his chest yet seemed to emanate from the top of his wise, grey head. As he sang he swayed, listening to a relentless drum beat he alone could hear. Slowly he raised his foot, replacing it as he raised the other. He continued to transfer his weight from foot to foot, slowly with great control: his voice, his body and his spirit in unison. The drum beat quickened: his feet obeyed. Stella saw his great spirit shimmering around his earthly body, a vivid purple light - as much a part of him as his wrinkled old skin. This was the first time in all the years she had known him that she knew him to be a holy man: a man who knew death, a man who communicated with the spirits, was intimate with them. The spirits were as real to him as Stella's dreams were to her.

Stella looked down at her own body. It too was bathed in coloured light, a subtle shade of Magnolia. Effortlessly her feet began to move, keeping perfect time with the stomping feet of Runs-With-The-Buffalo. She too was dancing the

Ghost Dance. The steady repetitive motion was trance inducing. Stella felt powerful. She felt imbued with wisdom: she now understood everything that the tiger had said. This was their gift to her. The old man and the tiger had given her the knowledge of a world beyond life, beyond death, and far beyond dreams. They had taught her how to love and how to trust.

Before telling herself to wake up, she vowed to remember both the feeling and her new name – 'Woman-who-dreams.'

*

Martina arrived at ten the next morning, along with all her worldly goods stuffed into three large black sacks and a couple of tatty Tesco bags. None of them contained any household things, any appliances, or indeed any groceries, which reminded Stella that they had not discussed food or the use of amenities. They had not agreed a workable rota for the kitchen or the bathroom, nor had they discussed a reasonable rent – any rent. Stella had no recollection of having discussed anything to do with money, or any of the practicalities which came with sharing a house. What she found even more alarming was the fact that this was Thursday not Friday. Moving day had been the one, the only, thing they had actually agreed on.

Full of apologies for arriving early, Martina explained, rather too graphically for Stella's taste, that her landlord had demanded rent in kind, leaving her no option but to leave there and then. She dumped her bags in the hall and aimed her coat at the rack on the wall. There was a slight creak as the screws on one side sprung from the wall, followed by a small plaster avalanche which landed on the heavily patterned carpet. Martina shrugged, stepped over her coat and pushed passed Stella into the kitchen.

"I'm dying for a cuppa."

Stella fetched a dustpan and brush and swept up the debris. She hung the heavy coat on the bannister and made a vain attempt to push the rack back into place. Martina was, meanwhile, busily opening the kitchen cupboards. Finally she found two mugs and placed them on the draining board. She filled the kettle to the top, without shaking it first to ascertain if it already contained enough water for two cups. She then moved on to raid the fridge, reaching round Stella who was emptying the dustpan into the pedal-bin. Before Stella could object, a new carton of milk was opened and far too much poured into each mug. After a quick raid, Martina had found the tea caddy and dumped a teabag in each mug, with the milk. The over-filled kettle spluttered, predictably, over the worksurface, before being poured on top of the drowned tea bags. Martina handed Stella a mug containing a pale ecru liquid, with a brown floating island bobbing in the centre. Stella watched as Martina heaped three hefty spoons of sugar into her tea. The wet spoon was then thrust back into the sugar, wetting it, caking the spoon and sending a hailstorm of partially dissolved white crystals rattling across the draining board and the floor. All the cupboard doors were, like Stella's eyes, wide open.

"What's up? Oh, don't worry. I always make it like that. It goes brown eventually. Honestly. It like, tastes just the same. Let's go through shall we? I've had a fucking awful day."

*

Stella spent a frustrating couple of hours trying to lay down a few rules. She explained that taking a lodger was a big move for her. Martina apologised. Stella continued, saying that they would both have to learn to compromise: she was willing to make changes if Martina did the same. She pointed out that swearing was not negotiable and Martina agreed – apologising yet again. She had got quite emotional, she even shed a few tears, which caused Stella to tread softly. This girl was obviously very vulnerable. Stella smiled and Martina smiled back. By the time they carted all her worldly goods up to Stella's old room, the two women had reached an amicable arrangement.

Stella was pleased with her first attempt at diplomacy. She congratulated herself on tackling a tricky situation with tact and authority. However her mention of a rent book had not been so well received. Martina persuaded Stella to play everything very casually to start with. After all, as Martina pointed out, this was a big step for both of them. Stella might decide that taking in a lodger was not really her thing. No trouble, Stella just had to say the word and Martina would simply move out – with no harm done and no ill feelings. Besides, as Martina explained, why get the taxman involved? So any legal contracts were put on hold for the time being. It suited Stella to keep things simple and, as long as they both felt the same, she could see no harm in it – though, of course when Martina made another cup of tea she would teach her how to do it the proper way.

Martina proved the perfect pupil. In the space of a week she was making tea just the way her landlady liked it, in a pot. She cleaned the bath, plumped the cushions, helped with the washing up and took the bed linen to the launderette. She learned how to hoover and dust, and even tidied up the front garden. The rose bush was pruned, properly, and the small patch of dirt was covered with bright fresh shingle, which reminded Stella of her 'avenue'. Although she said nothing, she wondered when the time would be right to tell her friend about her nightly adventures.

The only thing Martina did not seem to grasp was the fact that all this domesticity cost money. So far there had been no offer of rent and no contribution towards the housekeeping. Stella broached the subject a few times, but Martina would duck and dive round the issue with amazing dexterity, always coming up with a plausible reason to delay matters. It crossed Stella's mind that she was being manipulated, but such a notion was accompanied with hideous feelings of guilt. So she rebuked herself for being suspicious and uncharitable. Besides, Martina always managed to win her round. She was an engaging girl. Her innocence appealed to Stella, who was delighted to have found a friend. The house was alive with an unpredictability that excited her. And so she was prepared, willing to overlook any misgivings she might have, in exchange for a new life-style.

CHAPTER 11

A month later Stella was signed off from the doctor's and told that she could go back to work. She had not mentioned her developing relationship with Martina, deeming it to be none of the doctor's business. The prospect of being employed again did not please Stella as much as she thought it would; she had got used to her freedom. On the other hand it would be good to be independent again: sick pay did not sit well on her proud shoulders. It occurred to her that she could find a job for Martina, but when she suggested this it went down like the proverbial lead balloon.

"It's a great idea, but like, I couldn't touch birds – let alone dead ones. The thought makes me feel all peculiar." Martina shuddered and pulled a face that spoke volumes. "Given the choice I'd be vegetarian like – I could easily live without ever touching another bit of dead meat. I love burgers – but that's not real meat, is it? I've never said anything 'cos I don't want you to think I'm faddy – or picky like. So thanks and all that, but I couldn't work there - not if you paid me."

Realising the stupidity of her remark Martina began to laugh – at first a giggly, girly laugh which deepened until it rocked her whole body coming from somewhere in her belly. She was literally doubled over. At first Stella watched passively, she too then started to giggle. Soon they were rolling together on the sofa in fits of hysterical laughter, springs pinging in their ears, tears streaming from their eyes. It took the crash of the table lamp, its china base smashing against the coffee table, to bring Stella to her senses. About to dash off for the dustpan and brush she was stopped by Martina grabbing her arm.

"I've got a great idea, Stel. You go to work - I'll look after the house – play the little housewife – like do all the chores, the shopping – I'll even do the cooking. We'll make a great team."

Before Stella had time to consider the actual implications of Martina's proposal, she had agreed to give it a go.

For the next few weeks, number 9 ran like clockwork. Stella went out every morning and returned to find the house clean and tidy with something resembling dinner on the table. She gave Martina enough money to cover the cost of food and laundry and continued to pay the rest of the bills as usual. Martina did not share quite the same high standards as Stella, but she kept the house looking good. She was discovering that an immaculate house will keep clean for a considerable time with just the modicum of attention. Of course, she realised that at some point it would need a thorough spring clean, but not yet. During the day Martina had the place to herself and, apart from an hour or so while they ate their evening meal, she was free to do her own thing. Stella went to bed earlier than anyone else Martina had ever met, which suited her just fine.

As far as Stella was concerned life had reverted back to the way it had been before her mother died, with one noticeable difference: Martina loved to chat. She couldn't help herself. She was one of life's chatterboxes. It came as a surprise to Stella that this inane noise was a welcome addition to the house. She began to look forward to their evening meal. For the first time in her life she too wanted to talk; wanted to share her thoughts, thoughts in which her young friend seemed genuinely interested. Had the time come to broach the subject of dreams, she wondered - just a taster at first - enough to test the water. But, for some unidentifiable reason, the time was never quite right; she was tired after work or Martina was always catching up with some soap or reality show. After giving the matter a great deal of thought, Stella concluded that the weekends offered the best opportunities. She began to steel herself, preparing to approach the subject.

Both women slept a great deal at weekends. Martina would slump in front of the television and Stella would take to her bed, wrapped in her blue duvet and the comfort of her dreams. On Saturdays and Sundays meal times were very regular, but always casual. Stella preferred to take a tray to her room, while Martina remained fixated on the TV. So Martina was totally taken aback when, that Saturday afternoon, Stella appeared in the front room suggesting that they turn the television off and have a chat.

She asked Martina if she was sleeping well, telling her, for the umpteenth time, how for years the front room had been her room, and that she had always slept very well. Martina said nothing to discourage her, so she rambled on, explaining how often she dreamed. Again, receiving no rebuff, Stella swallowed hard and asked Martina if she ever dreamed. Martina shrugged dismissively, saying that she'd never once had a dream, or if she had then she couldn't remember it. There was no excitement in her voice, no recognition of the value of dreams. This wasn't the hoped for answer, but Stella took some comfort as the subject had not been dismissed out of hand.

Throwing caution to the wind Stella proceeded to tell her friend how important dreams were to her, how widescreen Technicolor they were, and how she could probably remember every single one she had ever dreamed since she was a child. Having revealed this much, Stella was just at the point of describing a specific dream when Martina aimed the remote at the TV and fired. Further conversation was impossible and Stella retreated filled with bitter disappointment.

*

Later Stella was woken by a very chatty, smiley Martina bearing a nicely made mug of tea and a handful of biscuits.

"Sorry about earlier. That was rude, but I was feeling bloody awful – you know what it's like when you want to scream at everyone? Well, like that – only more so! Anyway, like you got it. Sorry. Am I forgiven? Listen – what you were saying – about dreams and all that – you see I was listening – well I am interested. It so happens I've got this friend…"

Stella hardly heard the rest of the girl's chatter. Martina was interested in her dreams. There was nothing she had wanted to hear so much as that declaration. The door was open. Together they could enter the magical world that up 'til now she had never shared with anyone. Now she had a potential travelling companion. Her life was suddenly filled with promise.

"Hey, I'm talking to you. Do you want to hear about my mate or not?"

Stella apologised and Martina continued to tell her about 'this friend'.

"Look they're not a fortune teller – nothing like that. But they'll tell you exactly what your dreams mean. What do they call it? Analyse - that's it – they'll analyse your dreams. It could be a bit of fun. What d'you think? I'll text them. I'll come too. It'll be a right laugh."

Martina was chattering so quickly that Stella had a job keeping track of what she was saying. It seemed that this 'someone' could interpret dreams, explain why the dreamer conjured up certain images and themes, they could even surmise on their significance. Martina was sure she could get Stella a special deal – mate's rates she called it. Did that mean they were professional? Stella wondered if this was the right approach. Was this the sort of response she had wanted from Martina? It seemed far too premature to involve a third party - a stranger at that.

"…and it'll be so cool to like find out if your dreams mean something important."

The young girl was so enthusiastic. It had never even occurred to Stella that her dreams might mean something in a universal sort of way. To her they had always been self explanatory, which was sufficient for her. Each one told a story, took her on an adventure and stood on its own. Even if she dreamed sequels and prequels, they made sense in their own right. She could see that dreams might be reflections of real life, the mind's way of solving problems or looking at situations from a different perspective. It intrigued her to think that they could be messages, possible glimpses into the future. Of course her dreams were significant, she knew that. The idea of analysing them excited her. It scared her too. Martina was a natural saleswoman and was using all her powers of persuasion. She made it sound so intriguing that in the end Stella agreed to visit 'this friend', telling herself it was just out of interest – just as a bit of fun – just to please Martina.

*

That night Stella dreamed of her avenue. On waking, at precisely 4.44 she wondered how many times she had dreamed of it. She wished she had kept count; the number might be significant. These dreams were a part of her. Although each one was unique, they had a collective identity, an intrinsic similarity. It was always the same avenue, the same gates with the same poplar trees. Yet its atmosphere, degree of dilapidation or level of maintenance varied. The seasons altered, the weather changed accordingly. Stella's own mood and physical standing were equally variable: always refreshingly unpredictable. There was always some seemingly insignificant happening along the way. But, in the end, it was a journey, along the same path, leading to the same house. The house was paramount, always there, always waiting for her. That was beyond doubt. What's more it was always number one and she always knocked three times.

Oddly enough the dream affected her differently each time she dreamt it. Sometimes she woke up in a state of heightened excitement. At others she would be extremely anxious - at times even depressed. Another night would find her questioning and fearful, while yet another would leave her oozing with confidence, bursting with knowledge and wisdom. The one constant factor had been her knowledge that she belonged: she was a part of the avenue. Lately, however, it had been taking her much longer to reach the house. The journey had become hazardous. The goal was moving farther away, farther beyond her reach - fuelling her desire to have someone answer the door.

Portentous dread, fears that she would wake up abandoned or excluded now preceded each visit to the avenue. It was akin to falling out of love, breaking up with a friend, losing some essential ingredient to life. Emotions bled out of her whist she dreamed, leaving an anaemic vacuum waiting to be filled with overwhelming loss. For years she had racked her brain searching for the link that would connect her dream to life. She had searched her other dreams for a thread that might connect them to the avenue. She could not recall any films that might have triggered it. She could not remember any pictures in her childhood books that might haunt her subconscious. The only conclusion she could draw that made any sense was that there was no link. The avenue existed in its own time and space and she just belonged in it – full stop.

This explanation was no longer adequate. Why did she always wake up at precisely 4.44? And why did no one answer the door. She had lived with these perplexing questions for years, content to enjoy the dream for what it was; assured that in time an explanation would be revealed. But that was before her dream changed. What had been an intriguing, stimulating pleasure had become a source of anxiety and fears. Stella could no longer wait for the answers. Maybe this friend of Martina's could provide them.

*

Stella decided to take Martina up on her offer. They set out late on Sunday morning. Stella had wanted to go alone, but Martina insisted that she 'troll' along too, explaining that it was a difficult place to find and she could not remember the exact address.

They took the bus as far as the Livingstone Estate. It was high summer and the thin grass between the tower blocks was the colour of straw.

The vast estate looked equally dead. Martina marched on ahead - her Doc Martin's ringing hollow on the sun baked concrete paths that crisscrossed the yellow grass. Stella was just thinking that 'Estate' was an odd word to describe such a God-forsaken place, conjuring as it did for her wide expanses of green, dotted with lakes, spouting fountains, water-lilies and swans. There was nothing green in sight, except for the clumps of lager cans that seemed to thrive in the desert conditions. When Martina's purposeful stride came to an abrupt halt, Stella stopped too. Together they stared up at a faceless block of concrete, silhouetted against an unnaturally blue sky.

The lift did not work and the stairwell stank of pee. The stairs were daunting. Each flight had fifteen steps and it took three flights to reach the next level. The heat, already intense, increased with the altitude. There was nowhere for air to enter or leave, the stairwell trapped everything that entered it. Every dinner that had been cooked that week, every beat of every tune on every CD that had been played, every episode of every soap opera, every child's screech or cry – it was all there, stained into the concrete with the graffiti. They reached the third floor and Stella doubled over to catch her breath. When she looked up, one of the doors on the narrow walkway that stretched far to their left, was open.

Stella was expecting to meet a woman, probably of a similar age to Martina. Nothing prepared her for the rather fit young man in tight black jeans and matching shirt who stepped out to greet them. He spoke with a London accent, sounding well educated, certainly polite. He welcomed them, almost formally, into his flat. Stella said hello and held out her hand. He had the manners to take it – although it was clearly not the customary form of greeting on this estate.

Everything in the flat was black: the walls, the ceilings, the chairs, even the cushions. They were all covered in either black paint or even blacker cloth. The wealth of textures and shades was quite staggering and strangely soothing. The man, who was also black, introduced himself as Col. He pointed to the sofa. He suggested they had a cup of tea, which he served very sweet, without milk, in black mugs. Stella found it remarkably refreshing on such a hot day. This was a far cry from her magnolia world.

They spent a few moments in rather one-sided small talk. Stella guessed it was meant to put her at her ease, but she was not ready to lower her guard. Col switched key, his voice dropped and he spoke expressly to her. His voice was full of considered gravitas and dramatic pauses.

"Okay, Stella I want you to relax. Martina told me about you on the phone, okay?... I know about dreams, okay? ... I hear you keep having the same one, over and over... Not nice. Okay, maybe I can help you find out why it won't go away? Don't worry, that's fine. Tell me about it and I'll see if I can tell you what it means. Okay?" He paused, waiting for her answer.

Stella stared hard at him. He was sitting directly opposite. She had not really been listening to what he was saying as she had been busy counting the number of times he had used the word 'okay', but she nodded as though she had registered each and every syllable. His head was shaved and when he spoke his already narrow eyes became slits. They were never still; they flickered constantly from side to side. This might have been alarming had their almond, oriental shape not been softened by a fringe of luxurious black lashes. His black skin shone and Stella imagined him buffing it with chamois leather and oil when he emerged wet from the shower. She blushed at such immodest thoughts and took a deep breath. He certainly smelled very nice, but that was not enough to convince her to tell him the secrets of her dreams. She had been misled by smells in the past.

At this point Col got up and moved over to the window which was already wide open. No air entered, but the static atmosphere of the estate permeated the small black space. The heat became suffocating, Stella's head began to throb. Just as she felt she was going to pass out, a small gang of children raced passed along the passageway, their shrieks and inappropriate language bursting into the room, shocking her back to the reality, the absurdity of the situation. Who was this young man? How could she even consider confiding in a total stranger? Placing her mug carefully on the coffee table, Stella picked up her handbag. She had decided to leave.

Col, who still stood by the open window with his back to Stella, began to speak again.

"Okay, this is hard for you. You don't know me

from Adam and here I am asking you to describe your most precious dream to me, okay. You'd be crazy not to be spooked, but I really think I can help you. Think of it like going to the movies, seeing a great film then describing it to me, okay?"

Stella weakened. He obviously had not the slightest idea what her dreams meant to her, but he did seem sympathetic. Still clutching her bag to her chest, she swallowed hard before challenging him.

"Well, I wish it was that simple. But you see it's my film. I wrote it, directed it and I also star in it. It's personal - very personal. Anyway, it's different every time. The same - but different - if you see what I mean. What I mean is, I know it's the same dream but it's never exactly the same." What had meant to be a clear, statement of fact had become a garbled stream of nonsense.

"Okay... point taken. Well, you tell me what you dreamed when you dreamed it for the very first time. Just take me with you, just as far as you want to go. Listen, I can't hypnotise you. I'm not that clever, am I, Mart?" He laughed and the whiteness of his teeth lit the room. "Anyhow, like you say, you're in the director's chair, you can stop the action whenever you want. Mart, go get some fresh air. We'll give you a call when we're through. Okay?"

Martina shrugged and left the room. Stella heard the front door close. They were alone. Col smiled again.

"Just remember - the very first time, okay? No rush, I want to see every frame just the way you do."

He smiled, just using his eyes, and Stella had the strangest feeling that she knew him very well. She knew that telling him about her avenue, her tall trees and her house would be safe. It would be 'okay'. She leant back against the soft, black cushion, closed her eyes and stood in front of the gates.

*

Her dream was there, as fresh as if this was the first and only time she had dreamed it. This was her dream, the dream that had visited her throughout the years, remaining for most of them constant and unchanging, never varying, not even in the slightest minutiae, and she was sharing it. Each leaf, each stone, the whispering of the leaves, the dappled sunlight through the trees every detail was there as it had been the first time. Each time she had dreamed it had seemed like the first time. It was never familiar, or predictable. Her avenue led her on a previously un-travelled journey to the house, to number one, with its large brass oak-leaf knocker, compelling her to strike it three times. She felt her breath enter and leave, her heart pumping her blood, the warmth of the sun and the contrasting shade. She listened to hear what the leaves were telling her, the scrunch of her feet as they trod the gravel, the fading light as the day drew to a close. Nothing got forgotten. It was as though she was dreaming it again, but this time by sharing it she was giving it new life.

*

When Stella finished, she opened her eyes and blinked. The black room came as a total shock. She recalled being hypnotised at the doctor's. The return to normality had always brought a similar jolt. Yet, in contrast, this had been an incredible experience: beautiful, as exciting as an actual dream. Telling her dream to another person had not detracted from the experience: it had added a whole new dimension. Had her private inner world transformed into something with an external existence? Had the simple process of sharing it made it externally real to another like a painting or a book? Now that her creation was no longer hers alone, was it a virtual reality or was it a solid, concrete durable thing visible and tangible to others? A bond had been sealed between this strange young man and herself. She waited eagerly to hear what he had to say.

Col was looking out of the window. He had his mobile in his hand and thrust it into his pocket when he saw she was watching him.

"Okay? Just take a while to come back down. You got pretty spaced out. I could hear it in your voice. How many times have you dreamed that dream? Four times? Forty-four times? Four hundred and forty-four?" He laughed seemingly having plucked the numbers from the static air.

Stella swallowed hard. *'Why did he say that? I had not told him I woke up at 4.44. Or had I? Has he hypnotised me? Or is his choice of numbers pure coincidence? It makes no difference to the meaning of the dream.'* She had been dreaming about her avenue since she was sixteen. She dreamed of it at least once a week and she was forty now. Her mind began to swim.

"Thousands... It must be thousands." Her voice went into auto pilot, while her mind was calculating. '42-16 x 52 = 1352.'

"One thousand three hundred and fifty two... about."

She added the final 'about' for fear of appearing too obsessional. She thought she caught the flicker of a smile flash across the sober, black face, but she was not sure.

"It's changed now. My dream... it's not consistent... not always the same. Not lately. It was to start with... It was always exactly the same - the same, but fresh each time as if it was new, if you see what I mean? I knew I had dreamed it before, but I had no idea what came next. Can you understand that?"

"Sure. Okay, listen, before we discuss how the dream is morphing, let's take a good look at the original? I've got some ideas to throw at you, okay?"

"This analysing won't stop me dreaming it, will it?"

"It might, yeah. Is that cool?"

"No!"

Col laughed. "I get it. It's like an old friend? Don't worry we won't wipe it out. But when you realise why you are dreaming it, you may find you don't have to dream it anymore. You won't want to. You can move on. But, hey we're a long way from that. Okay?"

He laughed again, and this time Stella joined in, although she had no idea why.

What he said did make sense, she could see that. The avenue was a part of her life. It must mean something. But unless, or until, she knew what, how could she decide if she would still need it? Col laughed again. He had a loud infectious laugh. Once again his teeth shone, incongruous against the blackness of his surroundings.

*

Their session together lasted a lengthy hour. Col refused Stella's offer of money, saying he only did it as a hobby, and anyway he was doing it for her because she was Martina's friend. A pang of guilt hit Stella as she remembered the girl. Col had given Stella a lot to think about and she did not want to go home and be bombarded with questions. When he offered to call Martina, and tell her they were finished, she told him to tell her to meet her back at number 9. Stella thrust a twenty pound note into Col's hand and this time he put it in his pocket without looking at it. Without speaking Col placed his palms together and lowered his head to touch his hands. Stella backed out of the door hardly daring to breathe until she reached the safety of the ground floor. Had an elephant been waiting for her she could not have been more surprised.

*

Losing Martina gave Stella a few hours of freedom. She headed off for the park and the cool air which rose from the lake. The ducks were bobbing about enjoying the water, clamouring for food as soon as they saw a human. Stella popped a mint imperial into her mouth and, thankful that her usual seat was free, she sat down and began to mull over the morning's revelations. In the past she had adamantly dismissed the notion that one could read a dream. Now she began to question whether she had used this as a defence mechanism. Had she just been afraid of finding out what her dream meant?

Everyone knew the old clichés - a road meant a journey, or a discovery and a house meant home. But she had refused to believe that applied to her road, her house. She clung to the belief that there was nothing clichéd about her dream. It meant far more than those interpretations you could get from books or off the net. And Stella was pleased that Col appeared to agree with her.

Col's remarkable resemblance to the young prince gave his opinion an exceptionally high credence in Stella's eyes. His cool methodical approach had impressed her. His way of asking her opinion at every juncture and the way he never jumped the gun with stereotypical explanations was impressive. They had reached the mutual decision that her dream was a way of connecting the past and the present: her subconscious and conscious. Adding a second mint to her mouth she began to reflect in detail on the morning's revelations.

Much of what Col had told her was, with hindsight, common sense. The avenue was a journey of sorts. He described it as her need to explore alternative paths through life. That made sense. As did the fact that the gates were usually open, allowing – inviting - her to enter. This, he claimed, showed her willingness to explore. The green leafy trees were either new hopes, or a thirst for knowledge, and their height indicated that her aspirations reached up to the sky. 'The sky's the limit' were his exact words. The path was straight, steering her directly ahead, while the gravel could mean a natural practicality, or uncertain territory. He said to read it as a warning to be cautious. On the other hand the grass was all about self reliance.

The house represented her. That it was locked and unwelcoming spoke volumes. The fact that it was number one meant her ego was too strong and could lead to loneliness; a denial of that higher spiritual force that was probably what she was seeking. To knock on the door was an expression of her desire to be enlightened. To knock three times represented a subconscious wish, as in the three wishes granted in a fairy tale, or the saying 'knock three times and it shall be opened.' Stella had to agree that the number three did hold magical connotations. This reluctant admission made her feel rather childish.

By the time she was sucking her last mint, Stella had reached a conclusion. Everything Col had said was both logical and plausible. But, and it was this 'but' that settled it for Stella, he had failed to grasp the fact that her dreams were real. They were not some virtual check on reality. She refused to view them as anecdotes or parables for life. They 'were' her life. It made more sense for her to explain her life through her dreams rather than the other way around. Her avenue existed, as did the trees, the drive, the gravel and the house. They were waiting for her. Why else would they change and evolve? Dreams were not there to explain her waking life. They existed in a parallel universe. It was she who must accommodate them. They controlled her life, and she had to master control of them. It was a balancing act.

The fact that he was rooted in reality did not make his opinions any more important. Stella preferred to listen to the prince – she knew when he was lying. She decided not to see Col again and felt an immediate surge of relief.

Stella walked home from the park, taking the route past M&S. She debated whether to pop in and treat herself to a tasty snack for tea, but then she remembered Martina. What if the girl had prepared something for the two of them? This precious peace, this indulgent time for self introspection would vanish the moment she entered number 9. Stella was juggling her need for peace and quiet with her guilty hope that Martina would not be waiting at home, when she saw Anita enter the store. Her instinct was to run, to catch up with her: to tell her about her visit to the strange young 'Man in Black.' This was someone who would listen without interrupting, someone who would understand the importance of what had happened without judgment. She was debating whether to follow Anita when the doors opened and Anita walked out.

Stella ducked in through the next door. Her heart was thumping and her mouth felt dry. She watched Anita cross the road and walk away. The moment had passed. Setting off home she felt stupid and angry: angry that she had not had the courage to speak and stupid to think that this kind stranger might have taken the slightest interest in her private life.

Realising that she was exhausted she resolved to go home, make some excuse to avoid Martina's inevitable pestering and take herself off to bed, to dream.

*

They swam for days in deep water. Only the brightest rays of sunlight were strong enough to penetrate the depth, punctuating the journey with blinding darts of emerald refracting into zigzag lightening forks, breaking the silent darkness with unpredictable frequency. Eventually the swimmers reached the point where the river widened, opening to swallow the ocean. Two smaller rivers joined at the confluence, creating cross currents, rapid slip streams, which cut deep into the sandy bottom. Banyan trees thrust tangled roots down into the receptive mud, forcing the travellers to navigate a labyrinth of submerged undergrowth until, without warning, it fell away and the bottomless sea engulfed them.

The sweet water turned to salt and waves towered above their heads leaving their bodies to be pulled by tides urged on by a waxing moon.

They had been swimming for miles; the tiger always leading, his great webbed paws propelling them faster and faster towards an unseen destination, carrying Stella in his wake. The river journey had been hard, but the sea crossing was harder. She could feel the strength ebbing from the tiger as he carried them on. By the time they reached land the sun was low in the western sky.

Runs-With-The-Buffalo was waiting on the shore. He had lit a fire and prepared plates of meat and bread for them to eat. Stella embraced him and they sat down together to enjoy their feast. The tiger sat apart from them. He stretched his tired body close to the flames on the far side of the fire, as slowly he licked the salt from his feet. Stella noticed that his paws were no longer webbed. Thoroughly he cleaned between each pad with his rough tongue. Then noisily he began licking his long, black claws, grooming them until they glistened keenly with his spit. A vast yawn escaped his mouth curling his lip back to expose a lethal arsenal, heavily encrusted with years of brown plaque at their roots. Their circumference measured that of a grown man's thumb; the jaws which held them were powerful enough to snap such a man in half.

Having eaten her fill, Stella rose, walked round the fire and settled down beside the tiger, burying her face in the wonderful smell of wet fur which

rose from his steaming coat.
　"Why don't you eat?" she asked.
　"I only eat when I am hungry, or threatened."
　"Aren't you afraid of the fire?" She asked.
　"Yes, but this fire dries and warms me. We must not avoid everything we fear, for fear of avoiding the best of life. Life is not given to us to ignore it. It is our duty to be brave: to trust until that trust is betrayed. When the fire burns me I will avoid it. When you betray me I will eat you."

*

Stella was woken from her dream by an almighty crash. It came from her old room and was accompanied by shrieks of laughter and strange shushing noises. Someone was anxiously, unsuccessfully, attempting to be quiet. Clutching 'Old Faithful' Stella rushed out onto the landing. Although the sounds were muffled she was sure she could detect more than one voice. Stella drew her dressing gown even tighter than before. Swallowing hard, she threw the door open.

　In the rather inadequate light, she could see two figures tangled together on the floor, a knotted heap of bodies and bedclothes. The bed, her old bed, was tilted precariously, resting on three legs, the fourth having snapped off at the base. A bare arm, which she recognised by the butterfly tattoo to be Martina's, reached out and dragged the duvet over her head to cover her feigned embarrassment and her laughter. This vain attempt inadvertently exposed a very bare, black body. This was Stella's first sighting of an aroused male member in a full frontal position, and her shocked reaction merely served to increase the hilarity of the other two. Stella slammed the door. She did not get back to sleep that night, for fear she should dream of the young prince.

*

The next morning Stella finished her breakfast and, hearing no signs of life from upstairs, decided to investigate. Her loud knock on the door was greeted with a snigger. She knocked again and was granted permission to enter. The broken bed took centre stage. Martina was sprawled on top of it, wearing just a tee shirt. She appeared unscathed and totally unabashed. She blurted out an apology for damaging the bed, which might have ingratiated her in Stella's eyes if she hadn't immediately followed it with a loud, unnecessarily rude, complaint.

"That effing bed's so old it's a miracle it's survived this bloody long."

"You had a man in here last night, Martina. That's not on. And I have asked you before not to swear." Stella felt betrayed. She was trying not to appear prudish, but there were some things that were way beyond the pale. She regretted not having been more assertive, not having established more rules, especially one clearly stating 'no house guests after dark.' To Stella this had seemed patently obvious. She had assumed that Martina was the type of woman who did not need such instructions.

"Bloody cheek! Like it's your bloody fault, so don't try to shift the blame onto me. This bed is the pits. It's a liberty to expect a guest, let alone a lodger, to sleep on it. I could take you to the tribunal for like breaking the trade's descriptions thingy - if I wasn't so forgiving."

"I'm sorry. I'll get the bed fixed." Stella kicked herself, but she was not sure if it was for losing her temper, or for apologising. Martina had done it again. Stella was on the defensive.

"No way! I think we're talking a new bed here. Never mind. Get it sorted and we'll say no more. Okay? Go on give us a smile. Worse things happen at sea." Martina climbed over the distraught bed and gave the equally distraught Stella a token hug.

"Are you saying you didn't have a man here last night?" Stella blushed as she stammered out her question.

"I should be so lucky! You must have like dreamed it. Poor old Stel. Anyway, I'm off men at the moment." Martina climbed back onto the lop-sided bed and pulled the duvet over her head, leaving Stella wondering how she could have been so utterly mistaken.

*

By the time 'poor old Stel' arrived at work, Martina was up, dressed in 'Old Faithful' and planning her day. Col came round at about eleven and they drank the last of Stella's coffee. Taking advantage of the empty house, they took themselves off to Stella's room: a double bed being much more comfortable than a single one - a broken one at that. Most of the afternoon was spent testing the springs, Martina finding the fact that this was Stella's bed a total turn on.

As Stella climbed down from the 94 bus, blissfully ignorant that her privacy had been so wilfully invaded, Col was diving into a doorway opposite the bus stop to avoid being spotted, and Martina was lowering herself into an over full bath thus flooding the bathroom floor.

*

That evening, at Stella's instigation, the two women had a 'serious' talk. Stella tried to appear firm and express how displeased she was to arrive home to no dinner and an untidy house. Martina bit her tongue and played the contrite lodger for fear of losing favour. By the time they had finished their tinned spaghetti all was mended; all except the bed. Stella agreed to invest in a new divan, but flatly refused to replace it with a double one, which was what Martina was demanding. Martina did not share her satisfaction with her landlady's explanation that the front room was far too small, even for a four foot bed, nor with the simple fact that she could not afford one.

Stella retired to her bed with a cup of steaming hot chocolate made by Martina who, anxious that she may not have remade the bed to Stella's high standards, threw herself on it before Stella's critical eye could spot any wrinkles. Chattering loudly and inanely all the time Stella was in the bathroom, Martina promised to get up bright and early and cook them both a lovely breakfast. Bathed and ready for bed, the promise was accepted, but taken with a large pinch of salt. Having crumpled the bed sufficiently to allay any suspicion, Martina bounced off it, kissed Stella good night and wished her sweet dreams.

Stella sighed. She shook her crushed duvet, smoothed over the all too obvious creases, sighed again and finally slipped beneath it. The hot chocolate had gone quite cold, and Martina had been far too heavy handed with the sugar. Stella sighed for a third time. What she needed was a race across the prairie plains; to ride where the tall grasses came up to her pony's withers and the sun could be wherever she wanted in the wide open sky; a gallop to wipe away the memory of a tedious day.

*

Predictably, Stella breakfasted alone. She was long gone before Martina even thought about opening her eyes. It was midday when, wrapped in 'Old Faithful', the girl padded downstairs, lit a cigarette and, angry that there was no coffee, made herself a cup of tea. Eventually she phoned Col.

*

The sound of Stella's key in the lock took Martina by surprise. She had spent the day in bed and had lost count of the time. Luckily for her, Stella stopped to remove some unsightly leaves from the rose bush, which gave her just enough time to clamber out of bed and pull her jeans on. When Stella entered the hall Martina was leaning over the bannisters.

"Don't take your coat off; I'm taking you out for dinner. My treat, just to say I'm sorry if I upset you. My periods have been all over the shop lately and it makes me a right grumpy cow. Think of this as a small thank you for taking me in."

Within seconds she was fully dressed and downstairs. She grabbed her leather coat from the bottom stair and hustled Stella back out through the door before any objections could be raised. After being frogmarched up to the nearest burger bar, Stella found herself, having eaten her very first Macdonald's, beginning to relax. She settled back on the leather bench to digest her food and Martina's endless chatter.

"Listen, Stella, you'll love this. I had a dream last night - me - like I never dream. Well, you know that. It must be your influence or something 'cos I really did have this dream. It was so real and I could remember everything so clearly. Talk about weird! I was asleep in my dream, and I was like dreaming. Have you ever done that? Dreamed you were dreaming? It was truly weird." Martina did not pause or allow Stella time to answer. She had no intention of letting Stella interrupt her flow.

"So, anyway, I'm dreaming I'm a tiny baby, dressed from head to foot in pink and I'm sleeping in a cot, covered in a pink woolly blanket, cuddling a pink woolly teddy bear. My little hands and feet were all pink too! Honestly they looked like they'd just been painted! Then all of a sudden everything went black, but I could hear your voice calling me, and I felt really safe. Then I woke up."

The hairs on the back of Stella's neck rose up and although full of burger and chips she felt a cavernous void open in her stomach. Martina had only paused for breath.

"Like I said I never dream, well hardly ever, unless I've been eating cheese, or I've been watching a horror film. I had dreadful nightmares after I saw the Exorcist. Have you seen that? We could get it on DVD. It's a bit old now but it's really good, especially the bit where her head spins round." Martina was laughing loudly now, apparently lost in the memory of the spinning head.

"You don't look too good. Hope that burger hasn't like given you food poisoning. Shall we go? God, look at the time; it's way passed your bedtime. Dirty little stop out! You should be in the land of nod by now, dreaming sweet dreams of your own." With that she took Stella's purse and paid for their meal, then bundled her out of their cosy booth and back home, where she fussed and clucked, playing mother hen, finally tucking her up in bed. Martina kissed Stella on the forehead and crept out, turning the light off behind her.

*

Left alone in the dark, Stella's mind was racing. How did Martina know about the baby? Had she read her mind? She knew so many details – it could hardly be by chance. Was it possible to catch someone else's dreams, like one caught measles or chicken pox? Had Martina used a dream catcher? Runs-With-The-Buffalo had often spoken of them, but she didn't really know what they were, not exactly. It would have to be a pretty big coincidence for Martina to have dreamed her dream. What were the odds on that happening? She wondered whether to telephone Col, but decided against it. Instead she opted to bide her time, choosing to think of this as a one-off: a mere fluke. She resolved to sleep on it. Anyway, there was nothing she could do. She yawned loudly and let herself slip off to sleep.

CHAPTER 12

Directly after lunch that Sunday, Martina breezed out of number 9. She gave no hint as to where she was going. She left abruptly, without saying goodbye. Stella, alone for the first time in weeks felt a welcome sense of freedom – space in which to think out loud without being overheard. The business of the shared dream had been haunting her. Whichever way she looked at it, the same perplexing thought came crashing in. This thought was so alarming, so incredibly amazing, that she hardly dared entertain it. Nevertheless it kept gate-crashing her thoughts, 'What if?' 'Is it possible?' These thoughts were so absurd, so disquieting, that she did not let them move beyond the abstract. She vowed not to entertain them again. Unless – or until - she had more proof.

Firm in her resolve, Stella retreated to her parents' room. She pulled the drawer out from her hiding place beneath the bed and sat on the floor beside it. Slowly with reverence, she lifted the knitted blanket from the top, drew it to her face and breathed in. There was nothing, not even the imagined memory of a scent: not the hint of talcum powder, or the milky sweet smell of new life. Gently she smoothed the cover and laid it on the floor beside her. Next she took the card in her left hand while she stroked the fragile little prints with her right. She placed her hand next to the imprint. 'How could a hand be so tiny yet grip so tight?'

She thought she recalled the tenacity with which the baby had held on to her finger. She wondered whose finger that little hand gripped now; grown big, maybe bigger than her own.

Stella recognised that she was on dangerous ground. Once she stepped onto the quicksand of supposition she would get sucked down. A million questions suffocated her. The shifting grains of uncertainty clogged her nostrils; they blocked her ears, smothering any vestige of rational thought in her congested head.

'Had her baby been loved?' Stella hoped - she almost prayed - that her little girl had been brought up by people who showed her love. That she had been raised her in a nice clean house, sent to a good school, college, university even - all the while being a proper mum and dad to her. *"Maybe she was living somewhere as a successful, well balanced, happy young woman: loving and loved. Or, had she been mistreated? Had they, whoever they were, abused her? Had they taught her to fear and hate? Maybe she had been kept in a dark cellar or sent abroad to work as a slave in some distant country. Had she grown into an insecure, frightened, pathetic woman? Perhaps she was damaged goods by now; unable to trust sufficiently to form lasting relationships, condemned to a lonely unfulfilled existence. Had she grown into a miserable worn out woman living on the edge of life without even the stuff of dreams to fall back on? How can one dream if one has not seen happiness and adventure, even if it is only second-hand from the TV or from films? Maybe - and this was the worst maybe of all - maybe she had not grown up at all? "*

*

Stella read through the newspaper cuttings one more time. Of course they were engraved on her heart, but each time she re-read them she hoped they would offer her a fresh clue. There had been times when she hoped they would not be there; that the drawer would be empty, that she would wake up to find that it had all been a dream: the tiny hands had never existed and the little teddy had never been hugged and snuggled up to at night, under the pink knitted blanket. But there it was, in the black and white news print: 'Baby snatched in Livingstone Park.' The park was exactly the same today as it had been then. It was everything else that had changed; everything else had faded like a much-read, yellowing cutting from a twenty-five-year-old newspaper - or a dream.

Stella remembered how cold it had been that day in the park. If it hadn't been so cold she wouldn't have wanted a cup of tea. If she hadn't wanted a cup of tea she would not have been tempted when that woman had said "Go on, you get yourself one. I'll look after the baby. She'll be fine with me." Maybe if she had bought a coffee, instead of waiting for that stupid man to faff about opening a new box of tea-bags, she would have been back before... The bench was empty. There was no sign of a woman or a baby. The park was empty. The world was empty.

Stella felt the familiar void filling her stomach just as it had that day twenty-four years ago. She had gone straight to the police station. She remembered them being very gentle with her that first day. The questions they had asked were burned into her brain, she would never forget them.

"Where were you sitting? How far away was the drinks' vendor? What did the woman look like? Had you ever seen her there before? What was she wearing? Was she alone? Who else would have seen her?" ... etcetera, etcetera, etcetera.

As she answered the relentless questions, she kept telling herself to wake up, although she was wider awake than she had ever been - before or since.

When the police brought her home Stella overheard her mother tell them how sick her daughter had been. That 'poor Stella' had been under the doctor for months – that there had even been talk of sectioning her. Mrs Sankey said there was no baby, there never had been any baby; it was all a delusion.

Stella vaguely remembered being put to bed when the police left. That was the beginning of the difficult process which would eventually lead to her believing that her mother was right. She had already learned that her memory was not to be relied on. Now it was different. Now she had seen the proof. If she had known about those little prints back then she might have used them to prove, if only to herself, that the baby was real. Why hadn't her mother done just that? Instead another doctor had been called and Stella had been sedated to pass a drug induced, dreamless night of comfortless emptiness.

The next day her parents had gone out. Persistent banging on the door had dragged her, hardly conscious, from her bed. It made her break out into a sweat now, all these years later, to recall the hoard of reporters who had invaded number 9, armed with notepads, cameras and even more questions. Like the police, the press were very nice, but relentless, almost ruthless. They wanted to take photographs of the exact spot where the baby had been born, the place where the baby had slept. What had Stella been wearing? What did she wrap the baby in? They wanted to know who the father was. Did he know about the birth? Did he know the baby had been snatched? Could he have taken it? They ploughed on regardless of feelings, regardless of common courtesy, regardless full stop.

No one had shown any sympathy for how Stella was feeling. No-one had thought of asking her if she minded that her baby had gone. By the time they left she had felt utterly lost. She believed she was dreaming again and would wake up soon to find there was no baby, there never had been a baby; therefore there was no missing baby. She had memories of knowing that would be the worst irony of all: to be the butt of all those jokes about the idiot girl who didn't know if she had given birth or not. Nothing could be worse than that.

The police had returned the next day. This time

they took Stella back to the station with them. They questioned her for hours. The questions were the same as before, but the manner in which they were asked was far from gentle this time. Her parents had raised Stella to respect the police, to think of them as friends - there to help and protect people like her. She knew these officers did not want to help her. She could feel their anger. Her parents had been wrong.

The police were convinced she had fabricated the whole thing just to get attention. They told her as much. They demanded she produce the birth certificate. She did not have one. They demanded to know the address of the doctor who had treated her throughout her pregnancy. She had none. They demanded to know which hospital she had attended for the birth, which mid-wife had she had, who was the father, why hadn't she reported any part of her confinement or delivery? Why had no baby been registered? Could she in fact prove the existence of any baby? And, by the way, what was the baby's name? 'Poor Stella' had no answers.

She did not know about the little pink prints: proof of a tiny hand's existence, one that should have held hers. Sometimes, all these years later, she told herself that had she known, she still would not have shown them; she could never have let such sacred memories be defiled. She could never have watched those tiny pink prints trampled over by the feet of giants.

Her parents said nothing to her. They too were questioned over and over again. Mrs Sankey thought the whole dreadful business had brought shame on the family and continued to insist to anyone who asked that the whole thing was a figment of her daughter's imagination. At the time Stella had no choice but to accept her mother's word - the whole baby business was just another crazy fantasy, like riding on paint ponies and playing with tigers on hilltops of grassland.

*

The kidnapping, real or imagined, was never mentioned again - not at number 9. In time the whole thing died down. The press had exhausted the story of a loopy girl, who had concocted a dramatic story just to get her name in the papers. There was some talk of arresting Stella for wasting police time, but it never happened. It all seemed so very long ago now. Her parents were dead: they could not bear witness. So, after a while, Stella chose to believe what everyone else supposed - it had been just another dream. But at times Stella would remember. 'And that woman,' Stella thought, 'she must remember too.'

It was years later, just after her father's death, that Stella needed a copy of his birth certificate. Having exhausted all the usual places she remembered her mother's laundry drawer. There she stumbled across the little stash of treasure: the box, the prints, the blanket and the teddy, and the newspaper cuttings. They had slept there all those years, quietly bathing in the scent of lavender and old newspaper. That was a long time ago, but they still had the power to drag Stella down and hold her under, making her drown in her loss all over again.

    Life was altered from that brief moment of discovery. Stella's trust in her dead mother's honesty was destroyed. Suddenly Stella no longer knew what the 'truth' was. When her mother had died whatever 'truth' had existed had gone to the grave with her.

*

Now as Stella sat in her room revisiting her treasures, the guilt and the questions came back. They were still as potent as the first time she had seen them. With a shrug and a cynical laugh she packed her sacred relics away, trying to dismiss them as the buried past. She made a vow not to visit them again and marched downstairs to make an extra strong cup of tea. There was no tea: the empty box had been put back in the cupboard.

CHAPTER 13

Martina was still not home by five o'clock. It was the perfect evening for a walk; Stella reckoned that, if she got a move on, she would reach the park in time to see the sun set over the lake. Sitting on her bench, she was so glad she had made the effort. It was spectacular, impossible to tell where the sky finished and the water began – almost a spiritual experience.

Momentarily embarrassed at entertaining such frivolous, romantic thoughts, it occurred to Stella that, in her dreams, she often stopped to marvel at nature. The red sun slipping from the sky, as it was now, was melting to a state somewhere between liquid and gas. Everything it touched transformed, as though viewed through a veil the colour of lilacs and roses. There was nothing frivolous here. Runs-With-The-Buffalo would not be out of place standing beside her, and for a moment she sensed the breath of a great cat on her neck. The sensation was so powerful that she turned to greet the tiger.

"Hello. It's Stella, isn't it? We met in M&S – Oh gosh - it was a few weeks ago – I don't expect you remember me. It's Anita. Tell me, did you buy the pink sweater? It was exactly the same colour as the sky tonight. I bought one the next day."

Stella did remember.

"Sorry, I hope I'm not intruding. I hoped we would meet again, Stella. Beautiful, isn't it? I often come here at this time. It reminds me of a friend, someone I went to school with. We used to say we would live on the other side of the sunset when we died. I don't see her now, but I've been thinking about her a lot just lately, and especially now. " Anita closed her eyes and breathed in as if to absorb the whole scene physically and spiritually. Stella watched, envious of this woman's ability to lose herself so readily. Anita smiled, as if she could read Stella's thoughts.

"I've not seen you here before." She said.

Stella felt no urge to escape. She too began to smile although she had to swallow hard before she could speak.

"I usually come earlier and yes, I do remember you. I bought the blue one, and another navy one. It's for work you see." Stella felt she needed to add an explanation, afraid that Anita would think her too boring. They smiled at each other then turned their gaze to the final dying moments of the sunset until the warmth sunk below the horizon with the vanishing sun.

"Right – shows over. Shall we have a coffee or something to get rid of the chill? The kiosk's closed, but Costa's will still be open."

Delightedly Stella accepted the offer. Had she been brave enough she would have suggested it herself. As they left the park Anita pointed to a small, white Fiat.

"That's my chariot. Hop in."

There were no other cars in the car-park – Anita had rightly assumed that Stella was on foot. It had been a long time since Stella had been in a car. Anita helped her with the seat belt, chatting easily about the complicated trivia of modern life; seat belts being one of them. She drove confidently and, as she concentrated on the road, Stella concentrated on her. Their ages, she guessed, were about the same - early to mid-forties, but whereas Stella was thin, Anita was rounded. Her hair was a light, bright brown, naturally curly and thick, cut to fall in bouncy waves around her face. She wore a velour tracksuit – which Stella recognised was from M&S and she had a long flowing scarf around her neck. It was a look Stella liked – smart casual was how she assumed one would describe it.

Anita asked Stella where she worked, what she did, did she like it, was she married. Not probing, nosey interrogation just natural, easy curiosity. Natural was the apposite word. It fitted Anita: there was nothing false, nothing artificial about her. Having 'no sides' to her allowed Stella to relax: this woman posed no threat. Stella found her presence pleasing; almost reassuring. As the car turned into the High Street, Stella found her courage and suggested that they go home for a coffee. The invitation was accepted and the rest of the journey was spent discussing the inflated price of coffee at Costa's and M&S, and the ridiculous, equally inflated size of the cups - the two women were getting on like a house on fire.

*

Martina was still not home. Settled on the sofa in Stella's sitting room, Stella was debating whether or not to tell Anita a bit about her. Not, of course, the fact that they had met in a psychiatrist's surgery. More on a general level - about her being a lodger and such, but before she started, Anita interrupted her.

"Be very careful, Stella. There is danger around you – a young woman is involved. Don't trust her. She has the means to hurt you. She will betray you."

Like a bitch protecting her pup, Stella felt her hackles rise.

"I'm sorry. I didn't mean to upset you. It's just that if I am given something I have to pass it on. It's second nature. I'm psychic you see. I wouldn't have said anything if I didn't feel it was important. It's just a warning. Please, take it in good faith, offered in friendship and love."

Stella was annoyed with herself. No names had been mentioned. She had no reason to assume that the young woman in question was Martina. It was absurd to think Anita was referring to her. It was probably that new girl in the office. Her eyes were much too close together and she had seen her talking to the woman from accounts, who she already knew did not like her. Anita's delivery certainly held no malice. Whatever the source of her information, it seemed it had been said out of kindness.

"I'm sorry too. I shouldn't have jumped to conclusions. Why did you say that – about the girl? Who is she?"

"Sorry - I'm awful. I assume people understand what I'm talking about – when they haven't a clue.

My husband, Mike, gets so cross with me. It's just that if I sense something untoward I have to share it. And, I do feel you are vulnerable to some sort of exploitation." Anita's concern was written all over her face. She smiled in such a reassuring way that Stella had no doubts about her sincerity.

"You mentioned a young woman. Can you see her?" Stella was intrigued that was all, holding no fixed beliefs either way.

But before Anita had a chance to elaborate, the conversation was interrupted by the sound of Martina's key turning in the lock. The slamming of the front door reverberated through the hall, followed by something heavy - a leather coat maybe - dropping from the bannister to the bottom stair. The noise was rounded off by a loud expletive. Then, Martina burst in on the scene.

Her dramatic entrance was ruined by the presence of a stranger. As soon as she saw Anita she clammed up. Anita smiled, Stella welcomed her to join them, but Martina was jealous. Sharing did not come easily to her. As far as she was concerned this was her home, in which some strange woman was comfortably ensconced, sipping tea in her lounge, cosily chatting to her friend, while sitting on her sofa. She threw a sarcastic remark at Stella, something about not wanting to butt in where she wasn't invited and stormed out.

"Oh dear, I think that's my cue! Goodness, look at the time, I should have been home ages ago." Anita smiled sweetly and got up to go.

Stella felt embarrassed. She was also cross.

Who did Martina think she was behaving like that? Stella vowed to give her a strict talking too as soon as her guest had gone. Mumbling an apology, Stella rose to show Anita out.

"I'm sorry about that..."

"Please – no need to apologise. I've got kids of a similar age. They can be a nightmare. Let's meet up again. I've really enjoyed our chat. We could meet for a coffee in M&S – if we save up! What time do you finish work?"

With difficulty they agreed on a time and place; it was not easy to hear each other above the avalanche of rock music that was crashing down the stairs. Stella mouthed the word 'Sorry' and Anita laughed, mouthing back 'kids!' Stella stood in the doorway until the white Fiat had gone. Then she took a deep breath and assaulted the banana tree to have it out with her 'daughter'.

*

Life at number 9 became strained for a while. It was like living in a minefield where Stella had to tread carefully for fear of triggering an explosion. Martina had reacted badly to Anita's visit; it had produced an unwarranted hostility that alarmed Stella. She had tried to reason with the girl, explaining that as the householder she was entitled to invite anyone she chose to tea in her own house. But her statement met with what she could only describe as jealousy, bordering on possessiveness. After a brief slanging match when the no swearing rule was flagrantly ignored, Martina did a total about face. With a dismissive, "Whatever!" she locked herself in her room, remaining there for the rest of the night. Stella assumed that the girl was sulking and left her to it, but their row had upset her. As a result she slept badly, worried that cracks were appearing in what had, until now, promised to be a good a relationship.

*

Anita phoned Stella on Monday to confirm their arrangements. Stella finished work at five thirty. Anita started an hour later so they had agreed to meet at five fifteen. Anita worked as a psychic medium, which took her all round the county. But most of the time she worked in the Christian Spiritualist Church located somewhere off the High Street. It was within walking distance for Stella. But, first, she had to agree she would go.

When Stella quizzed Anita about her church, her questions made it patently obvious that her idea of spiritualism had got no further than a couple of Dennis Wheatley novels. Anita laughed. She promised that no one would spirit Stella away, conjure up the devil or sit in the dark asking, "Is there anybody there?" It was, as she explained, a simple Christian church, whose members believed in the continuance of life after death and contact with those already in the spirit world. It was the job of the medium, in this case Anita, to offer proof of the existence of the 'departed' to those who needed it.

The conventional church had played no part in

Stella's childhood. She could not remember a single display of faith at number 9. Her parents were not disrespectful of the church; she could remember the great interest her mother had shown when watching TV coverage of the Pope's visit to the UK. She had become visibly emotional when Pope John Paul knelt down to kiss the ground. Mind you, as she said at the time,

"It's not right; an old man bending down like that, with no one helping get him back up. He could catch all sorts, putting his mouth on that bit of old carpet. Goodness only knows how many people have walked all over it!"

She was not in the least bit interested in witnessing the world's religious leader paying his respect to her country. Even when her husband had pointed out that he was actually kissing a brand new, clean bit of carpet, and probably not actually putting his mouth anywhere near it, she simply shrugged, called it a nice gesture, and said a man of his age should know better.

Her parents often watched the carol service at Christmas and she recalled her mother enjoying Songs of Praise, but they never attended a live church. Stella was not even sure if she had been christened. She wondered what her mother would think of her daughter visiting a Spiritualist church. Maybe it would throw some light on the past? What if these spiritualists could contact her mother – she would have to answer Stella's questions then. Such ideas crowded into Stella's mind, bringing sensations which hovered between hope and horror, joy and fear. Then, just as she was weighing up the pros and cons of attending a service, she remembered what the tiger has said - fear was no reason to avoid life.

*

The church met in a small modern building built on the same spot where the old Co-operative grocery shop had once stood. There was a small arch around the entrance bearing the words, Christian Spiritualist Church. A notice board displayed the names of the president and vice president, whom Stella assumed to be husband and wife, but turned out to be mother and son. They apparently held services each Tuesday - afternoon and evening, and again on Sundays.

As Stella walked through the door, she was greeted by an elderly woman who introduced herself as Lillian. She shook Stella's hand with a firm comfortable grip, and welcomed her to the congregation, informing her that she was welcome to stay behind for a cup of tea after the medium had given her 'proof'. An electric organ played very softly and, for a brief moment, Stella was back in the crematorium at her father's funeral. She found a seat in the back row, pleased to see that she was not the only woman who had come along on their own.

The little hall was filling up quickly, which surprised Stella, this being a Tuesday evening and timed to clash with the most popular soaps. She had expected to find a few, rather sad, probably lonely people dotted along the rows, anxious to see, but not be seen. In actual fact the congregation appeared quite jolly. The organ played gently in the background and Stella watched growing numbers of church goers chattering readily to one another. It had more of the atmosphere of a social club than a church. A youngish, very large man, bearing a remarkable resemblance to Lillian, moved to the front and solemnly took his place in the centre of the low platform, which Stella later learned they called the rostrum. Lillian, his mother and also the president, sat on the middle one of three chairs behind him. Another woman joined them, taking the chair to the right of the older woman. Stella leant forward in her chair. It was Anita. Her presence gave Stella a sense of belonging. She felt important - not just another member of the congregation, but connected to the inner circle. The organ's playing rose to a modest crescendo. It was being played, rather well Stella thought, by a blind man, of at least eighty. Stella felt a sense of disappointment when the pleasant sound was replaced by the rather over-pious voice of the president's son.

It was difficult to concentrate on what he was saying; he was sweating so profusely. Stella watched his fat round face grow redder and redder, afraid he was destined for a massive coronary. What he was saying was infinitely less interesting than watching the next trickle of perspiration hit his striped shirt, which was changing to darker shades of blue with each outpouring. Sanctimonious sentiments gushed from him, as profusely as his sweat, until Stella could not watch him any longer. Without moving her head, endeavouring to appear interested, she turned her attention to her surroundings.

The church was in effect no more than a hall. There were twenty windows, set high so the only view they offered was a glimpse of sky, which ran down both of the long sides. At the far end was the platform - the rostrum. The whole thing was simple, almost austere, apart from the enormous leather-bound bible. A wide, lavish silk-embroidered bookmark, edged with golden fringing, lay draped across the bible's open page. It then reached down until it met the dark blue of the carpet.

Only the platform was carpeted, the rest of the hall had a bare wooden floor. Beneath the organ lay a yellow and gold sweetie paper. Stella wondered if anyone else had spotted it, and how long it had been there. She suspected that the organist had dropped it. Maybe there would be more by the end of the evening. It reminded her of her father who, when he wasn't smoking, continuously and noisily sucked on boiled sweeties. This reminder of why she was here came with the uncanny feeling of someone walking over her grave.

Behind the three chairs on the rostrum was an altar, or rather a long table which served as such. It was draped with dark blue velvet, overlaid with a smaller cloth of white lace. A simple wooden cross hung about three feet above the altar. It was all very tasteful, except for a badly painted 'abstract' concoction of red and yellow swirls, which hung directly behind the cross. Stella supposed that it was intended to complement the cross. In fact it did the opposite: it destroyed the impact. Stella recognised it as a typical symptom of modern society's lack of taste. She was pursuing this superior line of thought when she realised the rest of the congregation were standing.

An open hymnal lay in front of her, tucked into the rack on the back of the chair in front. The singing started badly, unsynchronised and far too weak, having been led by an uncertain cue from the organist. But, by the end of the first verse they were unified and in good voice. By the second verse Stella was singing along. She had forgotten (if indeed she had ever known) how therapeutic singing could be. When the hymn ended and they sat down, she found herself hoping they would sing some more before the evening was through. They said prayers, listened to a bible reading or two, and listened to the 'organ', while a list was read out for those in need of healing, Then came the time for the sermon. Only it was referred to as the address - the inspired address. As such it was delivered without notes and - if the president was to be believed - without preparation.

Anita stepped forward. She didn't go to the lectern, but chose to stand in the middle of the rostrum. Seeing her standing there all alone; waiting presumably for inspiration, Stella began to feel nervous on her behalf. There was no need. Anita appeared totally confident. Her address was well delivered, if a bit trite - rather too 'Patience Strong' - for Stella's taste. She would have preferred another chance to sing. But the congregation clearly loved it and when Anita finished Stella half expected a round of applause. There was none. Instead another prayer was said. Then they sang again. Unfortunately Stella's unfamiliarity with the hymn denied her the chance to sing along, which left her feeling rather cheated. A hush descended and the president rose, walked to the centre of the rostrum and announced that the guest speaker would now give a demonstration of clairvoyance. The silence was breath-taking.

Stella felt a rush of adrenalin. Her knees began to jiggle up and down in rapid uncontrollable jerks, her heels striking the floor producing annoying clicking sounds, exactly as her father used to do. Stella pressed her hands against her knees and the jiggling stopped. 'What was that all about?' She wondered.

Anita's head was bowed in deep concentration – or it might have been prayer. Stella studied her carefully. She was surprised to find that any cynicism she had been harbouring was allayed by what appeared to be a genuine display of sincerity. Anita gave out a natural quality, an air of no nonsense, of take-it-or-leave-it, the very quality that had so impressed Stella the first time they met. Stella sat back to enjoy the performance, surprised to find herself physically relaxing. Her shoulders dropped and her jaw loosened. Until now she had not realised how much tension she had been carrying.

Anita's eyes were still closed. She was like an insect putting out antenna, scanning the congregation: feeling for something - or someone - she knew was present. All the while she kept her eyes closed. When she did open them, her gaze settled on a middle-aged woman, in a black and white chequered coat. Stella had noticed that the congregation was made up almost entirely of women, middle-aged and worn; women who had encountered the knocks in life. There was only one man, apart from the son of the president and the organist, and he had the brow-beaten look of a man who was there because his wife had insisted he attend.

Stella could not hear everything that was being said: Anita spoke quietly, delivering her message without hesitation or embellishment. Judging by the woman's reaction, she predicted with considerable accuracy. The woman in the chequered coat thanked Anita for her words of comfort and Anita thanked her back with a simple nod, before moving on to her next recipient. This was a very large, loud woman, dressed in a strident yellow jacket. Her equally strident voice related, in graphic detail, the incident of her brother's death: the poor man had died earlier that year in a gruesome car crash. Anita comforted the woman with a few kind words then returned to her stance with her eyes closed. She told Stella later that too much information made for a bad reading.

Stella was just thinking it was all a bit boring when she heard the words, "I want to come to the lady at the back, the one in the blue scarf. Yes Stella, you dear. I have your father here." Stella had been chosen. Her immediate reaction was to flee. The irony of the situation struck her. She had come to the church in the hope of getting a message – some information to fill in the gaps she had created in her own memories. Now, faced with just such a chance, her fear took over. Her instinct to take flight was replaced by petrification, rooting her to the spot. Anita simply carried on in her natural yet professional way.

"As I look at this man, I want to cough. I have a lot of pain here." Anita put her left hand to her chest and breathed deeply. Her eyes were shut and she looked every inch as though she was in real pain. Stella was convinced that she saw Anita's face grow gaunt; her eyes sink back in their sockets and her normally pink complexion take on an unhealthy, grey pallor. Her voice also changed: it deepened, coarsened, as though her throat was dry and sore.

"He had cancer of the lungs. It was not an easy death. But he wants you to know he is happy now. There is no more pain. I can hear the rustle of cellophane paper; he ate a lot of sweeties, sucked them very loudly. Can you accept him?

Stella couldn't answer.

"A simple yes or no will do."

"Yes." Stella forced out a voice that surprised her with its loudness. "Thank you," she added, attempting a smile. It failed. Tears were streaming down her cheeks; her nose was running, and as she sniffed she searched in her bottomless handbag for a tissue.

Anita had not finished, she was merely pausing. Once she was sure that Stella was alright, she continued.

"I can see a long drive: an avenue lined with poplar trees. I think it might have been your family home, or his. He isn't telling me, just showing me. There's a big Victorian house: double-fronted, with a brass knocker in the shape of a tree, or it might be a leaf. Anyway, he is saying 'Knock and it shall be answered.' Does that make sense to you? He's gone now."

Stella did not remember the journey home. She did not bother to wash or to clean her teeth. She pulled off her clothes, letting them lie where they fell, and buried her shaking body beneath the duvet.

*

Stella was breathless when she reached the gates. They were open and a sign hung on them which read: "WET PAINT – DO NOT TOUCH". A tentative prod, with the tip of her index finger, assured her that they were in fact bone dry. The notice had obviously been there for some time. How long was it since her last visit? She remembered the daffs, but that did not mean anything; dream time paid no heed to real time. The avenue appeared to have undergone a complete make-over. The path looked pristine: freshly raked and weeded. The trees were in full, fresh leaf. They rustled, welcoming her back. 'It's summer' she thought. 'How nice.'

She had no memory of ever having lived here. Had it been in some previous life? Was that what this dream was all about? In which case, it wasn't so much a dream as a memory. Part of her wanted this to be her home. She wanted to belong here: to have memories of this place.

'Knock and it shall be answered.'

Had the trees said that? Stella looked at them, anxious to see them for the first time. This dream was different. Never before had she been revisiting – it was always the first time. The first time to enter the gates; the first time to see the trees; the first time to hear the voices; the first time to see the house: always a new experience, with the novelty and surprise of the unknown.

Eager to see the familiar through fresh eyes, Stella assessed her surroundings as objectively as she could. The trees were tall, very tall. Poplars, she knew they were poplars although she had no idea how she knew. She could recognise conker trees and pussy willow, and she could spot an oak because of the acorns. But ash, elder, and elm - they all looked the same. These trees, her trees, stood up like fingers pointing skyward. They were English poplars. For years she had thought of them as evergreen, but they weren't. Today she recalled having seen them in mid-winter, when they had let their leaves go. She had seen them standing naked and cold, bolstered by an absolute faith that they would be clothed again in the spring, brighter and full of the vital energy of the young. She tried now to picture them without their greenery, but she couldn't.

Stella ran her hands along the foliage. She let her fingers spread so that they barely touched the leaves beneath them. They responded with an instant stillness: a silence, but the second she let go they resumed their incessant nervous jiggling. Letting her fingers run on down over the rough bark, she knew she was feeling the age of the trees. They were older than her, much older, older than time. Stella knew then that she had known these trees longer than she had known her own life. But she had no idea how she knew all this.

As she walked on down the avenue the sun followed her. Each time it peeped from between the thick trunks of the trees it struck her with its warmth. The regular beat of her feet and the accompanying flashes of light made walking enjoyable. Her heart beat provided a steady percussion below the rippling leaves' string section. Stella stopped. The orchestra stopped with her and silence rose up like thunderous applause. The absence of wind was striking.

A blackbird landed on the gravel at Stella's feet. It was exhausted: its poor little heart jumping wildly behind a thin rib cage. It must have flown too far, and for too long. Stella bent down to examine it. The movement she had mistaken for a heart beat was the heaving and writhing of a hundred maggots. Disgusted by such an unwholesome object she lifted it gingerly by its unfolding wing and threw it away, hurling it as far as she could. But, no matter how hard she wiped her hands against her skirt, she could not wipe the memory from her mind. Poor little bird, it deserved a better end than that; being flung into a ditch to continue rotting, forever un-mourned and un-

loved.

Stella scrambled around on the grass until she found the little carcass and began to dig a hole on the bank of the ditch. While she dug, two beady eyes stared up at her. They were still bright: that horrid, glazed, milky blindness had not yet clouded them. One winked at her, a strange sideways wink, the lid moving across the eye, dimming it for a brief second before releasing the mischievous glint that had first caught her attention. The bird shook itself and rolled back up onto its spindly legs. The maggots withdrew before dissolving and vanishing from sight, but not before the quick yellow, beak had grabbed two or three and swallowed them whole.

Stella lay down on the grass so that her eyes were level with the bird.

"How did you do that? You're dead."

"Oh, come off it. Don't tell me you've never done that!" The bird began to preen itself and look around to make sure there were no maggots remaining.

"I certainly haven't. At least, I don't think I have."

"Ah, now you'd better decide if you're coming or going; migrating is a skill. Just go a bit farther each time. The knack is to know which way leads home. Practice makes perfect. It's easy peasy once you know. Bye."

With that the blackbird flew off, like a cartoon character from Uncle Remus, leaving Stella to continue her journey on down the avenue. Her thoughts were racing. This is my path. I have trodden it before; many, many times; some that I can remember; even more that I have forgotten.

Feeling uncommonly pleased with herself, she broke into a dance. Her feet gleamed as they tripped over the gravel, and she was delighted to see that she was wearing Dorothy's red glittering shoes which shone out against the bright path. Her arms linked with those of her mother and father, the three skipped along together, singing in harmony, as they followed the yellow brick road to the house.

Stella bounded up the steps, avoiding the crack on the fourth, and grabbed at the leaf- shaped knocker. Three loud raps...

*

Stella woke up at 4.44. Martina's coat was not in the hall, and when Stella peeped in her room was empty.

CHAPTER 14

The unmistakable smell of shepherd's pie filled the hall. Carefully Stella hung her coat on the half of the coat rack that still clung to the wall. With relief she saw the familiar leather mound on the floor, and stepped over it on her way to the kitchen. She half expected to see her mother standing by the oven - apron tied tight, her oven-cloth gripped in a white knuckled hand - the smell of the pie having taken her back ten years. But it was Martina, not her mother, who was busy in the kitchen. A quick glance into the sitting-room showed the table laid ready for tea. The pie sat in a Pyrex dish, browned to perfection. Martina picked it up with the towel and carried it through to the table. Stella followed her through still saying nothing.

"Hi Stel, sit yourself down. Brilliant timing! Brown sauce or ketchup? What d' you want to drink? Coke?"

"Water."

"Sorry, I forgot - Coke reminds you of your dad, right?"

"Where were you last night? When you didn't come home, I was worried sick."

Instead of answering Martina began to spoon large dollops of food on the two waiting plates. Stella tucked her chair under her, picked up her fork and began to push mince around the plate, as if inspecting it for foreign bodies.

"I was at Col's. Didn't think you'd mind as you were seeing your new friend, what's-her-name. Anyway you were out. Where did you go?" Martina spoke through a mouthful of mince.

Stella had just taken a forkful. She pointed to her full mouth and made it clear she was not in a position to answer. Martina waited. As soon as Stella swallowed, she pounced.

"So where did you go?" Martina was spooning her dinner into her mouth at a rate of knots. She had no problem speaking with a stuffed mouth.

Stella put her fork down and sighed. She turned her attention to the glass of water beside her and began to swirl it around slowly, watching the clear liquid take on the colours of the patterned glass as it turned. Again she said nothing.

Martina answered for her. "Of course, you don't have to tell me if you don't want to. But, like I thought we were friends. And that's what friends do. They like share things. Of course, like I said, if you don't want to tell me that's fine. Now you've got a new friend I don't suppose you need me."

Martina continued shovelling the mince and potato into her gyrating mouth. Stella stared at the open chasm in front of her. It looked as if it was haemorrhaging, the tomato sauce having turned the contents into a blood-soaked mush. Looking away, she turned her attention to her glass – sipping the water then twirling it around, before sipping again.

Stella had decided not to tell Martina about her visit to the church. Not because it had been so traumatic – but because she did not want to explain why she had gone there in the first place. Instead she chose to tell a little white lie.

"I went out alone. Actually I had some business to sort out – concerning my parents. I didn't ask you because a) it was personal and b) you weren't here.

Martina laughed. She had finished eating and pushed the empty plate away from her.

"Fair enough," she said, without a trace of animosity or jealousy.

Stella was relieved; lulled into thinking the whole matter had been dropped, when Martina floored her by adding,

"You didn't like your mum and dad much, did you."

"It's not something I think about. They were just Mum and Dad. What's to like or dislike?"

"How should I know? I never had a Mum or a Dad."

The single, blunt statement cut Stella like a knife. Martina got up and began to clear the plates. A rush of guilt swept over Stella: how could she have been so unthinking? At least she had known her parents. They had never abused her or treated her badly. In fact, if she bothered to think about it, she had a lot to thank them for.

"Sorry. I didn't think."

"It's okay. I don't think about it very much. Except… It's funny, but like I've begun to wonder what my mum would have been like. I like to think she'd have been like you, Stel."

The two women cleared the table in silence before settling back in the sitting room. Between them hung a whole conversation which one did not know how to start, while the other was waiting for the right moment. Both felt the mounting heaviness, the growing tension. When the weight of silence became too much, it was Martina who broke it.

"You know I told you about my dream the other night? Well, I dreamed it again the next night, exactly the same, pink baby and all that. Then, the night before last, I dreamed it again, only like it was different. I didn't know dreaming was like bloody buses, nothing for years then three come along together. Listen, see what you make of this. I was all alone, in a big room, sort of like a nursery and, like before, everything was pink. You remember Col's black room? Well, this was just like that only pink; everything was bloody pink and - how daft is this -made of wool. I can't describe it. It was as if the whole place had been knitted, yes that's it. Like even the bloody walls were knitted. Oh and there was a teddy bear. He was knitted too! And pink of course! Weird or what? But the weirdest thing of all was that I knew this room. Like it was my room, if you know what I mean. Only I'd never been there before. I hate pink. I mean really hate it. It's so chav. But in my dream I really loved it. Funny sort of dream. Nothing happened; it wasn't exciting, but I had the weirdest feeling that it meant something. Weird or what…"

She waited for a response, but none came. Stella's head was buzzing and she felt a lump somewhere deep in her guts. Or was it in her womb? It ached as if it knew it was empty.

Martina saw her flinch. It was almost imperceptible, but she spotted it.

"Then like last night I had another dream. Listen, I hope you're not cross with me or anything – for staying out – and not telling you. I didn't mean to worry you. Anyhow, where was I? Oh yeah, this dream. Well, it upset me. I mean like really freaked me out. I didn't tell Col, I thought I'd much rather tell you. In fact, I nearly came back to you I was that upset. You'd have loved that! Me bursting in in the middle of the night! Where was I? Oh yes, my dream - I was like looking for something. I'd lost something – no - it was more as though I'd lost someone. I felt so lonely. It was like I was the thing that was lost? Yes, that's exactly how I felt. I was lost.

"It was horrible. I was blubbering so loud it like woke me up, and you'll never guess what? I really was crying, sobbing like a blinking baby; just like I used to when I was in the home. You know, old enough to know you've been dumped, but too little to know why. Abandoned, that's the word. I'd been abandoned. Aren't dreams crazy? Silly question, you should know- you're always dreaming. Maybe I should have told Col about mine. He kept asking me what was wrong. What d' you think? You never told me what he said when you saw him. Did it help? He's a bit of a wanker, but like he's shit hot on dreams. Oops, sorry."

Stella had nothing she could say. Nothing made any sense to her. Her mind switched to overdrive. How could Martina know about the baby? It could be just a freak coincidence, but too many factors aligned with her personal story. Martina smiled. "Let's have some coffee, ay?"

Returning from the kitchen with two overfilled mugs, which she slopped onto the coffee table, Martina continued with her story.

"Well, it's not much of a dream by your standards, but then I'm like new at this lark. I suppose it could be just a memory, after all I was abandoned wasn't I? Anyway, I thought it would interest you. I mean like it was so real; it made me cry. Are your dreams always that real? I can't wait to have another one. How often do you dream? What's the matter, Stel, did I put sugar in yours by mistake?"

Rising slowly, Stella picked up her mug and left the room. She was going to bed. Martina said "Good Night", muttered something about "sweet dreams", and lit a cigarette. Thinking twice about the smoke, she crept down the hall and through the front door. In the safety of the fresh air she lit her fag and let out a loud bellow. It soared in the sulphur light where it mingled with toxic wisps from her Benson and Hedges. At the same time she raised two fingers in the direction of next door's curtains, just in case.

*

As if satisfied with dreaming by proxy, Stella's own dreams began to dry up, leaving her hungry for any titbit that Martina threw her way. Her personal dreams were never part of their discussions. In fact they were not so much discussions as discourses, with Martina taking the role of lecturer and Stella passively playing disciple. Like any keen student, Stella began to question her tutor, not openly, but privately when she was alone. At first she was simply looking for connections between Martina's childhood and her dream, but gradually her interrogation progressed, probing wider issues; seeking connections between her own past and that of this comparative stranger who had dropped, from the blue, into her life.

*

Dreams were fast becoming the only subject up for discussion at number 9. Martina had gone from a non-dreamer to having nightly adventures, all of which involved the avenue house. Gradually new factors were introduced, but Martina starred in them all. In one version she was dressed all in pink. In another she was held by strangers, separated from her mother by a glass wall. Always she was a baby when the dream began and grown up by the time it ended.

Stella said nothing during all these revelations, partly because she did not know what to say, but mostly because she was terrified of the obvious conclusions. She herself had only an occasional dream, in which her loyal friends Runs-With-The-Buffalo and the tiger would appear. They were a comfort, but offered no explanation. Martina's dreams worried Stella. At the same time they thrilled her. It was obvious that there must be some rational link between herself, her dreams and those that were visiting her young friend.

*

That night, when Stella was fast asleep, the door to her room was flung open by Martina. A quick glance at her the alarm clock made the hairs on the back of Stella's neck rise up, prickling her skin with a rash of chilling goose bumps. Martina hurled herself at Stella, crying with such vehemence, that Stella felt tempted to slap her face. It took an immense effort to prise the hysterical young woman off her, grip her by the shoulders and give her a good hard shake to ensure she was quite awake. After a while her sobs died down and she began to tell her tale.

"I've had another dream, Stella. It was so real. Christ, I've just got to like tell you about it before I forget it. Sorry, is it still the middle of the night?" All the while she spoke she was scanning the room apparently looking for a clock. Without a second glance at the bright green figures on the ever accurate digital face behind her, Stella repeated the words she had just spoken silently to her soul.

"Four, forty-four."

Martina almost smiled. "Sorry Stel, but like I need to talk - do you mind?" She was imploring, her voice a semi- tone below sickly.

Stella patted the side of her bed and Martina placed herself dramatically -'composing' herself – all the while reading Stella, checking on her timing, before beginning her story.

"Well, it started the same as before, all pink and

like me a tiny baby and all that. Then there is this like loud banging at the door – three knocks actually. I wake up, only when I wake up I'm still asleep, if that makes sense. I mean like I wake up in my dream only now I'm not a baby. I'm me, like fully grown and everything and not knowing I'm dreaming. I don't know – it's all a bit confused. Anyway, I get up and go downstairs. I know I'm at home but like I'm not here. And it's not the children's home. I don't know where I am. I'm in this huge great house, some mansion or other, old and spooky, with a bloody great staircase. Anyway, in my dream, I know the house really well. It feels like my house, so I assume I must live there; I must do 'cos like I know my way around. So, I go down to the door and undo all the bolts. God, there are hundreds of them. Bolts, chains, deadlocks, you name it. This door had the lot. Anyhow, when I finally like open the bloody thing there's no one there. That was odd too because like, even though it had taken ages to get downstairs, the last of the three knocks ended just as I opened the door. Like there was a time warp between the first knock and me getting to the door, I'm not kidding, it was a big house! Anyway like I said, there was no one there, not a soul. So, I go outside and like snoop around. I'm on this drive - all scrunchy – oh, what do you call it? Like Brighton beach…"

"Gravel. It was a gravel drive." Stella's voice trembled as she offered the suggestion to Martina.

"Yes, gravel. I never was any good with words, but like there's no sign of anyone, no footprints, no tyre tracks, nothing. I was just going to snoop about a bit to see if I could find who had knocked when I woke up. I mean like really woke up. Honestly, Stella, it was a fucking, whoops sorry, great barn of a place. And I, little old Martina, lived there. Like how bloody cool is that?"

*

Stella stopped gaping, but still sat staring in silence at Martina. This young woman had just described the other side of her own dream to her. This proven connection between the two of them was irrefutable. Their lives were linked not just for now, but possibly for eternity. Thinking her brain would explode, Stella got up, calmly edged passed Martina, and took herself to the bathroom where she sat down on the loo grasping her head in her hands. Her hands were getting wet. She didn't realise it, but she was crying.

CHAPTER 15

The bus pulled into Brighton, at that precise time when day meets night. Martina jumped nimbly from the platform and grinned at the driver. With a hefty shrug, she humped her knapsack high onto her back and turned out of Pool Valley, heading straight for the beach. The sea met her ears long before she saw it. Even before that, its salty tang had reached her nose. The swoosh of the waves followed by the dragging of pebbles as the tide hauled itself back to where it belonged - with the rest of the sea. This was familiar music: the repetitive surge and retreat had imbedded itself in her brain since childhood. Endless days on the beach, skimming stones, charging then retreating from the relentless waves: her mind flooded with a pleasant nostalgia.

From the Palace pier came the vulgar noise of the old town. It rang loud and predictable; the screaming of kids on the rides, the laughter of people having fun and getting drunk, all mixed with the sound of the sea: the Brighton symphony.

Martina sat near the water line on the darkening beach, now cleared of the earlier sun seekers, skimming pebbles until it was too dark to see if they bounced or sank. Stuffing a pleasingly smooth stone in her pocket, she climbed awkwardly back up to the esplanade, her Doc Martin's disappearing in the loose shingle. Defying traffic, her leather clad figure crossed the Stein, passed the tiered fountain with its gaudy lights, more visible now that all natural light had gone, to march back along the London Road. By the time she had reached North Road, her legs and back ached -tired from the weight of her rucksack. It was all up hill now until, nearly at the top, she turned left. Three houses more and she had arrived.

*

The lights were still on at number 25. They would be watching the telly or having a last drink before bed. They never sat up late. Running a B&B meant an early start. The vacancy sign was in the window. Did that mean business was not so good? Or was it still too early in the season to have bookings? Martina didn't really care. She rang the bell, leaning on it just a little too long for good manners and watched as the hall light extinguished the dark.

"Good Heavens!" The exclamation came from a large middle-aged woman whose dyed black hair framed her face like a helmet. Instinctively a hand ending in long pink nails reached to pat the helmet, to adjust her appearance for the guest. The helmet shifted in solid formation before settling back in the centre. This well-rehearsed performance was accompanied by a metallic jangling together of charms, swinging and clinking, as they dangled from the large gold chain which cut into the woman's puffy wrist. Aiming her voice over her shoulder she called out, "You'll never guess who it is, Bill."

A reply came from inside the house, abrupt and

gruff.

"I know. It's Marian. I can smell her from here. Tell her to get lost. There's nothing left for her here, she took it all last time."

Martina pushed passed the woman, calling out as she approached the front room.

"Nice to see you too, Dad!"

Martina looked around the little room. Little had changed in the three years since she had last been home. There was a different clock on the mantelpiece and the arm chairs sported new cushions. Other than that, it was exactly as she remembered it. Her mother had disappeared into the kitchen as the smell of hot oil began to permeate the air, totally overpowering the white orchid and lavender which puffed out at regular intervals from various dispensers dotted around the house. Her father watched suspiciously as his daughter's eyes surveyed the contents of the room. From the kitchen, a chirpy voice tried to deflect any potential hostilities with an over enthusiastic cheerfulness.

"Have you had your tea? You're in luck dear; the back single is empty until Friday. How long are you staying? It doesn't matter. I don't want to pry, dear. Put your bag down and take that heavy old coat off. I'm cooking your favourite, egg and chips. It is still your favourite isn't it, Marian? I'll fetch it in on a tray."

Her father was still eyeing her up and down. His narrow eyes disapproved and his voice was even more disparaging.

"Lean pickings, this time girl. I see you've

spotted the new clock. Can't think what happened to the old one! My grand-dad's that was... Antique... Worth a bob or two... There's only one thing worse than a common thief and that's a family one: a thieving junkie daughter who only cares about her next fix!" He picked up his paper, shook it hard and went back to reading.

The well-rehearsed words slid off Martina's leather back like water off one of Stella's ducks. She replied by raising her middle finger in silent salute. The smell of frying from the kitchen was calling her, so she left her father to the remorse and anger which swept over him in alternate waves. Her mother had laid a tray. Removing one of the settings already laid out for the guests, she placed it on the table and motioned for her daughter to sit down.

"It'll be nicer in here. He'll come round in a while. It's just a bit of a shock, you turning up out of the blue like this. Nothing wrong is there, Sweetheart? You can tell me. I won't say a word. He doesn't have to know." She put an arm around her daughter and placed the plate of egg and chips on the tray in front of her. The ketchup was already on the table in readiness for tomorrow's full English.

"Thanks," Martina mumbled through a mouth already stuffed with chips. She greedily snatched at the cool air. "You make the best chips in the world. But they're like too bloody hot!" Her words were garbled and her hands flapped frantically in front of her burning mouth.

"Well they've come from a hot place!" her

mother laughed, as she placed a glass of cold water on the table. This happened every time she cooked chips for her daughter. She smiled, as she battled with a nostalgic lump in her throat.

Martina gulped down the cooling liquid. "Never learn, do I?" She felt her mother's curiosity rising. Better to attack before the inevitable barrage of questions hit. "Don't worry. The police aren't going to be banging on the door at any minute. I'm clean. I know dad won't believe me, but like I haven't used for over a year."

The two women sat quietly in the kitchen having already communicated more than usual. One was suffering from bolting her egg and chips too quickly, whilst the other looked on: a smile of resignation on her face. It was the smile of a woman who was easily pleased: someone who expected very little from life, yet was always disappointed. To have her child back safe and well was nice, and she was not going to spoil things by raking over the past. Besides, she had not forgotten her daughter's temper. Violence was always possible if Marian felt crossed, found out, or cornered. Finished with her meal, Marian pushed the plate away and leaned back, tipping her chair recklessly onto its back legs.

"I'll have a bath now and get an early night. The back single, you said? My old room, ah, how sweet! I'll like help myself to towels. See you in the morning. Don't wake me; I don't want to eat with the rabble!" Her chair crashed back onto the lino and, grabbing her bag, she climbed the stairs, humming some unrecognisable tune.

Sweet Dreams

*

Mrs Smith cleared the tray, washed the eggy plate and reset the table for breakfast. Taking a deep breath, she patted her hair again, sending it wobbling to the left this time. After another deep breath, she sailed into the sitting room where her husband sat reading the Evening Argus. She poured him a top up from his bottle of lager, refreshed her gin, then sank into the arm chair opposite, waiting for him to say something. When he finally opened his mouth it made her jump.

"I've told you, I don't want her in this house, Rita. God in heaven, woman, what is wrong with you? Don't you ever learn? That girl is evil." Doug spat out the words and her face crumpled as they landed. Slowly he eased himself up and moved across the room to perch on the arm of Rita's chair. The chair creaked and Rita sighed as his large arm wrapped around her. She let her head fall against his beer belly, no longer mindful of her hair.

Her sigh contained the pain of the past twenty five years. Broken trust, lies, violence and heart break: all of these had resulted from sharing their lives with their daughter. The two of them sat together for a while, without speaking or moving. If a stranger had entered the room, they might have assumed this couple were the recipients of some dreadful news: bereavement, or a terminal disease. There was no rejoicing, no indication that their prodigal daughter had returned to the fold, unrepentant and unwelcome. Her father had no desire to kill yet another fatted calf.

*

It was two whole days before Martina surfaced from her old room, dumped a pile of washing on the kitchen floor and stormed out. As the door slammed, Mrs Smith sat down at kitchen table. She was close to tears. After some time she pulled herself up to the fullness of her considerable height, marched purposefully into the sitting-room, eased herself down in front of the sideboard where she remained - kneeling on the green and brown shag pile. She opened the cupboard, her rear end sticking out inelegantly, as she reached to the back of the bottom shelf from where she pulled out a well thumbed photo album. With her free hand, she raised the dog-eared book over her head, sliding it onto the top of the unit. A mild expletive escaped her lips as she felt it push past the fruit bowl scratching the polished surface as it did so. It was with some difficulty that she pulled herself up, until once more she stood upright.

Wiping the scratch with the sleeve of her cardigan, she swore again. Then clutching the book to her well-upholstered chest, she returned to the kitchen, carefully wiped her already clean hands on a piece of kitchen towel, and opened the album. Spread before her was her record of a life: a life which made no sense to her puzzled brain. Not being a woman of faith, she often questioned the purpose of life; not in any great philosophical way, just out of curiosity really. 'Had any of it been worthwhile? Did the good times outweigh the bad? What was the point of it all?' Before her spread an account of a life lived with honesty and faithfulness - and of another that wasn't.

The first four pages were filled with tiny black and white images of her with her mother and father, her with her sisters and the family dog, her in school uniform with no front teeth. There were lots of her with her best friend Anita. There was a picture of her grandfather and grandmother standing outside their little house in Manchester with a baby in an enormous pram. There was even one of her maternal great-grandmother looking like something from an ancient history book. The one of the entire Smith family, on Brighton beach, had been taken just after she had got engaged to Doug. And there was a whole page of wedding pictures, taken at the registry office in the Stein. Her fingers could not resist reaching out to touch the radiant, slim young couple in the centre. Life had been full of meaning and promise then. Where had it all gone? Her hand went to her face and she wondered when she had grown so big.

Not prepared to waste the morning regretting every chocolate biscuit, every gin and lime that had passed her lips since then, she gently turned the page, smoothing it with her left hand as her right wiped away a tear before it dropped and marked the paper.

This page contained photos of Marian as a baby. Quite adorable: a tiny porcelain doll and a long awaited addition to the family. They had taken her picture at every possible opportunity and the rest of the album was full of snapshots of the child. Marian's first cot, Marian in her pram, Marian in nappies, nightdresses, bunches, plaits, Easter bunny ears, tinsel halos and witches' Halloween hats. Each snap showed a happy, normal infant. None displayed a hint of the tormented, troublesome creature that lurked behind all this innocence: programmed to wreck the lives of her unsuspecting parents.

Mrs Smith thumbed the pages until her eyes stopped at a photo of a tall sullen girl wearing a brand new blazer and hat. That was when it had started, she thought: when Marian had started secondary school. It was then that things had begun to go seriously wrong. They thought it was adolescent moodiness at first. The girl became sullen and rude. She hated anything to do with the family, and went to great lengths to avoid them. She stole food from the fridge, which she ate secretively in her room. Hygiene went out the window. She began to dye her hair: first orange, then purple, then black, until she settled for black with a stripe of the colour of the week. The walls of the bathroom bore the Technicolor history of this particular phase. Even now, the smart cream and brown tiles held a slight memory of magenta, leaving Mrs Smith wondering each time she cleaned them just where she had gone wrong.

Had she known how innocuous, how innocent, all this was compared with what was to come, she would willingly have turned back the clocks and returned to their life then. With the onset of puberty Marian became more deceitful - prone to fly into ugly, unpredictable rages. These outbursts worsened, each one putting the fear of God into her mother. The malice was always aimed at her, although the poor woman could not for the life of her think why that should be. Thankfully the outbursts were short lived, but alarmingly frequent.

Mr Smith grew first to distrust, then to dislike his daughter - this, despite being out at work most of the time and ignorant of her most outrageous escapades. Mrs Smith tried hard to convince herself that it was natural teenage behaviour. She never told tales, but became through necessity a master at telling white lies. Had she been aware of the full extent of Marian's waywardness she might have been driven to extreme action herself. When she believed Marian was upstairs doing her homework, or tucked up safely in bed, or staying over with a friend from school, the likelihood was that the girl was in the centre of town getting up to things that way out-stripped the realm of teenage pranks.

From the age of twelve Marian was adept at climbing out of her window. Once free, she would hurtle further and further out of control. The crowd she mixed with were much older than she was and certainly not the type of friends a parent would want for their young daughter. She never brought friends home, at least not when her parents were in. As she got older, she absented herself more and more from the family home, deigning to put in a presence only when she was hungry, or in need of a change of clothes or money.

By the time she was fourteen Marian was bunking off school most of the time. She was into petty crime and smoking cannabis. By fifteen she was expelled and on hard drugs. The Smith's family life, which never resembled a game of Happy Families, had become a ride on a roller coaster with the devil's daughter at the controls.

*

Mrs Smith stroked her album, letting her fingers caress the contents at arm's length. There were beds to make and shopping to be done. She wondered if her domestic obsessing was what had driven her daughter away. Was it the predictability of it all: the excruciating boredom of everyday life? 'Kids today want excitement and thrills', she thought as she cradled the book, rocking it like a baby. Then with a deliberate snap she shut the past between the protected pages. Marian would be twenty five this year; she was not a child. 'Anyway,' she thought, 'boredom is no excuse. I spent most of my childhood being bored. Christ, I've lived most of my life being bored; there are worse things in life than a little tedium.' Counting her blessings, she eased herself out of her chair, and turned, to find Marian standing in the doorway, watching her.

"Hi, Mum. Did I make you jump? What's that? Not those old photos again! Never fucking give up, do you?"

"I've got to get on. Your father'll be back soon, wanting his dinner." Mrs Smith brushed passed her daughter and took herself upstairs, where she could take solace in smoothing scented bed linen and replacing the lavender potpourri in the airing cupboard. When she dared to venture back downstairs, Marian was nowhere to be found.

*

Tuesday, Wednesday, Thursday and Friday went by with the house free of Marian. Come Saturday a peace that passed for normality descended on the B&B. The rooms were full, all but the back single, which Mrs Smith kept vacant, just in case. That evening, lost in the romance of Strictly Come Dancing, the fragile peace was shattered. Marian, drunk, possibly high, burst into the room and promptly threw up all over the green and brown carpet. Her father stormed off to the pub. Marian passed out in his chair, leaving Mrs Smith to clean up.

An hour later - with Marian tucked up in the back single - the living room was heavy with the synthetic smell of lavender and white orchid, this time mixed with an organic undertone of vomit. Retreating to the less noxious atmosphere of the kitchen, Mrs Smith sat at the table nursing a large gin and an even larger headache. Between each sip, her teeth ground against each other, exacerbating the pain that now filled her heart and her head. Uncharacteristically not waiting until her husband and all the guests were safely home, she refilled her gin and took her self off to bed.

*

Next morning Marian made a messy coffee and decamped to the sitting-room. Slumped in her father's chair, one leg slung over the arm - having retuned The Archers to a heavy rock program - she idly watched her leg as it swung in time to the pounding beat. Her head thrown back, she joined in with the lyrics, drowning out the sound of her father's return. The first she knew of it was the hefty slap that sent her leg crashing to join the other one. Mr Smith reclaimed his chair without waiting for his daughter to vacate it. The gauntlet was thrown.

As he slammed the radio off Marian rose, poised to accept the challenge, and her mother entered the room.

"Why do you always do this the moment I turn my back? It's like living in a bloody war zone. Well, enough is enough!"

Mrs Smith had lost count of how many times she had held it together, often by the thinnest and feeblest of threads. Whether it was something in the look that Doug gave her, or in the stream of abuse that her daughter let loose, this time was the last straw. Mrs Smith erupted. The explosion was nuclear.

The room was still standing, but nothing in it would be the same again. Mr Smith, his mouth open, was cowering behind his chair with his daughter cowered behind him, a look of abject terror on the face which she pressed into his cardigan. It was the closest the two had been in decades.

Not quite sure what she had done, or indeed how she had done it, Mrs Smith calmly removed her apron and took herself off to the Norfolk Arms for a large gin. She burst into the saloon like John Wayne - Gloriana, Britannia, Liberty all rolled into one. Triumph radiated from her - so much so that the other regulars kept the gin flowing all evening; her own purse and handbag having been left behind. By the time the landlord called 'Time', she had to be escorted home by Judy and Bert from across the road.

Nuclear whiteout was replaced by equally devastating fallout. This was the end of an era. The next day, Marian was striding down North Road in her Doc Martin's with no sign of a tail dangling between her legs, but with the knowledge that an important battle had been lost. It was the last the Smiths would see of their daughter Marian. Martina was back with a vengeance, to be found less than an hour later under the Palace Pier, nursing an empty beer can and a desperate craving for a fag. As she hurled a fistful of pebbles into the grey sea, she vowed that this was the last time Marian would ever come to Brighton. She had only got two pounds for the clock and nothing for the charm bracelet. Her father had been right. Now, with no fags, no credit left on her mobile and no money, she had no option but to hitch back to London. 'The Girl without the Kalashnikov' hoisted her knapsack high on her black leather back, before pointing her thumb in the direction of home.

CHAPTER 16

Stella hated to admit it but the house was horribly empty. All evidence of Martina had vanished with her disappearance, carried off in the knapsack she toted wherever she went. There were no skimpy knickers dripping over the bath. No dirty dishes crowded out the sink. The rings around the bath had gone. The rapidly diminishing bath-cream remained as it was, as if frozen in time. No heavy leather coat made a hazard of the bottom stair. Number 9 Maple Street showed no trace of 'The Girl without the Kalashnikov'.

Stella managed to get to work each day but it was a struggle. Routine was all that held her life together. Arrival home after her shift brought nightly disappointment. She had got used to the strange girl who had bounced into her life, only to bounce out again, leaving no clues as to where she had gone or for how long. When two days and nights had passed without so much as a word, she toyed with the idea of reporting Martina as a missing person. But the memory of her past experience with the police dissuaded her. Instead she rang Anita.

*

Anita called round early that Saturday. She was horrified by what met her. Stella had made an effort: she was wearing some lipstick and her new bright jumper, but it was not enough to disguise the distraught wreck she had become. Anita's first reaction was to offer some healing. Reluctant to admit her ignorance, Stella refused, insisting that she was fine, tired, maybe even a little run down, but not ill.

Anita did not need psychic skills to pick up on the negativity that engulfed Stella – but they were immediately engaged - honing in on the cause of such destruction. It was clear to her that another person was involved - the obvious candidate being Martina. Over coffee Stella had told Anita that she was not related to Martina, but was in fact her landlady. The news came as a relief as Anita had been dreading the unpleasant task of warning a woman to beware of her own child Cleary there were strong emotional ties between the Stella and the girl - ties that bordered on the maternal. Experience told Anita to tread very carefully. It would be so easy to alienate Stella. The tell-tale signs - shutters and emotions tightly shut - were already apparent. Anita was a caring woman. She was also stubborn and determined. Willing to put herself in the firing line to save another, she had often met with hostility, taking the flack in order to prevent an avoidable disaster. Anita knew she was going to have to approach the subject obliquely, possibly applying a certain amount of deception, in order to get the message across. The fact that she was dealing with a friend made her double her resolve. One thing was for sure: she had to warn Stella of the potential danger that was so clearly, and rapidly, approaching.

Getting Stella to relax was in itself a challenge. As the afternoon progressed, the wall of resistance weakened. Eventually Anita was able to breach it and tune into the source of such discord. Her initial assumptions had been correct. Martina was at the root of it. Anita was just weighing up the least damaging way to broach the subject when Stella herself provided a way in.

"Martina's gone AWOL. I'm worried sick. She left no note, no contact number – she could be lying dead in a ditch for all I know. I really don't know what to do."

Anita offered up a small prayer of thanks. The way had been opened for her, but she would still need to tread with care.

"I'm sure she'll be alright. Martina is perfectly capable of looking after herself. She'll be back soon enough. I'm sure I'd know if something untoward had happened. I'd feel it." She studied Stella's face. Her words of comfort appeared to have had some affect so she continued. "No. my dear, it's you I'm worried about. There's so much pain around you, Stella. Please let me help you."

Far from receiving comfort Stella was picking up negative vibrations. Was she correct in thinking there was a drop in temperature each time Martina was mentioned? To have an open discussion about her was not an option. Evasive action was called for.

"I know you don't like Martina, but none of this is her fault. It's my fault. I get confused. We had a row, well not a row exactly. Something happened... something very odd. I don't want to talk about - it it's too personal - I don't understand it myself, not fully. But Martina and I are… I can't explain it – it's amazing – quite astounding really. I think she feels it too – this strange bond or whatever. Anyway I handled the situation badly. I can't sleep, I get very edgy. Now she's gone and I miss her. That's all I want to say. I really don't want to talk about it anymore."

"Listen to me Stella I think you are quite ill. You need positive energy around you and Martina's influence is very negative. You really mustn't trust her, she is too manipulative. Maybe her going is all for the good."

As Anita was speaking Stella stood up. Anita knew she had gone too far, too fast. In a vain attempt to repair the damage she added,

"If you want listen to me, will you listen to your guide? You already know him."

Stella was ready to call the whole thing off. She had not asked for this advice. All she had wanted to know was whether she was related to Martina. She wanted to shout at Anita. To voice her thoughts in an authoritative way, 'This is getting out of hand. What with hints of threats, warnings - and who was this so-called guide? Why haven't you mentioned him before - at the church? Eh? Where was he then?'

But of course Stella could say nothing. Instead she listened with amazement as Anita continued, her soft voice uttering words that threw Stella completely off guard.

"He says his name is Runs-With-The-Buffalo, he looks wonderful, full eagle headdress and magnificent beads round his neck. He is very old, but strong - wiry. His voice is fabulous, nasal, deepened by the years – I could listen to him for ages."

Stella's mouth stayed open. Anita's eyes remained closed as she went on to describe the old chief. It was him. His headdress of eagle feathers, the beads and medicine wheel that hung round his throat, his narrow sun-scorched eyes. Stella closed her own eyes – hoping to get a glimpse of her dear friend.

"He is chanting - singing - and stomping out the rhythm with his bare feet. He is calling you 'Woman-who-Dreams'."

As she spoke Anita's own voice grew deeper. Her face became longer, her nose narrowed, her eyes remained closed but behind the tight lids were the piercing lasers of Runs-With-The-Buffalo. Stella could feel the presence of the old chief as vividly as if he was touching her. He was speaking, not Anita, his familiar, commanding voice.

"You have not called to me lately. Remember me. I am with you always, on the plains, in the park, by your side. Learn to know who your friends are. Do not give your trust too readily. Friends should not betray each other lest they get eaten."

Anita opened her eyes and looked at Stella. Her face once again rounded, smiling.

"That doesn't make sense to me, but he says you'll know what he means."

Anita took a sip of her tea, although it was quite

cold by now. She was not about to give up. Moving nearer to Stella she placed her arm around her. Stella stiffened and moved away.

"I am so worried about you, Stella. You do trust me, don't you? I'm your friend. Please, just hear me out. Then, I promise if you don't want to hear anymore I shall keep quiet. I shan't say another word." Anita took the silence as tacit approval to continue. "Martina is damaged, she's dangerous. I don't know her life history, but she is bent on some form of revenge. Please, Stella, just be careful. Don't let her fool you – especially where money is concerned. Have you been signing any legal documents? Don't do anything without checking with your solicitor. Martina is…"

"Shut up. Shut up. I'm not listening."

Stella had jumped up. Her body shaking - her hands clasped firmly over her ears. But she could not block her thoughts. 'Just who does this woman think she is? This isn't why I asked her here. I thought she wanted to be my friend. The last thing I need is another 'Inquisitor.' I should never have got involved with this stupid woman or her church. She's the one I shouldn't trust. She knows nothing about Martina. She has no right to say such things and in my house - Martina's house."

"Please go. I want you to leave now", was all she managed to say.

She left out how much she hurt: how she resented her space being invaded. How she detected a derogative tone whenever Anita mentioned Martina. It was insulting. All she wanted now was to be left alone. Fatigue washed over her, it took all her energy to remain standing. Stella sighed, and her eyes pleaded with Anita to go.

"I can't leave you like this. I'm sorry if I've hurt you, but we need to talk things through."

Stella's reaction turned from resentment to hostility. "I told you to go."

By now she was standing by the front door which she held wide, her body turned to a frosty shadow partially obscured by the glass. A pang of guilt struck as her eyes made brief contact with Anita's. They were moist, brimming over with concern, pleading to be forgiven. The last thing Stella wanted was a display of tears.

"Call me next week – we can talk then. I'm really tired. I just want to go to bed."

Anita sniffed as she rummaged in her bag for a tissue. She sniffed again. When she spoke her soft voice was imploring.

"I'm away all next week. I've got a booking in the West Country. God, that's such bad timing. Listen, Stella, why not come with me? Take some time off work. A little holiday will do you good. It would be lovely – time to get to understand each other better... grab a little sunshine... breathe some sea air. Just leave a note for Martina – she's perfectly capable of looking after herself for a while."

Stella shivered with the drop in temperature.

"Just go. Call me when you get back if you still want to."

The door closed leaving a woman standing on either side - one crying, both nursing regrets.

Sweet Dreams

*

Anita tipped the contents of her bag onto the passenger seat. Finding the elusive Kleenex she wiped her eyes, blew her nose, then secured her seatbelt and drove to the top of the road. Here she stopped, made a three point turn and drove back to number 9.

Anita sat outside for sometime, trying to pluck up the courage to ring the door bell. The whole afternoon had been a disaster. She should never have said such things, especially not to someone as vulnerable as Stella. Anita did not retract the content of her message: Martina was bad news. But she could kick herself for being so tactless. She knew what Martina meant to Stella. What had she been thinking of? Her delivery had been all wrong - its lack of prudence unprofessional. Determined to put things right Anita got out of the car and walked briskly up the path.

The curtains twitched at the window of number 7. Anita smiled politely as they fell back into place. Her hand went up to the bell, but something made her stop and place her ear to the door. She could hear Stella's voice loud and clear. A heated conversation was taking place. Embarrassed at the thought of eavesdropping, Anita retreated down the path. She assumed Martina had come back. Possibly – hopefully the two women were having it out in an open frank discussion – withdrawal seemed the most diplomatic action. Maybe her message had got through? Was Martina being challenged, receiving her marching orders? She hoped so. Clinging to this glimmer of optimism Anita got back in her car and headed home to discuss the whole sorry business with her long suffering husband.

*

As the front door shut on Anita, Stella tried hard to convince herself that the previous hour or so had not happened. Her thinking - at best confused, at worst chaotic - left only her with only one certain fact. She was under threat - but from whom? There were only two candidates, Martina and Anita. And, as Stella correctly deduced, Anita was hardly likely to put herself in the frame. The 'appearance' of 'Runs-With-The-Buffalo' had unsettled her. Had she imagined it? Where had he come from? Her head could not accept that Anita had 'summoned him up'. The old chief had not mentioned Martina by name. If the girl was so dangerous he would have said so in no uncertain terms. Stella knew he was never one to pussyfoot around. 'Surely' Stella thought, 'the only possible explanation is that I concocted the whole thing: I dreamed it... which leaves the vital question unanswered. Why?'

It unnerved Stella to hear Martina described as dangerous, whether imagined or real. She had to admit that the girl was irresponsible, inconsiderate, and at times lazy. But bad behaviour was not the same as malevolence. It was true that since their shared dream their relationship had changed. That strange experience had triggered extreme emotion on both sides. It occurred to Stella that Martina may have wanted – might have needed - to talk it through. Had she been unsympathetic? After all Martina had shared on intimate moment with her which, as Stella knew better than most, was not an easy thing to do. She now feared that her own impulsive reaction could have been taken as tantamount to running away. To abandon a vulnerable young girl, to leave her confused and scared, just because she, Stella, was incapable of facing her own inadequacy was inexcusable. Stella felt unworthy of Martina's trust.

Even with her limited reasoning Stella could see that her own mental withdrawal was as much an act of evasion as Martina's physical retreat. In their own way both had behaved in a cowardly fashion. On reflection it was clear to Stella that Martina's flight was the direct result of her own selfish action. She had forced Martina to react. The thought of being abandoned, yet again, had proved too painful. Or had her leaving been an act of vengeance? Was it the girl's only way of conveying her desolation, her sense of abandonment, the self loathing, the self judgement: the negative emotions that had marred her life? Or was she simply acting out of spite: out to hurt the only person she could hold responsible? In the face of all this Stella could hardly blame Martina. The guilt was hers and she would take her punishment with good grace.

*

What began as a silent soliloquy developed into an imagined dual, Stella's arguments being countered by an imaginary Martina who parried then thrust back. As the fight developed Stella began to externalise her thoughts, to talk out loud, taking both sides of the argument, a device which denied her the ability to foil any weak strokes by ignoring them. Stella could not see her own suit of chainmail, but she recognised Martina's preferred protection: a suit of emotional armour which, like her thick leather coat, she used to keep people at a distance. Her tendency to shout and swear pushed them still farther away. Stella found she was enjoying the fight. Shouting back – something she had never dared do face to face - peeled the layers away. It was wonderfully cathartic.

Years of pent up frustration were unleashed. Inhibitions were drowned out by the decibels Stella's liberated voice generated. When the battle ended it left Stella satiated, her throat sore, her body exhausted. Mentally she was refreshed. A window in her mind had opened, allowing fresh air in. It was time to run a nice hot bath and wash the day out of her hair.

As she climbed the stairs Stella decided that if - when - Martina came home, they should have this candid discussion for real. She concluded that Anita had been too presumptuous in overstepping the line. But it had not been malicious and was not worth losing a friendship over. They could all start afresh, on a permanent, meaningful footing - just as soon as Martina returned,

When Martina had been missing for a whole week, Stella began to fear she was never coming back. Their imagined talk, their shared dream, these were never far from Stella's thoughts. At night Stella willed herself to visit the avenue to see if it had been altered by Martina's visit, wondering if so, in what way it would have changed. The question, the hope fermenting in her brain was electrifying. 'What if Martina is waiting at the gates? What if Martina opens the door.'

*

Stella's power to control her dreaming stopped the day Martina left. Now, if she slept at all, it was in fitful bursts. What dreams she had came in confused snatches. Without the ability to wake at will, she would wake involuntarily, often at an inauspicious moment which splintered her dreams into disjointed fragments. Not knowing who had taken control of her dreams became a constant source of worry to her.

Martina was never far from Stella's thoughts. The incident of the shared dream had provided a link which she felt would never be broken. Although they had not discussed it, Stella felt sure that should they, they would discover its significance. Maybe her dreams, their dreams, were trying to tell her something far more direct and concrete than any dream analysis could deduce.

Her visit to Col came flooding back. That black room, his constant use of the word 'okay', his whiter than white teeth. Stella had liked him, he was easy to like. She remembered he was Martina's friend, and took some comfort from the thought that Martina might be staying at his flat. She recalled what Col had said to her. His analysis had been interesting, but that was all it had been. She had no desire to allow him to encroach further on her privacy. Anita's interest had been different again. That too had felt unwanted and, although well meaning, intrusive. With Martina it had been different. Only Martina had displayed an intimate knowledge of Stella's private world, a knowledge that no one had imparted to her. This fact Stella had found startling at first, then gratifying and now - dare she admit - desirable?

Stella gave serious thought to this conundrum. The solution when it came was like a lightening bolt. She and Martina shared the same 'other' world. They occupied the same space- maybe not always together - perhaps on different planes – like parallel universes waiting for the right time to converge. Martina was present in Stella's 'other' world, perhaps she had always been there. It was shared territory now. It thrilled her to think that they had both been there, walked there, both belonged there. Others had merely glimpsed it through another's eyes. That was the difference: the difference between spectator and participant. They were worlds apart.

Such irrational thoughts – wholly cogent to the

thinker – began to weave convoluted paths in Stella's brain: paths often shadowed by high fences, leading to blind alleys blocked by dead ends. At other times they lit up like the road to Damascus, awash with blinding revelations: Stella's own shadow offering the only distinction between light and dark. It was all of little consequence to Stella. She had stopped pinching herself long ago: what difference was there if she was awake, asleep, dreaming or dead? 'What had happened to her control? Had she passed it on to the next generation in the form of Martina? Indeed had she ever been truly awake or was life one long dream? Questions like this gnawed away at Stella's sanity both whilst asleep and when awake. Her unique logic told her life was an hallucination. She found little evidence to prove otherwise. But this personal reasoning brought another unwanted conclusion with it – It meant that Martina was also a dream. There was no trace of Martina; ergo she did not exist.

*

Stella's mind continued to rock on a seesaw from total delusion to a basically functional sanity. The stress of constant mental turmoil eventually took its toll: Stella's downward spiral was rapid. Not eating, hardly sleeping and never resting, she became physically, as well as mentally, ill. What little flesh she had melted away: a fact noted by everyone at work although no-one commented to her face. But then hardly anyone spoke to her at the best of times. Her clothes hung on her: the only way her skirt stayed up was with a belt pulled in tightly around her waist. Her skin, always pale, took on an unhealthy pallor and her lips were cracked and drained of colour despite a smear of lipstick. Her appearance became so startling that 'The Woolly Hat' actually offered her seat to the 'poor young woman', telling her, in no uncertain terms to:

"Get yourself to a doctor, dearie, and tell him to give you something for that anorexia."

*

It was true she was hardly eating. Nothing stayed down long enough to make the effort worthwhile. Her stomach churned constantly vying for dominance with a persistent headache. Nothing had happened to dispel her mistrust of doctors leaving Stella resigned to suffer in silence. She refused to answer the telephone or open the door to anyone. It was only her stubborn independence that got her to work each morning.

Then on Friday morning she passed out at the bus stop. Someone called for an ambulance which carried her off to Milford General.

CHAPTER 17

The hospital insisted on keeping Stella in order to carry out various tests. At first she remained oblivious to her surroundings, but after a couple of days taking regular food and medication she was sitting up and taking notice. They put her in an unbearably noisy open ward which to her horror had men in it. Nurses flapped about and orderlies rattled trolleys from which they doled out inedible breakfasts, elevenses, lunches, teas then suppers, and finally night time beverages. If it wasn't food it was pills and potions dispensed by robotic nurses in what seemed to be a chaotic and potentially lethal fashion. There were mawkish 'Hospital Friends' who appeared from nowhere selling sweets, newspapers and sordid, tawdry paperbacks; adding their own wheeled contribution to the constant rush of noise and confusion.

If the days were bad, the nights were worse; every sound magnified by the pretence of hush. Stella remembered the peace that existed beyond the hospital walls and prayed to be sent home to die quietly in her dreams. Sleep was impossible: dreaming was out of the question. The man opposite rang his bell all day. He also rang it at regular intervals throughout the night, alternating periods of deafening snoring with loud whispered complaints that he could not sleep because of the noise. The woman to her left went to the loo every five minutes which involved a mammoth production number on each occasion. And the man in the corner was – well Stella was disgusted and refused to turn her head in his direction after her first shocking revelation. The whole hospital thing was a nightmare. Stella was in a bad place with little hope of relief.

*

The familiar voice - such abuse could only come from one mouth – was a tonic. For once Stella did not recoil at the expletives; they were music to her ears. By the time Martina appeared, Stella was eager and expectant.

"Stupid, fucking cow!"

She turned and raised her middle finger in the direction of the nurses' station. Then mimicking the nurse she shouted,"'No flowers in the ward. They're not healthy!'"

She laughed and addressed Stella in her own voice, "Ha! You can have flowers at your funeral, like when it's too bloody late, but when they might actually make you feel better someone has a fucking rule banning them!" Having got her angst out in the open, Martina turned her full attention to Stella.

"God Stel, you look fucking awful!"

Martina peeled off her signature scarf, unwinding it with broad sweeping gestures. But she remained cocooned in leather as she plonked herself on the edge of Stella's formally neat bed. Stella recalled how surprised she had been at the weight of that coat the first time she had lifted it. Since dislodging the rack, the coat had lived either on Martina's back or on the bottom stair in the hall.

Holding her hands up, Martina fended off Stella's inevitable rebuke. "I know, I know, 'don't swear.' Seriously though, what has happened to you? You look half dead."

Martina flung her leather-clad arms around Stella.

For a split second Stella recoiled, then allowed herself to melt into the hug.

"I can't leave you for a minute without like something dreadful happening. What's wrong with you? Do they know? When can you come home? I got such a shock when you weren't in your room. The old biddy next door told me they'd taken you to hospital. So what happened?"

"You spoke to number 7?" In all her years of living in Maple Street, Stella had never exchanged a single word with the woman in number 7.

"Yeah, why?"

"Nothing, it doesn't matter." Stella felt as though she herself had come home. All the fears and anxieties of the past week evaporated leaving no trace of their existence. In an instant everything was back to normal. Martina was home. "It would seem that I'm anaemic – I'm suffering from a lack of iron. They're giving me a course of injections. Then, if my blood count reaches a certain level and stays there, I can come home. Anyway, more to the point, where have you been? I didn't know if you were coming back or what to think. I was really worried." Stella pushed Martina away, only gently. A second hug would have been too much: her skin ached and her body felt too fragile to withstand Martina's bear like enthusiasm.

"What do you mean, 'if?' Of course I've come back! It's my home isn't it? Like you're the only family I've ever had!"

*

On the Monday night, three days after Stella's being taken to hospital, Martina had arrived back unannounced. Anxious not to wake Stella – deeming this no time to have a row – she had climbed onto her bed and within seconds was fast asleep. Martina had made a lot of decisions since that empty beer can hit the grey English Channel.

*

Martina took out a cigarette and began to search her pockets for a lighter. Stella frowned. She peered around to see if anyone else had noticed. They hadn't. She smacked Martina's arm playfully.

Martina was right: Stella did look 'fucking awful'. Her skin was sallow and dehydrated. Her already wispy hair looked thinner, duller and was in need of a jolly, good wash.

"I missed you, young woman."

"Missed you too!"

*

For the rest of the visit neither uttered another

word. In this comfortable silence Stella took time to study her young friend. Martina was slim to the point of being bony: an elongated frame, not dissimilar to Stella's, just a tad taller. Her hair was black, obviously dyed but probably naturally dark, cut longer on one side than the other, so that it hung down over the left eye, causing her to squint. When it really annoyed her she would shake her head with a defiant toss; a mannerism destined to last far longer than the hairstyle. Stella smiled at this thought. She sensed vulnerability, which she guessed was an ingredient to their unlikely bonding. Martina's clothes were odd; to Stella's conventional eye they were bizarre. Nothing matched, yet they presented a unity, which was precisely the effect Martina wanted: a scruffy mishmash of textures and shapes giving the overall impression of a hurried visit to the local charity shop: a pretty accurate appraisal. However, Stella knew, from the length of time Martina spent in the bathroom each day, that this was no haphazard look. Each layer was carefully applied, from the skimpy pants that dripped on the line above the bath each night, to the top layer of mohair and leather. Each finger joint bore at least one silver ring – some heavily ornate, others delicate and romantic.

Over the months Stella's disapproval had mellowed into an acceptance of this way-out style. Not with a fondness that made her want to emulate it, but with an admiration of the 'freedom of spirit', the blasé assertiveness that it displayed. The fact that they shared the same home gave

Stella a feeling of partial belonging to an alternative modern world - albeit by proxy.

Martina's welcome return promoted a need in Stella to know more about 'The Girl without the Kalashnikov'. She knew Martina's name, and that she had also been a patient of Dr Devant. She knew that Martina had been abandoned at birth, that she had been brought up in a children's home and that she hated porridge. She had no idea how old she was, or when her birthday was or what ambitions she had, if any. Without making a conscious decision, Stella was putting herself in the role of mentor: an older woman who could guide Martina through the traumas of life, to be there if needed. In short she wanted to play mother.

If Martina had possessed the ability to read Stella's mind she would have been delighted. Not that she wanted another mother. 'The one in Brighton was more than enough!' But this was exactly the hook she had been fashioning and now poor Stella had swallowed it. Moreover fate had played straight into Martina's hands. An immobile, vulnerable Stella would be so much easier to manipulate. Her hospitalisation was a God send.

Martina resolved to make her self indispensable and worm her way further into Stella's no-longer-so-reluctant heart. Taking a deep breath, she replaced her frown with a beaming smile, a pleased to see you, 'ever-so concerned about you' smile.

"I'll come back tomorrow with some grapes. The old cow can't complain about them!" Martina left, throwing a kiss to Stella and a Nazi salute to the nurse.

*

Stella was right in thinking that she knew very little about this girl. Martina had landed in her life, with such force, that Stella had not known what hit her. The emotional vacuum in which Stella lived her entire waking life offered no protection from manipulative invasion. Stella, for her part, had presented as a sitting duck. Martina, always on the look out for just such a target, had pounced. Her own life had hit rock bottom. She was jobless, virtually penniless and homeless. She had in her own words, 'run out of suckers to sponge off.'

Enter Stella. The first time Martina saw her at the doctor's surgery she marked her out as a soft touch. Well dressed - so obviously reasonably well off. Under treatment – so probably vulnerable. And with the unmistakable look of a loner about her. At first Martina thought small; the odd free coffee, maybe a lunch, or a cash hand-out or two. But Stella was perfect. Played correctly the sky was the limit.

By the age of twelve, Martina had become an expert con artist. Now in her twenties she had honed her art to such perfection that she was ready to go for the big one. She could not believe how very easy it had been so far. With little or no effort, here she was with a free roof over her head, all expenses paid. If she played her cards right there was no limit to what she could milk out

Stella. The house would be worth a tidy sum: enough to provide a cosy future. All she needed was a little more information, a little more trust, and a little more time – a commodity she had in abundance and Martina knew she could take Stella for everything she possessed. She would continue to woo her then fleece her.

*

Vanishing from Stella's life for a while had been part of Martina's master plan. She had needed Stella to miss her. The tactic had worked. It was plain to see that Stella was scared of losing her friend again. All Martina had to do now was to make herself indispensible. She made a point of visiting Stella every day. The hospital staff assumed she was family and so nothing was said to discourage this. Stella responded by eating more and making a remarkable advance to recovery. After another long week Stella was released into Martina's care.

*

As the taxi pulled up outside number 9, Stella looked up at her house. The exterior had remained unchanged for decades. Farther up the street some frontages had been stone clad, with added porches. There were potted box trees - clipped and trained outside number twenty one, next door (11 not 7) sported tropical palms. At number 15 an incongruous pair of stone lions stared at each other as they crouched uncomfortably on the gateposts that were far too small. Over the years the road had become increasingly affluent. Not yet gentrified, it had definitely gone up in the world. None of the older residents survived, apart from number 7, whose curtains twitched their welcome as the two women walked up the front path. What had once been cheap, overcrowded housing for poor working folk had been snapped up by a more prosperous generation. Now known as 'Desirable Residences', they fetched silly money.

Once inside her own 'Des Res', Stella was helped upstairs by Martina.

"Let's get you settled and comfy and I'll bring you a nice cup of tea, just how you like it. None of that muck they called tea in that awful place." Stella stopped outside the back room.

"No, not there. I've like put you back in the front. I thought the new bed would be more comfortable and there's more to see from the window."

Martina navigated her patient into the front room. Stella felt a sharp pang of annoyance. 'How dare Martina take such a radical decision without consulting me? This is, after all my house.' But, too weak to argue, she obediently followed her leader. 'No doubt, Martina has acted with the best of intentions and it really doesn't matter that much. Except... '

"What about my clothes... all my personal things?"

"Don't worry, Stel. They're all here."

Stella cast her critical eye around the small,

familiar room. It was cleaner and tidier than she expected, and indeed, when Martina opened the wardrobe, there were her clothes neatly hanging in line, with her sensible shoes stacked beneath them.

"See, just how you like it." Martina was laughing, chatting inanely, as she helped Stella out of her coat. Next she began to attack the buttons of Stella's blouse.

"I can do that, thank you. I'm not an invalid."

Stella knocked Martina's hand away and instantly regretted having been so brusque. She was still smarting from the presumption of being moved. Then, not wanting to appear ungrateful, she added,

"Sorry. But I'd prefer to do that myself. I'm just very tired. Maybe I'll have a little sleep. It was impossible to get any rest in that place - like trying to sleep in Piccadilly Circus." She attempted a weak laugh. "A cup of tea would be nice though." She thought for a moment then added, "I don't suppose Anita has been in touch?"

"No." The answer came back short and swift.

Stella had hoped for a postcard – something to break the ice. Hiding her disappointment she muttered "Oh well, never mind." Adding a brighter, "I'll say night-night then. And, thank you, Martina, I don't know what I'd have done without you. You're a good girl."

When Martina placed the mug of tea beside the single bed Stella was already fast asleep. Smiling as she closed the door, Martina vaulted down the stairs two at a time to retrieve her lighted cigarette from the tiled work-top. She stifled a laugh, licked her finger and rubbed, half heartedly, at the unsightly nicotine stain. The pile of postcards from the West Country, and the many letters that had followed had been disposed of in the wheelie-bin at number 7. The numerous phone calls had finally ceased when Martina told Anita Stella never wanted to see, or hear from her again. Martina took a drag on her cigarette, rubbed again at the brown mark, and congratulated herself on a job well done.

*

The effort of getting up and dressing, the taxi ride, and the exertion of going back to bed - compounded by the emotional upheaval of having been ousted from her own room - had exhausted Stella. The moment she was left alone, she disappeared beneath the covers, still in her underwear, and fell into her first proper sleep for ages. At last she dreamed of her avenue, but not as she remembered it. This dream took her to an alien place – a place too menacing to visit even in her dreams.

*

The gates creaked, their lack of oil resisting every effort she made to prise them apart. Her frail body echoed their groans, recognised their thirst, sympathised with their lack of moisture. Her lips were cracked and scabby, and a thin moan escaped as she strained to open them – hardly knowing where her lips ended and the gates began.

Exhausted she leaned against a stone pillar. The ivy reached out, its thick black stem encircling her, tying her to the post, its brittle leaves scratching her naked body. As she wrenched herself free she watched her shadow lengthening out before her. Alongside it a companion shadow, smaller, fainter linked hers with a hand that barely touched. Stella tightened her grip only to find her hand was empty, apart from a trickle of dust: ashes that fell to the ground to lie in a pile at her long, bare feet.

No wind disturbed the little pile, no air moved; the trees stood silently watching her, their tall bodies bent over until the topmost branches lay on the dusty gravel. Stella dared not reach out to them, sensing that they too would disintegrate: turn to powder at the slightest touch. Her feet were brown with dust. The grass had turned to straw and the two thin shadows pointed like fingers towards the house nagging her to proceed, to finish what she had started.

The house was in darkness. If she had not been there before she would have been lost, but she knew the step. Counting them blindly, she avoided the crack on the fourth. Her feet recognised the Victorian tiles, the shattering of the clay, the splitting of the glaze as they broke beneath the pressure of her shadow was new. A wreath of dried flowers and ribbons encircled the veiled oak leaf which her companion wraith reached up to grasp. Stella covered the smaller hand with hers and prepared to strike.

A wind, as cold as a grave, blew across her

face. It tugged at her flesh ripping it from her bones, tearing her hair from it roots. She let the oak leaf fall as her hands and arms flailed against the attacking air. Then, all at once, it was over. Stella opened her eyes. She was alone. In front of her stood the gates, locked and obscured by thick, dense undergrowth. She was on the outside looking in. There was no avenue, no lines of trees. No dream. On the gates hung a notice, 'BEWARE OF THE TREES'. From somewhere in the distance, beyond the gates, Stella heard three distinct raps – someone was knocking on a door.

*

Stella was screaming and very thirsty when she woke. No one came, but her clock told her it was four forty-four precisely.

*

Martina persuaded Stella she needed to take complete bed-rest until she regained her strength. She explained all her actions with such devotion, such sincere warmth and concern that Stella believed everything. Yet, despite such attentive nursing, her health was not improving. If anything it was worsening. Martina consoled her by telling her everything was under control. She said the doctors did not want to see Stella until the end of the month; all the mail was opened and sorted by Martina so Stella had no way of verifying this. Not that she cared. It was all too much: 'Dear Martina, best to leave things in her capable hands.'

Number 9 was fast falling to rack and ruin. Slowly, slowly, day by day, it was becoming a tip. The girl told herself that tomorrow she would blitz it, but of course tomorrow never came. And, anyway, so long as Stella stayed upstairs, what difference did it make? Martina calculated that a month, two at most was all she needed to complete her plan. Stella's health, like the house, was going rapidly downhill; Martina was making sure of that. She monitored Stella's medications with the vigilance of a professional nurse. It was all too easy for her to switch the prescribed pills for Aspirin, or slip a little sugar lump doctored with LSD courtesy of Col, into the starvation rations she fed her patient.

With every dose Stella thanked Martina for her diligence of care. Manipulating the poor woman's mind was proving to be a doddle. As planned, Martina was making herself indispensible, ingratiating herself, literally worming her way into Stella's heart, until the inevitable would happen. 'Well who else is the stupid cow going to leave it all to? It's so fucking simple. A few more dreams, a few more hallucinations and bingo!'

Under normal circumstances being ordered to stay in bed would have been bliss for a dreamer like Stella, but the deluge of uncontrolled nightmares that poured from her subconscious mind was drowning her in terror. Hideous misshapen happenings distorted her brain and drained her: mind, body and soul. Physical weakness made her thinking fuzzy, while creating damp shadowy swamps where her worst fears could spawn and grow. At first she had wondered why she felt no benefit from the copious tablets she swallowed each day. Now she just took whatever was handed to her, without question, hope or memory. She no longer slept, but merely drifted in and out of consciousness, further fudging the fast dissolving line between dreams and reality.

*

Stella had always believed that her dreams ran on in a continuous story, somewhere beyond her waking life. This personal logic told her that although she was unable to enter her own familiar dream world it was still being played out without her. She began to fear that she might not be able to catch up if, and when, she managed to tune back in. It was like missing too many episodes of a soap opera: too long a gap and your favourite characters might have left, replaced by strangers acting out an unfamiliar story-line. Even worse if, as in Stella's case her favourite character was herself, and she returned to discover she had been written out.

'What had happened to Runs-With-The-Buffalo? Where was the Tiger? Had he been shot by Col or the prince? Was the avenue still there? Was it waiting for her or was it being haunted by another dreamer? Had Martina taken her place? Irrational thoughts blocked out any vestige of reason. Stella became convinced that she was now dreaming someone else's dreams, and that this other person had usurped her place in her own - enjoying the company of her many friends. The question was 'How could she get back to her world – the one she had begun to share with Martina? These were the fears which now haunted Stella: fears that she dare not share with anyone. And hidden among these was her greatest fear of all: 'What if Martina was not a figment of her imagination, but the creation of another – some unknown person?'

*

Having made sure that Stella had taken her medication, Martina tucked her in, wished her 'sweet dreams' and left her in the sulphurous half light of the small bedroom. Stella lay awake, fighting off the urge to sleep. She listened to the night sounds from the street below. The last bus always deposited a few stragglers, mostly drunks who kicked a can or two across the road, before heading off to the estate on the east side. Tonight there was one who lingered on, singing 'My Way' over and over again, as he tried to gain his bearings and find his way. Stella was grateful to him; watching his antics gave her contact with the tangible world. But, eventually he found the way. He left, weaving into the night, leaving Stella all alone in a jaundiced silence.

A quick glance at her clock told her it was gone one o'clock. She slid her feet into her slippers, drew 'Old Faithful' tightly around her, and staggered to the door. Her hands were weak and it was hard to turn the handle. Before she pushed it open she breathed in then placed her other hand on the door jam - partly to steady her as she was wobbly and afraid of falling - mostly to enable her to open the door without making a sound. When she was ready she pushed gently, but it resisted her. From across the landing she heard the sound of snoring. Martina was fast asleep. She pushed a little harder, but still the door would not open. When at last it dawned on her that the door was locked, she sat down on the floor with a loud bump. 'Why on earth had Martina locked her in?'

It took an hour of knocking and banging, exhausting her entire reserve of energy, before Martina was dragged from her sleep. When the door opened Stella literally fell out.

"What on earth do you think you're playing at? What did you think…" Throbbing filled her head, her thoughts tossing around like clothes in the spinning drum of a washing machine. The floor rose up to meet her and Martina only just caught her before she collided with it.

"What am I going to do with you? I only did it like for your own safety you silly cow. I'm fed up with finding you downstairs, fiddling with the TV, or trying to make tea and toast at all hours. You can't be trusted with a kettle of boiling water. Like, honestly, you almost set the house on fire a few nights ago. Trying to light the gas fire you said. Ha! Then last night I found you half way down the road, like in your nighty. Anything could have happened." She spoke sweetly, attentively as she led Stella back to bed.

"You were fast asleep. I read somewhere that it's dangerous to wake someone up when they're sleepwalking. So I thought, right I'll lock her in, then she can't get up to any real mischief. Honestly, Stel, why else would I do such a thing? Like I'm not a bloody monster - I really care about you." Martina plumped up Stella's damp, crumpled pillows and suggested she got them both a nice cup of tea.

Stella's head was still whirring round and her mouth was as dry as a bone. She ran her tongue along her teeth; they felt soft. Her tongue didn't belong in her mouth; it was too big and stuck to the roof. Martina was fussing over her, punching at her pillows, prattling on about tea and sleepwalking.

It was scary for Stella to admit it, but there was some logic to Martina's story. With no way of proving otherwise, Stella had little option but to believe her.

Martina reappeared, carrying refreshingly sweet tea. Stella apologised. She thanked her friend for taking such good care of her. She even heard herself agreeing to the suggestion that it might be a good idea to continue locking the door, at least until this somnambulistic phase was over. Having explained the word to Martina, Stella allowed herself to be settled back into bed. Martina was full of smiles as she blew a kiss before turning the key in the lock behind her.

Stella shuddered. Instinct told her that something was wrong, why else did she feel like a prisoner? Had she the power to see through wood, she would have witnessed Martina punch the air in triumph and known that her instincts were right.

Within minutes the drugged tea began to do its job and Stella slipped effortlessly off the cliff into a psychotic world of chaos.

CHAPTER 18

Stupefied and sedated, Stella did as she was told. Three times a day she swallowed bitter pills. Then in a rare moment of clarity (or an increasingly frequent moment of paranoia) she stopped taking them. It was easy enough to store them hamster-like in her cheek, only to spit them out into a tissue when the coast was clear. After a pill free week her brain was more alert. Her panic attacks diminished and the delusion that she was being fixed with a pin began to fade. Even the jaundiced room appeared brighter. Stella began to get up and sit in a chair for an hour or two each day, watching the comings and goings in the street below. Gradually it dawned on her that she was not dreaming.

In time she felt brave enough to venture downstairs. Stella waited until she heard the familiar slamming of the front door and watched, from her prison window, her leather cladded warder stride across the road, presumably on a fag finding mission to the corner shop. Stella reckoned she had at least a quarter of an hour before Martina returned and - as if fate had decreed it - Martina had neglected to lock the bedroom door. Stella knew this might be her only chance.

Clinging to the bannisters, angry at her legs' reluctance to support her, Stella edged her way down the stairs and into the living room. As she dragged herself over the wrong facing leaves she crossed her fingers and held her breath prepared for the worst. Nothing could have prepared her for what awaited her: the tip which had been her orderly home. Resigned to passive acceptance, she dismissed any fury with a click of her mental mouse. How could she react otherwise? Each movement was a challenge. She had not realised quite how weak she had become. After a mammoth effort, armed with pens and a note pad, Stella dragged her exhausted body back up the stairs. Aware she could not attempt to avoid the wrong leaves yet again, she counted each step twice – once for encouragement and once for safety's sake - until she reached the thirteenth.

Stella planned to write herself a script, commit it to memory, so she could go into her next dream prepared - in total control. This strategy had worked before so she could see no reason why it would not work again. Just as Stella pulled her duvet over her wasted body, she heard Martina return. With her writing weapons stashed securely beside her, Stella waited for night to fall.

*

For most of that night, Stella sat up writing - scribbling and scratching out until she was sure her work was done. When she was finished there was at least an hour of darkness left - a whole hour before she would wake: before 4.44. Stella closed her eyes and gave herself up to her dream.

*

The gates stood wide open, welcoming. They had missed her as much as she had missed them. She had on her new blue sweater and peacock scarf and in her hair - which had been washed especially for the occasion - she wore her highland terrier slide. Sunlight darted through the poplars dappling and scattering light like so many reflections from a glitter ball in a ballroom. Stella felt young again as with a carefree spring in her step she skipped along keeping time to the tune in her head.

'Onward Christian so o o oldiers... marching as to oo... war..."

Today she would reach the house. Today she would knock on the door with the heavy knocker in the shape of an oak leaf and at the third knock the door would open and the secret of the house would be revealed. It was written. She read the words again – just to make sure.

Of course she was nervous. (She had purposely written a degree of trepidation into the plot; it would be stupid to expect such a momentous occasion to pass without a few hiccups; but she was programmed to stay in ultimate control of her emotions while still allowing a contained amount of spontaneity. She wanted to be free to experience the unexpected, to enjoy the excitement and go with the flow. So far the flow was good.)

"With the cross of ...."

There was a gentle breeze encouraging the trees to shake their leafy tambourines to complement Stella's hymn with a little amusing timpani.

When she reached the blackbird's grave, she stopped, placed a small posy of violets on the mound and patted it. The earth opened as if responding to the knock and the occupant popped up.

"Hello. Thanks for the flowers. Nice thought. How are you? You look different. Brighter. Is this a special day? Is it your birthday? Or maybe it's your death-day?"

Stella jumped back. This was not part of her script. How dare he ad-lib like that? She knew what she had written, or at least she thought she did.

Another voice, again unscripted...

"Have you lost the plot again, Stella?"

"What are you doing here, Mum? Go away. You'll ruin everything, you always do." Stella looked around her but there was no sign of her mother, just the hint of a laugh coming from the trees.

'No, not the trees, please not the trees' thought Stella. Standing tall she shouted at them.

'You are supposed to be on my side today. This isn't what I planned - it's not in the script. Now I'll have to wake up and start all over again.'

The trees shimmied and shook, they threw their heads back and their leafy throats screeched with uncontrollable laughter.

"We never were on your side. We stand on the side of the avenue, my dear. We are partisan bystanders."

Stella pinched herself. She demanded in a loud

voice that she wake up at once. She screamed the order at the top of her voice. Nothing happened. There was nothing left but to start again. Turning herself around she prepared to march back to the gates only to find that the avenue turned with her. Time and time again she turned to face the entrance, to start her dream again, but it was impossible. There was no way back. Whichever way she turned, the house lay ahead and the gates were miles behind. Stella set her jaw, resolved to stand her ground. She knew she was dreaming, therefore she was asleep - therefore she would have to wake up - at some point. If she kept her head she would survive. Closing her eyes as tightly as she could she clasped her hands to her head and held on, waiting for the nightmare to end.

"*Why am I not in your dream? Didn't your parents teach you anything? It is very rude to exclude your friends from the important events of your life, and there is nothing more important than one's death. I'm deeply wounded. I thought you liked me." The tiger was standing with his back to Stella. His body language was unwelcoming and his voice was cold and grumpy.*

"*Your American friend is too upset to come along uninvited, but he might put in an appearance if you ask very nicely." His voice softened as he turned to face her.*

Tentatively her fingers reached out to touch the tiger's coat. It was wet and warm, smelling of campfires.

"*I am sorry. This dream is mine. I have to dream it alone. It is linked to my past and my future too," she said.*

The tiger smiled. His great teeth flashed in the sunlight, firing searchlights high into the trees. On reaching the peaks the beams bounced back again to spotlight the two friends as they stood centre stage. The trees fell silent, enthralled by the performance; they enjoyed a good show, a memorable play. Stella bowed, relishing the limelight, but the words that came from her were not scripted; they were not even her words: they came from the tiger who spoke his thoughts through her.

"Past, future, it is all one. I am always with you, invited or not, the thread is unbreakable. Runs-With-The-Buffalo, even the blackbird, we belong in the same world. When you were little, you knew this. You never doubted that your dreams came from another reality. You had no desire to control us - you knew that would be wrong. Have you forgotten that you can no more control dreams than you can control life? Go on, Stella, walk on down your avenue and discover what you already know. It is waiting for you. We are waiting for you. Go on Stella, be brave. It's easy."

With that the tiger vanished. The audience of trees shuffled, some of the leaves began to ripple. Others took their cue, joining in until their applause drowned out all other sound, except for the scrunching gravel as it moved aside for the marching feet of the brave soldier who strode on purposefully down the avenue to meet her fate.

*

At four forty-four Stella woke up alone in her single bed. She was still alive. She had knocked three times as usual before waking up. Nothing had changed. The house had appeared the same as always, standing at the end of the avenue: aloof and alone. Its door still displayed the oak-leaf knocker, still calling to her, daring her to knock. No one had answered the door. It surprised her to find that she was quite relaxed about that. In fact she felt better than she had for many weeks. Tomorrow she would demand that her door be left permanently unlocked. She would get up and go downstairs, with or without the approval of 'The Girl without the Kalashnikov.' And what's more, she would tackle her about the state of number 9.

*

The next day a letter dropped on the doormat as Stella's somewhat shaky foot reached for the bottom stair. Feeling encouraged at having conquered the stairs again, she threw a challenging glower at Martina who had already pocketed the envelope. Reluctantly she handed it over to Stella. It was addressed to Ms S. Sankey. It was from the hospital asking why she had not kept any of her appointments. It mentioned 'serious consequences' if further appointments were missed. Stella read the letter aloud demanding to be told how many more had there been. Martina shrugged and stomped off into the kitchen where she retrieved a couple of mugs from the pile of dirty bowls, plates, pots and pans festering in the pile that filled the sink.

"That's the first. Honestly, why would I want you to miss your appointments? "

Stella was leaning against the door frame staring at the chaos that was her kitchen.

"I know … it's a tip. Sorry. I do wash up - once a week - saves on water and soap."

Too weak to argue Stella sighed. Tomorrow she would make an appointment and sort things out with the hospital. She took herself into the lounge. Martina rushed ahead clearing the sofa with a quick sweep of her arm and stuffing a cushion under Stella's head. Stella let her heavy head sink back. She sighed again. There was hardly enough energy in her to breathe, let alone tackle this. Nothing short of a blazing row would convey her anger and disgust, and that was out of the question. She satisfied herself by sighing again. Just coming down thirteen stairs had been exhausting. Her main concern now was how she was going to get back up to bed - missing the right facing leaves in the process (three times was pushing her luck too far).

*

Outwardly Martina appeared calm, inside she was fuming. She had never meant Stella to see the house in this state. She cursed herself for being careless. 'Why had she let her out? How difficult was it to confine a crazy invalid to her room? As for letting her read that stupid letter, well, that was unforgivably irresponsible.' Her mind was racing as it tried to come up with another strategy, one that would get her back into Stella's good books. She knew deep down that all she needed was a sense of proportion. This was just one little set back. She was still the top cat with plenty of time left to play with her mouse. The meagre promise of a nice cup of tea never failed to placate Stella – it would not be difficult to win her round completely – finally.

Satisfied with her line of thought, Martina swept into the kitchen. While the kettle boiled she stuffed some of dirty dishes into the nearest cupboard. Meanwhile her brain was working overtime. By the time the tea had brewed to a suitable shade of brown she had rethought her plan of action. All she needed to do was take Stella on a trip down memory lane, courtesy of her dreams. But before she could do that she needed some vital information, and she knew exactly where to go to find it. A rather smug Martina stirred a couple of strong sleeping pills into Stella's perfect cuppa, before presenting it to her prisoner and escorting her back to her cell.

*

With her lighter in one hand and her phone in the other Martina waited impatiently for Col to pick up. Absentmindedly she flicked at the orange Bic lighter, the flame sparking or not by random chance with each neurotic jerk of her thumb. It was obvious that Col was either half asleep or high when he finally mumbled some obscenity into her ear. She dropped the overheated lighter and spoke through the unlit cigarette which dangled from her lips.

"Listen. Have you still got that tape?"

"What fucking tape? Don't you know it's the middle of the sodding night? Fuck off, okay!'"

"The silly cow's dreams... You did like tape her didn't you? Like can you remember what she said?"

"Dah... No... anyway, I told you... it was all crap, okay? Why?"

"I've like had an idea. It'll blow your fucking mind. Come round now, she's out for the count. Oh, and Col bring the fucking tape with you!"

Martina flipped her phone shut and lay back on the sofa with her arms behind her head, her legs stretched out, feet crossed as her left foot tapped neurotically waiting for Col to arrive.

*

When Col finally turned up, Martina was by the open door, smoking. Having snatched the tape from him she bundled him straight back out into the street. Martina did not like to be kept waiting. Besides the last thing she wanted was distraction, especially from someone who would undoubtedly expect a share of the proceeds. What's more, he was crap in bed. No, Col had served his purpose by hacking into Stella's accounts. He was now redundant. Martina preferred to work alone. She smiled as she shut the door on him.

Back in her nice double room, Martina listened to the tape, rewinding and replaying bits over and over while she took notes. After performing a little war dance, Martina crept into Stella's room. The patient was indeed 'out for the count', the drugged tea having done its work. Removing the heavy drawer from beneath the bed she dragged it back to her room and began sifting through it.

Martina knew the contents of Stella's secret drawer by heart. On one of her early forays she had discovered it 'hidden' under the bed. Its value as a source of insider information had been obvious from that first sighting – although it was not until this moment that she had recognised its true worth, or how best to use her find.

The things that lay buried in this hidey-hole made her shudder. She loathed the feel of the discoloured tissue paper, so old and dry it crackled and tore at the merest touch. The pink baby prints made her flesh creep – the thought of those wrinkled feet and hands forced down on the paper: babies were so not her thing. The hand written inscription below the prints read, "Baby girl. Born 09.12.1985." The coincidence never failed to shake her, although she had seen it at least ten times. This was one thing she did not have to memorise, or fabricate. She had been born on the same day, in the same year. They could have been her unused feet and hands pressed into paint and held down on the paper. She looked at her own hands, half expecting to find that they had turned the same shade of pink. Then she chided herself for being 'so fucking stupid'.

The Clarke's shoe box still contained the hand-knitted teddy. Martina did not un-wrap it; it too was cocooned in desiccated tissue beneath a baby's blanket made from the same itchy nylon wool - destined never to rot or decompose. It set her teeth on edge. The whole thing was, to Martina's unsentimental mind, macabre.

Beneath all this tat lay the thing Martina was after: a brown manila folder. It contained four newspaper cuttings each meticulously cut out and held together by a paper clip. The whole thing was then wrapped inside a local paper. The very first time she had rifled Stella's secret booty she had very nearly dismissed them as just extra packing. But, as soon as she read them she had known they would be invaluable when the time was right. And this was the time.

The clippings dated from January 9th 1986 until February 14th 1986. They reported the alleged kidnapping of a month old baby. The first time she read them she had skimmed over the contents. Now she needed to study the details, memorise the facts to prepare her case. Once again the weird coincidence of the dates struck her. She had been barely a month old when the baby was snatched.

*

The germ of Martina's plan had been sown the moment she first found the cuttings. After just a cursory glance she knew they were the perfect ammunition. This was her game. She knew every twist, every turn, every trick in the book. Luck had nothing to do with it: it was a game of skill and one that she was destined win.

Martina calculated that it would take a minimum amount of persuasion to con Stella into believing she was her long lost daughter. All the pieces fitted. Martina was tall and skinny, genetically similar to Mrs Sankey. According to some old photos she had seen there was an uncanny resemblance. The coincidence of the birthdays was a convenient bonus. Of course Stella had no idea of Martina's scheme, or her insider knowledge and secrecy was paramount.

Martina planned to drip feed this suggestion into her prisoner, little by little, drop by drop, until she overwhelmed her with the coincidences. Once she had convinced her – and this Martina had to confess was the genius of her plan – she could sit back and watch the roles reverse as Stella tried to persuade her as to the veracity of her own lies. Martina grinned in anticipation of the Oscar winning performance she would give. At first she would feign amazement: reticent to even contemplate such a premise. Gradually – always pretending it to be against her better judgement – she would be forced to bow down before the wealth of evidence – evidence that she herself had concocted. It was a work of genius. A good con knows their mark: Martina knew Stella. She knew her to be a caring woman, lonely and desperate to give love and be loved in return. Stella's guilt would be working in Martina's favour. In the final scene the 'abandoned daughter' would forgive 'her mother' and they would live happily ever after. Except of course they wouldn't.

Getting Stella to alter her will would be a

doddle to a consummate schemer like Martina. Of course, Stella would have to die first. That, in Martina's book, went without saying. She took mock comfort in recalling what her erstwhile mother, Mrs Smith, always claimed, "You can't make an omelette without breaking eggs." And to Martina Stella was just another egg.

Martina had to concede that her new plan would take a little longer that her original one. It was more dangerous, but that made it a lot more fun. Maybe that was why she preferred it. She congratulated herself for not involving anyone else. Col would forgive her soon enough and if not it was of no consequence. Ditching him had minimised the risk - and eliminated the need - to share her 'inheritance'. She licked her lips: the golden goose was nearly cooked.

*

For the next few weeks Martina was charm itself. She brought Stella downstairs at mid-day and took her back to bed at teatime. She cooked her patient's favourite foods and made copious cups of tea, including that disgusting camomile muck to help Stella sleep. If Stella liked something then so did she. If Stella disliked something it became anathema to her. Softly, softly she charmed her way into Stella's lonely heart's club, but in order to complete the first phase of her attack she first had to get Stella's health back on track.

Firstly she needed to win back Stella's trust. She apologised profusely for having neglected the house. To prove her repentance she cleaned the place form top to bottom, bought four new mugs from M&S to replace the stained, chipped ones and generally appeared to have turned over a new leaf. But it was not enough to get Stella to forgive her antagonist. Martina realised that she too must appear a victim. She had to appeal to Stella's maternal instincts which in turn would pave the way for her final pounce. She needed a scapegoat and who better than Col. As soon as the decision was made she knew she had picked the perfect victim, what's more she could 'kill two fucking birds with one stone!' Martina started a smear campaign to reduce Col's status from 'charming young man' to 'cheat, junkie and thief'.

Martina played her cards brilliantly. Having helped Stella downstairs, settled her on the sofa and presented her with her new mug of perfectly brewed tea, she artfully hammered the final nails into Col's coffin.

"I've got a confession to make, Stel." Martina's voice contained a mixture of contrition and indignation. "You know I was seeing Col. Well, anyway, it doesn't matter 'cos like, we're finished. I found out he was dealing – drugs and stuff. Then one day I caught him like going through your things. The little shepherdess - and the boy - they've gone. I'm so sorry. I don't want to make out he's all bad. He can be so nice when he's clean, but, well, I didn't want you to think, like, I'd broken them. Of course I'll replace them if you want. Col can't. He's in prison. Someone must have shopped him - probably for the best. How much do I owe you?" With that she burst into tears.

Stella was too overloaded with information, sympathy, shock and disillusion to do anything but shrug and tell Martina not to worry. How could she stay angry with her when life itself had dealt the girl such a cruel hand? Stella sipped her tea and slid beneath her blanket. Life was indeed hard.

*

At last they received a new date for the hospital. Meanwhile Martina, absolved and smug, diligently administered the correct medication and dosage. This time, her paranoia abated, Stella swallowed every pill. Diet too played its part and by the time the hospital car came to collect them Stella was almost back to her normal self. The appointment went better than even Martina had dreamed it could. Stella was told to convalesce for a few weeks then go to her GP for a final check up and all being well she could return to work.

The next few weeks went exactly to plan. The relationship between the two women blossomed. Stella began to trust her nurse and listen to her advice. For the first time in her life she truly appreciated the existence of another person. She felt happy. She was even dreaming happy dreams. It was weeks since she had visited the avenue; a fact which would have appalled her just a few months back. Now she saw it as a sign that life had changed. 'Maybe I did die that night? That boring, insipid creature I had inhabited has been laid to rest and I am reborn as a newly energised being. The blackbird has done it, so why can't I?' In Stella's eyes things were looking up. She was learning to trust. Was learning to love going to be her next lesson? If so, Stella was willing to give it a go.

Martina had a free reign to pursue her objective. She peppered their conversations with stories of her dreams while listening enraptured to Stella's own tales. Each time she 'dreamed' she dropped another tasty morsel for Stella to swallow: the one about the pink footprints turning to blood as she walked across the newspaper carpet was, she thought, a stroke of genius.

It was time for Martina to start phase two. The elimination of Marian was about to begin. Martina closed her eyes and pictured herself ascending bodily into heaven, returning as the child-saint Martina. She smiled. Another trip to Brighton was called for and this time poor Stella was going to be taken for a ride.

CHAPTER 19

The train pulled into the noisy confusion of Brighton Station. Feral children swarmed, wild with the promise of a day beside the sea. Their careless parents remained impervious to their antisocial anarchism. Endless holidays washed over Stella's feet in alternate waves of nostalgia and dread; she had not been to a beach since childhood. Miserable picnics with her mum and dad, dried-out sandwiches full of sand and tinned salmon; such pictures rotted in caves that she had not visited for years. She hardly ever ate sandwiches now.

These sour, if distant, memories had at first prompted her to refuse Martina's initial suggestion of a day out. However, the newly styled Martina, all smiles and promises of fun and fresh air, wove such an enchanting picture of a trip to the sea that Stella had begun to look forward to it.

Following the crowd, they found themselves in Queen's Road and, after a short bus ride, they stood side by side on the promenade by the old Fish Market. The vulgarity was electrifying. The smell of hotdogs and burgers pervaded the air negating any whiff of ozone. Stella's mum had always bleated on about the efficacious scent of the ozone, although as a child Stella only ever caught the sickly peppermint smell of freshly made rock, and the inevitable vinegary tang of fish and chips. Today the air was filled with frying onions and ketchup.

Martina looked remarkably cool in her black jeans and Doc Martins. Her leather coat flapped in the breeze that wafted from the expanse of sea onto the crowded pebbles. She listened to the familiar scrunch of stone on stone as the pebbles competed with each other for space. Sunbathers lay in various stages of undress. Martina gathered her coat around her, proud not to be confused with the rabble.

The two women clambered between the half-clad bodies until they stood on the water-line, in imminent danger of wetting their toes. Martina was grinning from ear to ear. Something about the place stirred her and Stella felt a pang of fondness as she watched her childlike behaviour, skimming pebbles (with surprising skill) across the water's surface.

A mother, watching her little darlings paddling just off shore, shattered the charm - her outburst leaving no doubt as to what she thought of Martina. One of the children held his head and began to scream even louder than his mother. Stella was pretty sure none of the stones had actually hit the child, but the danger of the situation was brought home in an alarming manner. From further up the beach other onlookers joined in, mostly taking the mother's side, and from the Banjo Groyne a gang of youths began shaking their fists and saluting the air as they chanted their support for Martina.

The bystanders assumed Martina was Stella's daughter: old enough to know better but not too old to be chastised. It was mortifying for Stella. The embarrassment worsened when Martina swopped pebbles for abuse, hurling it at anyone who cared to listen, with equal accuracy of aim. There was no way Stella could pacify her. By now the whole beach was divided into warring camps. Fearful of the consequences, Stella grabbed Martina by the sleeve and began dragging her towards the pier. Reaching a safe distance she suggested that they had an ice cream to cool themselves down. Martina's aggression turned to satisfaction. Ruining the family picnics of hundreds of day trippers placed her over the moon. She celebrated with a second extra-large whip, and a double helping of chocolate flake.

After a fish and chip lunch, Martina suggested that Stella should have a rest. She got her a deckchair on the promenade, bought her a magazine - one with plenty of puzzles in it, and settled her down for a nice, quiet snooze in a shady spot with a good view of the sea.

"I'm off to the arcade," Martina announced, "I shan't be long. If like you get cold, go into that hotel and get a cuppa. I'll meet you in like half an hour. It's three-thirty now. Let's say four. Okay?" In fact it was only just two pm, but she was pretty sure Stella would not bother to check.

With that Martina was gone. The thought of a half hour's gentle snooze in the afternoon sun sounded perfect to Stella. Trying to keep up with such a whirlwind was quite exhausting – although she found the sun was still surprisingly high and warm. Stella relaxed back into her blue canvas sling and immediately fell into a deep sleep.

*

The bus dropped Martina at the end of Gardener Street. One more turning and she was outside her parent's house. The timing was perfect. It was a Wednesday. Dad would be at the club and this was Mum's day for a shampoo and set. Mrs Smith always went to the same little backstreet hairdressers: Yvonne's, although it was now called The Cut Above. Checking that she was not being watched, Martina nipped over the fence at the back of the house. She removed the key from beneath the flowerpot and let herself into the kitchen. The table was laid out with eight places for breakfast, and a tray was prepared with two cups and saucers for their tea. Martina snorted disparagingly. Routine was everything to Mrs Smith. For once it suited Martina very well, anyway this was no time to sneer; she had important work to do.

What Martina wanted lived in a box file, in the bottom drawer of the sideboard next to the photo album. The box was still there. In it she found a bankbook, a cheque book, two credit cards - their numbers written on a sheet of paper beside them - and a library card. All the family documents were crammed into a bulging manila envelopes, in separate bundles held together by elastic bands and carefully labelled under the headings 'certificates', 'policies' and 'other'. It was the former that she was after, but she pocketed the bank book, cards and cheque book as a bonus.

In one of the bundles were her mother's and father's birth certificates. There was even one for her mother's mother, along with a death certificate for the latter and a couple of wedding certificates for her parents and her maternal grandparents. The one document she wanted was missing. Why was there no register of her birth? Quickly rifling through the 'policies' revealed nothing. However, in the category of 'other' she found more than she had bargained for.

Gradually the shock of her discovery abated, but dark, resentful anger remained. It boiled and seethed in her brain inducing a taste for revenge.

Having calmed herself down she went upstairs to wait for her parents to return, make their tea and settle in their arm chairs for their afternoon nap. They were so predictable. She heard them come in. Listened as her mother took the tray into the sitting room and waited until she was sure they had finished their second cup. Then she came down. They did not argue with her, or get up to say hello. It all made a nice change really. In fact by the time Martina closed the door behind her the house was quite quiet. The only sound was soft background chatter emanating from the 30 inch TV in the corner of the living room. Oh, and the faint crackle as the chip pan sparked into life and the boiling oil expanded to spread with alarming speed across the lino, up the curtains and along the ceiling.

Mr and Mrs Smith were sitting where they always sat, in their armchairs, facing the television. The Rohypnol she had put in their tea had rendered their bodies useless. By the time the Fire Brigade arrived there was nothing left of the little guest house. Mr and Mrs Smith were both burnt to a crisp.

*

The stream of foul language, emanating from the foyer of The Ship Hotel warned Stella her companion was back. They caught the five-forty to Victoria, having had tea together in the hotel then made the entire journey home in silence. Stella assumed that Martina had lost all her money in the arcade. She did not approve of gambling, not even the lottery. If she was right she hoped it would teach the silly girl a lesson. Stella despaired at Martina's profligate attitude to money. It was not until they reached Croydon that she realised Martina was not just sulking; something untoward had happened during that brief hour of separation in Brighton. Once back in the safety of number 9, tea made and slippers on, Stella broached the subject.

"You can tell me anything, Martina. I'm not going to judge you. I'll stand by you if you've done something silly. Or if you need help, of any sort, I'll do what I can."

"I don't want any help. I'm like going to bed. I want to be on my own." It was rage that reddened her eyes, not tears as Stella had assumed. They flashed like the eyes of a she-devil as she filled the doorway before beginning her deliberate ascent up the thirteen stairs. She mounted them as a hangman might climb the steps of the scaffold, with solemnity and purpose. Her world had turned upside down. Yesterday she was the product of Mr and Mrs Smith. Now her scam had become a reality. The revelation had numbed her. She was in a state of raw shock.

Stella did not know what to do. Her instinct was to follow Martina: to comfort her and offer a shoulder to cry on. Her head told her to respect the girl's wishes and leave her alone. Her head won. She left her alone for an hour before she counted the stairs herself. A few minutes later she was tucked up in bed trying, unsuccessfully, to sleep.

*

There had been no sleep going on in Martina's room either. Papers lay strewn over the bed. They had been pushed, prodded, sworn at, shuffled and torn in her futile attempt to draw a different conclusion. She did not know if she was angry, disappointed or delighted at her apparent change of circumstances: her emotions were as confused as the scattered papers. Throwing her leather coat on top of her pyjamas, she stomped downstairs to the kitchen where she found Stella.

It was the early hours of the morning. The only sound was that of the kettle winding itself up to boiling point. Filling her mug Stella prodded at the tea bag, watching the water turn a reasonable shade of brown. Meanwhile Martina stirred her four teaspoons of sugar round and round in her favourite 'Winnie the Pooh' mug, the spoon removing a thin layer of glaze with each vicious twist. The resounding clang of her abandoned spoon as it hit the metal sink acted like a starting pistol, shocking the two of them out of their torpor. Martina's reaction was to burst into floods of tears, her body shaking with the release of pent-up rage. Stella offered her refuge in her arms and for a while they stood together, neither sure what it was that they had to give each other - neither sure what they needed to take.

The rest of that significant night was spent in what Stella deemed to be a heart-to-heart exchange. She had never felt needed. No one had ever trusted her with their dark secrets, with or without an ulterior motive. The trust this young woman was placing in her came not only as a precious gift, but as a revelation. It had not occurred to Stella that other people had doubts; that they too were afraid of life. Until now the world had been peopled with, often stupid, yet always self assured creatures. She had thought of herself as the one person who did not fit; the square peg in the round hole of reality: the law of survival of the fittest dooming her to failure. Now she had a soul mate, a person who also knew what it was to be excluded. As she listened to Martina, her heart opened up and she allowed their spirits to merge. It was a religious, life-changing experience.

Methodically Stella cleaned her glasses, before placing them back on her nose. It would take all her powers of concentration to grapple with the crumpled papers Martina thrust into her hand. After a short tussle they were, thanks to her methodical efficiency, straightened, sorted and sitting in three neat piles. Only then did she begin to read them in detail. The reason for Martina's rage was not apparent from their content. They seemed to be in perfect order, legally binding and self explanatory.

"Well, like what are they? Like what does it mean?" Martina was standing over Stella, hopping from foot to foot with anxious anticipation.

"They're your adoption papers. They explain when you were adopted and where - who your adoptive parents are and why there is no conventional birth certificate." Studying them more closely, registering dates and details, Stella pulled her glasses off, wiped them and replaced them. She looked straight into Martina's eyes.

"According to these you only spent a few weeks in care. I thought you were in homes most of your life. Where did you get these? Did you get them in Brighton?" Stella wanted to push for answers, but something in Martina's attitude warned to her to back off.

"Yeah, well, like I lied. I don't even remember being in a home. But, like that's not the bloody point. Those bastards let me think I was their daughter. For nearly twenty-five years I thought they were my mum and dad. They always hated me and I hated them. God, like they must have really regretted the day they picked me! Ha! Serves them right. I knew I didn't belong to them. Oh, Stel, if only you knew what they were like. They had it coming, the lying bastards." During this short speech Martina had whipped herself up into a tantrum. As she spat out the last word she collapsed onto the sofa. The loud twang of a breaking spring shot through the silence snapping the tension at the same time.

"What did you mean – they had it coming?" Stella was quite calm as she asked her question.

Martina scored a direct hit with a cushion and the question was left unanswered.

*

That was the night that Stella told Martina about the baby. She showed her the little pink prints and the woollen blanket and together they cuddled the teddy. Years of guilt poured out with her story. She explained how, at times, it all seemed like a dream, while at others it was so real it tore at her, ripping at her insides until they were raw. She explained how her mother had told her she had taken the tiny bundle to the hospital. How she had waited until it was safely inside before returning home, empty handed. Stella explained how her body still ached from the emptiness, the loss.

Of course this was all just words. How could Stella convey things that she herself had not been prepared to face? As she told her story she kept her eyes fixed on Martina. The girl appeared quite composed. At one point Stella thought she detected a hint of sadness around the eyes, but the ugly anger previously displayed had gone. The abuse that she thought she deserved was not apparent. There was none. Instead Martina's arm slid around Stella's waist and her black head leaned against Stella's shoulder. They sat like this in their shared silence, totally at peace, until the dawn – unaware that they were both thinking and wishing the same thing.

*

Guilt was not an emotion on Martina's radar. What she had done in Brighton had been risky, satisfying and necessary. Her 'parents' had deserved it. They had lied to her. Her life had been built on a deception of such monumental proportions she had been forced to react in a way which, to her mind, was totally appropriate. In fact she had to admit she had got a tremendous buzz out of it, and congratulated herself that taking Stella along as an alibi had been her greatest stroke of genius yet.

*

Several days later two policemen called, looking for a Miss Marian Smith. Stella, in all honesty, denied knowing anyone of that name. She spoke with such integrity, in blissful ignorance, that they took her at her word and left. When they left she realised her mistake. She remembered the name on the adoption papers. She rang the station and called them back. Of course she told Martina who was livid. But they were already back, knocking on the door again, before she could tackle Stella for what she perceived to be an act of utter betrayal.

Martina, AKA Marian, need not have worried. An hour later they had gone again. All had been revealed. An unfortunate accident with a chip pan:

all too common and avoidable. Both Mr and Mrs Smith had died from smoke inhalation. Stella mumbled something to the effect of 'dear God' while Martina shifted from one foot to the other. The police explained that she would not have to identify them - there had already been post mortem which was quite normal in a case of sudden death and all that. The younger policeman explained that the bodies had been so badly burnt identification had been done using their dental records. Martina stared blankly and shrugged. She showed no emotion at the thought of her parents being cut up and examined... or being dead.

The older of the two policemen was gentler. He went to inordinate lengths to assure Martina that her parents had not suffered. He described them as having been found in their chairs "as if they were still watching the telly". He explained that they would have been overcome by smoke long before the flames reached them. A verdict of accidental death had been given. Martina was in the clear: an orphan again, but due to inherit a sizeable sum this time.

Stella sat very quietly throughout and when the police officers left she escorted them to the door. Checking that Martina was out of earshot, she asked the older officer if an exact time of death had been recorded. He told her it was half past four according to the clock on the mantelpiece - precisely the time she and Martina were having tea together. For some reason Stella took great comfort in this, but could not understand why. She thanked the police and closed the door, poking her tongue out at the quivering curtains of number 7.

By the time she got back to the living room Martina was watching morning television. Stella thought better of tackling her head on about the accident. Shock was a funny thing. You could never tell how someone would react. She decided it was best left until later. There were a few things she did not understand. Why hadn't Martina told her that her parents lived in Brighton? She couldn't have been to see them. She was only gone for twenty or thirty minutes. Had she wanted to see them? Did that account for her strange behaviour and the ruckus at the hotel? Why had she lied about her childhood, saying she had spent it in a children's home? Questions, questions, one day she would ask for the answers, but now was not the time to intrude. Not while Martina was in mourning.

*

When the next morning came it was quite obvious that Martina was either in a state of total denial or completely unaffected by the death of her parents. Stella wondered if more had gone on in Martina's childhood than she was prepared to let on, but this was still not the time to pursue it.

Martina cheered when she calculated just how much she would inherit. She would be rich. Stella tried to encourage her to let her grief out, but Martina had none. The guilt and anger Stella had felt when first her mother then her father had died had twisted in her memory until she convinced herself she had been far more upset than she had. She concluded that Martina was made of sterner stuff - or that there was a reason for her celebratory approach to their passing. Stella began to imagine scenes of abuse, neglect and rejection. This had to be the explanation for such cold, detached behaviour. It was unnatural. Had she had access to Dr Devant's files Stella might not have been so surprised. She might also have proceeded with rather more caution. But the artful Martina had succeeded in worming her way into Stella's heart, where the ice had already began to melt.

CHAPTER 20

Martina's mood was black. She just could not come to terms with being adopted. Her immediate reaction to the Smith's deception was one of having been betrayed. It was no mean feat to accept the fact that her parents were not what they had claimed to be. At first anonymity swamped her. She drowned in her loss of identity so much so that Stella feared for her sanity: already a fragile, insubstantial thing. Martina, never a creature of consistency, would display ugly, unpredictable mood swings; one minute soaring as high as a kite only to plummet at the drop of a feather. This emotional see-sawing continued for weeks, expressed by manic extravagance followed by sullen listlessness or violence. The moods cast their own shadows over number 9.

The silver lining was the gradual dawning that from nowhere Martina had been given a totally blank canvas on which to paint her self portrait. This realisation led her to adopt a more even keel, less manic than normal. Now that her origins were hers to define, her imagination took her off on wonderful flights of fancy. One minute she was the daughter of a Duke, a King even, certainly a man of noble birth. The next, her father was a mass murderer, a notorious jewel thief or a famous playboy. She determined that her mother must certainly have been beautiful, not a fat, painted seaside landlady: possibly a gypsy, maybe French, or Russian; an actress, or the madam of a successful brothel? She kept all these wild fantasies to herself, wary that they betrayed a childishness that embarrassed her. There was only one fantasy that she really wanted to believe, one she most wanted to be true. She really wanted Stella to be her birth mother.

It made sense. The timing was spot on.

*

In the beginning Martina had played her hand close to her chest. Only occasionally had she broached the subject of dreams in the early days, always taking care not to overstep her mark for fear of alerting Stella's suspicions. Everything had gone to plan. Martina had dropped a tiny crumb and each time Stella had swallowed it: as though it was a choice morsel, salivating with anticipation, before gobbling the next, until she was almost begging for another. Stella had never tasted the poison: Martina had been too clever. At first the only dream they had discussed was the pink one, repeated over and over until Stella felt she had dreamed it herself, but then of course she had. The story was interspersed with episodes from Martina's childhood. Tales of neglect and abuse, beatings and torture poured from her, leaving Stella guilt ridden and maternally protective towards the poor unfortunate creature. Now Martina had, rather dangerously, begun to believe her own lies.

She no longer recognised that she was lying

when she concocted, then described, all her carefully rehearsed dreams to Stella. She became convinced that she had actually dreamed each and every detail. She believed they came from her subconscious mind: a store of knowledge, a mine of distant treasured memories. She had actually been wrapped in pink. Her tiny hands really had clung to that teddy as though her little life had depended on it. Sometimes, when Stella was out, she would sneak into Stella's room and take him out of his box holding him against her nose, breathing in her birth and rekindling memories that had never known the warmth of life.

*

Stella had seen the date of Martina's adoption. She could put two and two together. It was not beyond the realms of possibility that they were mother and daughter. Yet the chances of such a coincidence were extremely unlikely. The whole circumstance of their meeting, the unlikelihood of these two disparate women forming an alliance, was so bizarre it rendered nothing inconceivable.

This was not the first time the idea had occurred to Stella. She had nursed it many times, always dismissing it as fanciful. Stella was too practical to harbour such hopes, yet she had to admit at her most vulnerable, when life stretched ahead as a long lonely road, that she longed to claim Martina as her own. But, to sail into unchartered waters was folly. This was the stuff of day-dreams and she refused to embark on such a reckless journey, especially as the destination was so unclear.

But, Stella reasoned, there was no harm in pretending. No harm in sweet make-believe that the tiny wet thing that had dropped out of her almost twenty-five years ago was Martina. Why not? They were both desperately lonely. What possible harm would it do to assume the role of loving mother and loving daughter? She had more than enough to give, materially speaking. It might be good to share it with someone.

*

There was of course one way to prove without a shadow of a doubt whether or not they were related, and that was to undergo a DNA test. But this was far too clinical, too absolute. It could take them into dangerous territory emotionally. Stella did not want proof (or disproof.) Not like that. Some intangible force, possibly the deeply concealed, closely guarded, romantic side of her nature, made her want to leave the truth understood rather than proven. Besides, if they were mother and daughter the bond would make its self apparent, the unique bond between mother and daughter being too strong to fake.

During this period of uncertainty, Stella thought back to her relationship with her own mother. Where had their bond been? Had she ever analysed what she had really thought about her mother? Was she brave enough to go further and consider what she actually felt about her? Thinking about her childhood brought a sense of sorrow in the form of compassion for the woman who had given birth to her. Her mother had clothed, fed and protected her. She could never once recall her mother shouting at her or hurting her. Her memories centred on the constant preparation of food, the incessant line of washing draped around the fire: tasks performed willingly by the woman who skivvied in other people's houses, or served thankless customers at a checkout till, packing luxuries in their bags that her own family could not afford.

Never once had she heard her mother moan about her father's thoughtlessness, his total lack of domesticity. His ashtray was always emptied and cleaned, the sweetie wrappers always gathered up and thrown away. The house he came home to was always fresh and tidy, with its cushions plumped and his carpet slippers waiting by the fireplace (even in the heat of the summer when there was no fire). This magnolia woman supported them through the years; silently, boringly and loyally. She kept them and the house. This was Stella's inheritance; a well kept house, and the colour magnolia - invisible, serviceable and unmemorable.

She had no recollection of her mother's touch. The more she tried to recall it the more she recognised its absence. Only the odd dabbing, none too gently, of Dettol soaked cotton wool on grazed knees or a rough rub down with a coarse towel at bath time. Her mother had not been a tactile person, and had raised her daughter to be similarly remote. Stella wondered if it was too late to learn how to hold a hand, to blow a thank-you kiss, to give or receive a cuddle before bedtime? Such gestures had been taken as read, not acted out, when she was a child. The words 'love' or 'thanks' were not in their vocabulary. It would be nice to have one last chance to say them, and seal them with a kiss. Was Martina her chance to let her own mother know she had been loved?

Her mind went to her avenue. She longed for the trees to accept her back. She wanted to hear the leaves sing instead of taunting and teasing. More than anything she needed to discover what lay in store for her at the end of the path. Surely she had been patient long enough? Surely the time had come for the occupants of the house to answer the door and share their secrets with her? The more she thought such thoughts the more she knew that this dream was what connected her to Martina.

This line of thinking convinced Stella that the only person who could unlock the door to number 1 was Martina. She had to find a way to take her with her down the long avenue, not as a shadowy wraith, but as a creature of substance. Together they could discover the truth.

*

The GP gave Stella the all-clear later that week. For Martina this meant no more medical busybodies checking on Stella's health. Martina had made sure that Anita was unlikely to reappear having foiled all her attempts at contacting Stella. It had been far easier to remove her from the scene than she had anticipated – the two women had obviously had an argument about something and all Martina had done was build on the ill feeling. She laughed as she recalled her last rebuff – Anita standing all concerned on the doorstep. She could see her face now, hurt and rejected, as she heard, in no uncertain terms, that Stella never wanted to see her again. With a simple slam of the door, the woman was history.

For Stella the news that she was fit for work meant no more medication and no more sick-pay. 'The chickens' were calling. No doubt 'The Tie' would be delighted. He would say all the right things; how nice it was to welcome her back to the fold etcetera, but she did not relish the thought of returning – not now that she felt so needed at home.

*

The path stretched on as far as the eye could see. Stella blinked away the snow that stuck to her lashes. The weightless flakes fell silently, obeying an instinct of memory which let them drift slowly, submissively to the ground where they lay hardly aware of their fall. Stella watched as they settled one on another until a deep layer of light spread around her. The world was changing; all reality was being erased and replaced by this hushed, colourless domain.

The avenue was asleep beneath a blinding white blanket. The snow balanced on the railings and spikes of the gate, raising them higher, softening the stern black iron into a fairy-tale structure of snowflakes and icicles. It seemed a crime to break the spell by moving them, but Stella could no longer resist the magic world the gates offered. They understood her apprehension. As she made to touch them they swung open in a gentle arc, causing no disturbance to the snow, which silently buried the ivy, the stone, and the iron.

She walked through and the gates closed as silently as they had opened. The whole world held its breath - noiseless beneath a duvet which smothered the slightest of sounds. Even the trees were quiet, their uniformity exaggerated by their homogenous coat. Thick rooted trunks sunk further into the spotless ground weighted down by the pristine layer of snow. Stella looked up into the branches that swayed as they competed to reach the sky. There was no sky; only a solid firmament of whiteness which promised to deliver more and more. Stella wanted to count the individual flakes, but before she could touch them they became one. The weight of the world descended on her. How could something so light be so grotesquely heavy?

The path was barely visible, and the trees bent low under the yolk of their burden. The ditch was filled. The blackbird's grave had not been spared; interred in snow it merged into the landscape - unmarked and un-mourned. Stella willed herself to rise up, so that her feet were an inch or so above the uniform ground: she could not be the first to defile such perfection. The heavy air was filled with falling flakes. There was no wind, the snow relying on the soft pull of gravity to tell it where to fall. Everything had surrendered to the weight of the mass.

Through the dense cloud Stella glimpsed a hint of gold - pale and liquid; not enough to melt the snow, just enough to offer a glimmer of hope. A sound, too faint for the natural world, imperceptible in the reality of life, descended on the silence. Stella turned and looked back. A line of footprints stretched back to the gates. Someone was following her, but there was no sign of anyone.

The house rose ahead of her, silent, swaddled in its own weight of white. The steps were clear. Someone had scraped the snow and ice away. The blue and brown tiles shone out brighter than she had ever seen them. As she climbed the steps she counted them. There were ten. She took care to avoid the crack on the fourth. They were so familiar: she knew she had seen them before. The oak-leafed door knocker gleamed, someone had polished it. It reflected a face, distorted, buried in the convex metal. It smiled at her but Stella did not smile back. She took the leaf in her right hand, her left hand behind her back, her fingers tightly crossed. She raised the knocker and prepared to strike. One... Two...

*

The third knock was Martina - just before she appeared in the doorway. She was as white as the snow in Stella's dream and tears streamed down her naked face. Without her makeup she looked like a child, a distraught child, in desperate need of love and comfort. Stella looked at her clock. It was four forty-four and as she stared at it the time clicked on to four forty-five. She held out her arms and the little girl fell into them, clinging so tightly that Stella felt the breath being sucked from her. Placing a gentle kiss on Martina's forehead, she prised herself away; touch was still too intimate. She wished she could display the same skills now as she did in her dreams and float above such physical displays of emotional ineptitude. She patted the girl's hand as a gesture of sympathy and suggested they make a cup of tea.

Martina continued to cling like a limpet, while she sobbed out her tale.

"I was standing by some gates, like I don't know where they were... never seen them before... but the strange thing was they were buried beneath a ton of snow. Then I think like some idiot must have opened them or something because all of a sudden I'm in a bloody avalanche. It wouldn't stop. There was tons of the stuff and it wasn't white, fluffy stuff, there was nothing Christmassy about it. It knocked the air out of my chest. Like my lungs began to explode and the snow turned scarlet with blood. Honestly, I saw my lungs like laid out in front of me - only for a second - then the snow covered them too. I couldn't breathe. There was no way I could get out. It was so heavy, falling faster and faster, like getting thicker and thicker by the second. I decided to dig down.

"Then it all got a bit crazy. There was this blackbird. Well I don't know if it was a blackbird as such, but it was a bird and it was black. Anyway, it was all wriggling with maggots. It stunk to high heaven and it crawled onto my hand, put its little head on my palm and went to sleep. I threw it down and it like crawled away into a hole. I almost felt sorry for it... almost. God it stank!"

Martina ran from the room, holding her hand over her mouth. From the bathroom came the sound of retching. Stella slid out of bed and wrapped herself in 'Old Faithful'. Her feet found her slippers and slid into them. She was only half awake and unable to think straight, but it occurred to her blurry mind that either their dreams had transmitted from one mind to another, or there was a definite world where dreams existed; a parallel universe that they had visited almost simultaneously. Calling out in the direction of the bathroom, Stella announced she was going to make the tea, and padded downstairs. Her head was reeling. By the time Martina joined her, she was sat on the sofa with her head in her hands.

"Sorry. I didn't mean to wake you up. I think I was still dreaming when I knocked on your door. I mean, when have I ever bothered to knock?"

Stella pushed the Winnie-the-Pooh mug towards the girl, who stood shivering in her thin T-shirt and pants. Stella's immediate reaction was to offer her 'Old Faithful', but Martina smelled of vomit and a fresh stain covered the front of her top. Stella staggered upstairs and, deciding not to risk her own duvet, snatched the double one from her parent's room. They sat for ages huddled under it, sipping their tea. It was disgustingly bitter and

Stella realised she had made it with two separate teabags, which was just not like her.

"Can I tell you the rest? I really need to get it off my chest."

"Alright, if you think it will help. I had a dream too. I think... never mind I'll tell you later." Some primeval fear caused the hairs on the back of Stella's neck to rise up, like a dog that senses danger. She went quiet and sipped her tea while Martina continued with her story.

"I felt sorry for the bird. It had the most appealing eyes - it winked at me. I never knew a bird could blink, let alone wink! Well this one could. Its eyelid moved sidewise – weird - and it could cry. Great big tears rolled down its little face and all the maggots like disappeared! So did the pong, thank God! It was quite sweet then. It began to speak. It told me it knew me; that it like knew exactly who I was and why I was there. I asked if it was dead and it said something really like odd. 'Aren't we all' How weird is that? Then it like flew back down into its hole and all the maggots crept back inside it. It was fucking... oops sorry... bloody gross." Martina stopped and took a glug of tea, wrinkling her nose in disgust. Removing a teabag with her fingers, she looked with astonishment at Stella.

"Sorry. I'm not properly awake yet." Stella's own tea tasted foul. She closed her eyes and sighed.

"You're angry, aren't you? Sorry. I shouldn't have woken you. I'll go back up and leave you in peace." Martina rose to go only to find Stella clinging on to her sleeve.

"No. Go on. Tell me about the house. Was that under snow too?"

"It was your avenue, wasn't it? Ha! Of course! I remember now. The tall trees and the long path. It was all there, but like covered in snow. I don't know how I got out. One minute I was buried alive, the next I was floating above the ground. That's dreams for you! But I don't need to tell you that! The path had been walked on or rather it was like being walked on as I floated over it. There were footprints appearing beneath me, not mine, but they followed me. When I looked back they came from the gate but there were none ahead of me. It was as if they were mine, but like I said I was like off the ground so I couldn't have made them. Anyway they were too big for me. Does that make any sense to you?"

"Yes." said Stella. "Did you get to the house? Did you knock on the door? Did anyone answer?" The questions tumbled out of her with such rapidity that the words made little or no sense to Martina.

"Steady on, mate. Like whose dream is this anyway? No. I didn't reach any house. No, I didn't knock on any door, and no, I didn't see anyone. Suddenly I was back at the gates, standing next to the dead bird's grave. There was a rose bush, flowering in the snow, yellow and pinkish just like the one by the front door – only much healthier looking. I think that poor thing is dying." Martina took another swig from her mug and pulled a face. "God, this is disgusting!" She got up and stretched her long thin body, arching back as she yawned loudly. She shook her head like a dog, scratched at her already tousled hair, then snatched the whole of the duvet and shuffled off to the kitchen.

Stella heard the kettle spring into life followed by Martina's voice forcing its way out through another loud yawn.

"Funny, but it doesn't seem so scary now I've told you about it. In fact it sounds rather pathetic. Can't think why I got so worked up. Silly cow! Do you want a decent cuppa? Did you say you had a dream too? What was yours about? You weren't like following me down that fucking avenue were you?"

Martina's laugh was loud and infectious, but Stella's mind was too preoccupied. She was trying to remember if she had knocked at the house. She had, but only twice – the third knock had been Martina hammering at her bedroom door. She knew she had never told Martina about the blackbird. She had never told anyone. Nor had she mentioned the grave. The rose bush was also new. Where had that come from? Declining the offer of yet more tea, Stella dragged herself back upstairs. She counted each of them and threw a backward glance at the frosted window. It was about time she checked those snowflakes.

*

Back in her own room Stella pulled out her bottom drawer. Lovingly her fingers ran over the blanket and squeezed the teddy as a baby might squeeze one's finger. It was time to find out what had really happened that night. Had she given birth or was it all the dreamed up fantasy of a sexually frustrated young girl, grown now to become a dried-up spinster? If her mother had been around she could have asked her for the answers. As it was she would have to look elsewhere. As she brushed her teeth and pulled back her hair, she had an idea which seemed to offer a solution.

First thing in the morning Stella made a phone call.

CHAPTER 21

Anita's absence had been a constant source of grief for Stella. Their parting had been awkward and Stella regretted having been so rude. She tried to find an excuse for her behaviour, citing her concern for Martina or the fact that she had been unwell, but she knew she was lying to herself. Her behaviour had been inexcusable. Fear of rejection had prevented her picking up the phone and apologising. Now the time felt right. She needed to discover the truth.

*

The front patch had been weeded and the rose bush had received some much needed attention in the form of a bag of John Innes, a hard prune and a jolly good feed. The brass figure 9 had received a rub over with Brasso, and the frosted glass was polished so that all five hundred and fifteen snow flakes sparkled like freshly fallen snow. The inside of the house had also undergone a thorough clean, and a vase full of yellow spray chrysanthemums sat in the centre of the dining table. Casting a critical, satisfied eye over the room, Stella crossed the hall, and stood behind the door waiting for her guest.

They shook hands tentatively. Then, realising the occasion called for more, Anita threw her arms round Stella and hugged her. It was a simple gesture, but enough to close the gap that had opened between them. What was even more remarkable was that the embrace felt totally natural to Stella; the damage of their last meeting was repairable. Stella ushered her friend through to the sitting room, grateful to have the past put behind them so readily.

Mistaken in her belief that she had made the first approach, Stella found Anita's opening remark a little odd.

"I'm so glad you agreed to see me at last. Are you alright? I've been really worried about you."

"Well, yes" Stella retorted, "Although you were right, I have been quite ill. I didn't think you wanted to see me as you didn't get in touch."

"I don't understand. Didn't you get my letters – all those postcards I sent? When I called round and Martina told me you didn't want to see me anymore I realised how much I had upset you. I wanted a chance to explain. I can only apologise if I hurt you in anyway."

"You spoke to Martina?" Stella's surprise was written all over her face.

"I phoned. I phoned several times... She didn't tell you, did she! I called round too, but she told me you wouldn't see me or speak to me. She said you never wanted to see me again."

"Martina said that?"

"Yes – I'm afraid she did. In the end I decided to take the hint as they say. I'm afraid I chickened out. Oh Stella, I was so relieved to get your call yesterday. Was it my 'get well' card that prompted you? Only, the last time we met you looked so dreadfully ill, I was scared something awful had happened to you. All the time I was away I had such a strong feeling that you needed me. If you hadn't called I probably would have popped round anyway – I can be very stubborn."

Stella stood staring at the kettle which seemed to be taking an age to boil. At no point had Martina mentioned Anita's calls. Had Anita's letters gone the same way as the hospital mail? Would Martina stoop that low? Even allowing for the fact that she had been ill, Stella knew she would have remembered seeing any postcards. One could be mislaid, but several... Forcing back her anger - her disappointment with Martina, Stella placed the sugar bowl on the tray, a smile on her face and carried the tea into the sitting room.

"You did get my little card didn't you? It had a picture of a Native American – a Lakota chief - I thought it was appropriate." Anita smiled back at Stella who was pouring the tea.

"Yes, I mean no, I..." Stella had more important issues to pursue. "Listen before we go any further, I didn't get a card. I knew nothing about any letters, or postcards, or your visit. I'm so sorry. I really thought you didn't want to see me because I had been so rude. I wanted to call you, I tried to, but I was scared you'd slam the phone down on me. I'm so very, very sorry..." Stella stopped as her voice began to break.

"I'm sorry too, but I'm here now."

The two women sat in silence drinking their tea while the spectre of Martina hovered in the air around them - the proverbial elephant in the room.

It was Anita who acknowledged her presence first.

"Please don't be cross with me, Stella, but can't you see just how naughty Martina is being?" She picked her words carefully, determined not to make the same mistake as last time. "It's probably because she is jealous. She's very young, although I think it goes deeper than that. I'm afraid to broach the subject again because of last time, but you really must be careful. I only want to help you. Please let me help. Don't push me away again."

Stella knew that Anita was right. Whichever way she approached the problem she found Martina. There was no way round her. Anita was here at her request. Stella had asked her here in the hope that she could use her psychic powers, or just her sound common sense, to look beyond the tangled mess of problems and find a way out. Stella swallowed hard. It would be asking too much of anyone to plunge into such treacherous waters without any means of navigation, something to warn of rapids and rocks. If this meant telling Anita the whole story, then that was what she must do. She had to find out the truth about 'The Girl without the Kalashnikov', however painful. Stella wiped her glasses, cleared her throat and began to speak.

"When I was sixteen I had a baby…"

*

Stella talked on into the night. They sat there in the dark, neither wanting to break the flow by turning the light on. She told Anita everything: the rape, the birth, the possible kidnapping, and finally her meeting with the strange young woman she called Martina. She left nothing out. All the mystery surrounding Martina's birth was laid bare. Her conflicting tales about the home and her adoption: Stella told it all as honestly and fully as she could. She described her dreams, her relationship with her dream friends, her confusion between dreams and reality. It all poured out. The dam had been breached. There was no stopping until the reservoir was drained. When she was done, she rose quietly, walked into the kitchen and poured herself a glass of cool refreshing water.

The light was on and Anita was sitting on the sofa smiling at her when she returned. Everything looked so natural.

"I know how hard that was Stella. I'm so proud of you. I know there are hundreds of questions you must want answered. I can – I will help. Your mother wants to help too, but she says this is not the time. You must discover the answers for yourself or they will mean nothing. She is holding out a rose for you, a peace rose... just like the ones by the front door. It's very late. We are both very tired. You need to rest and I must get home. Trust me. I will help you."

*

It was past midnight when Martina came back.

Their row was spontaneous and inevitable. Furious at being excluded Martina, who had obviously been drinking, began hurling abuse at

Stella who surprised herself by remaining totally calm throughout the tantrum. However, forearmed with Anita's warning, she rebuked Martina for being manipulative and controlling. She accused her of interfering in her personal, private life. She told her that she would not tolerate her mail and phone messages being tampered with and demanded to know where all the cards and letters from Anita had gone. The fight continued for at least an hour before the fury eased to a mere bickering which, in turn, dwindled to the odd snipe. Both women were shaken by the amount of venom they had generated between them. Fortunately the fight had cleared the air and Stella's head, leaving her hopeful that tonight she would dream. It would be just like old times.

*

The tiger was directly in front of her. Stella stood perfectly still, mesmerised by the light that shone from him. A million pinpricks of light swayed with each graceful move of his body: a galaxy of tiny stars whose fibre optic light only exaggerated the intense darkness of the hall. This was the first time Stella could remember the tiger visiting her house. It was a great honour and the tiger knew it. He turned, hardly able to fit the narrow space, his huge shape brushing each of the walls in turn. His tail remained tucked between his legs until he stood with his two front paws on the stairs. Now he lashed it freely, flicking Martina's coat aside as though it were a twig. Stella noted that he had carefully placed each paw on a left turning leaf. This impressed her as he had not taken any time to study the pattern or count the leaves.

"Have you a question for me? Stella." He did not turn to look at her as he spoke forcing Stella to move along the hall until she could look up at his head. He towered above her, hot breath pouring from flared nostrils, and his proud Roman profile tilted upwards to the landing.

"How many snowflakes are there on the window?" she asked.

"Five hundred and fifteen."

"How do you know that? It took me ages to count them."

"I am not you." With that he leapt into the air and vanished.

Stella ran up the stairs to find him. She wished she had asked a more useful question, but it was too late now. There was no sign of him; just the musty animal smell one associates with a circus, or a zoo. She climbed into her bed and turned off the light. The glow from a thousand tiny bulbs rained down on her. The tiger was floating high above her, far higher than her ceiling.

She watched his underbelly heave as he breathed in and out, rhythmically and heavily as if he was swimming. She counted the bubbles of air from his nostrils – five hundred and fifteen. The silver balls rose, floated off into space, popping loudly as each one burst, only to form a thousand and thirty more. Her body, grown as weightless as the bubbles, drifted up to join them as, united with the tiger, she travelled out to the night sky and far,

far beyond.

Directly beneath them stood number 9 - the front patch with the rose bush and wheelie bin still visible despite the great distance. She watched as the rose began climbing like a giant beanstalk, up and up, winding itself around her. The thorns ate into her flesh and her blood soaked into the yellow blushed petals, making them heavy; unable to cling to their branches, they dropped back down to the sad patch of earth from whence they had come. Martina stood there clad in her leather coat, her Kalashnikov slung over her shoulder. She was leaning against the front gate, under the toxic street lamp, covered in red petals; their colour leeching out in rivers of blood, down her body and into the culvert by the 94 bus stop.

The drain stank of sewage. The gates swayed as the engulfing water lapped around them, sloshing between the iron rails - beating itself into waves of anger as it fought for its freedom. Stella shook the railings, grasping them in her hands and using all her might to free them. They would not budge. The weight of the water held her fast, trapping her against the iron. She was alone, frightened, she didn't want to be washed away without ever knowing the answer.

Stella cursed herself for wasting the tiger's time with such a fatuous question. From far away came the faint sound of his laughter. It was then that she saw the fire. Two silhouetted figures, their screams drowned out by the roar of the flames, writhing in agony as the greedy fire licked their bones and shrivelled their skin before turning it to crispy

Peking duck. The skulls exploded simultaneously, two eggs cracking to release the boiling brains and free the souls. Stella watched them rise up into the heavens and heard angels singing, "Onward Christian Soldiers" in a shrill, discordant choir.

By the time she got back into the hall, she had dried out, but the stench of the drains, burnt flesh and dead chicken clung to her. Martina was still stained scarlet but smiling. Stella could still hear singing, although the angels had long gone. It was Martina's voice: her hymn full of profanities and expletives. Stella threw back her head and cursed out loud that she should be this bloody girl's mother.

*

Although the altercation had fizzled out, an altered atmosphere hung like a ghost in the house. It warned Martina to watch her back, to ingratiate herself, to try to win back the Brownie points she had squandered. She did not understand her fall from grace: diverting a few phone calls and a sprinkling of white lies hardly warranted such a reaction – at least not in her book. Stella felt totally justified. She had no doubts as to the seriousness of Martina's crimes. She continued to mull them over, trying to forgive, but not able to forget. Eventually Stella had reached a decision. The ethos of the house needed to change.

*

Sweet Dreams

When Stella picked a couple of her precious roses to replace the wilted chrysanthemums, and began obsessively to dust and polish an already clean house, Martina knew something was happening. Eventually Stella confessed that Anita was coming to tea. Lacking the nerve to actually banish Martina, Stella pleaded with her to make herself scarce. Meeting a stubborn refusal Stella tried bribery, offering the girl twenty pounds to go to the cinema. Martina pocketed the money but stayed put. Tired of trying Stella told Martina she could stay, but only if Anita had no objections, and only if she kept as quiet as a mouse.

*

Anita, true to form, arrived promptly. Stella ushered her into the sitting room, where tea had already been laid out. True to form Martina appeared and glowered from the doorway. Balanced on one leg, the other foot pressed against the door frame, her leather coat pulled tightly round her middle she looked exactly as she had when Stella first saw her - 'The Girl without the Kalashnikov'. She stayed put - like a spectre at the feast - casting her sinister shadow over the proceedings. Anita tried to draw her into the conversation. She failed. She tried to ignore her. She failed again. In the end she told her, in no uncertain terms, that she could not possibly tolerate such negative energy in the room. She must change her attitude or go. Martina let out a loud snort and trounced out. The foundations of the little house shook as the front door slammed - it was a miracle that all five hundred and fifteen flakes did not flutter to the ground. The curtains at number 7 twitched twice -once as the door crashed - and once again as, without Stella's knowledge, Martina crept back in.

Anita smiled. "Good. That young woman needs help. I know you are very fond of her but you need to look to your own health first, my dear. You're not strong enough to cope with all her issues. But I think you already know that... deep down. Anyway, my dear, how are you? You look much better: a lot calmer."

Stella told Anita she was indeed feeling a lot stronger, much improved. Stella went on to describe how she had taken Martina to task and felt more in command as a result. She began to pour the tea, anticipating a positive reply from her guest. This was such a normal conversation it amused Stella to be an active component in it. When she looked up Anita was crying.

"I'm sorry, Stella. It's not you, my dear. I've just had some terrible news. An old school friend of mine has died. Do you remember I told you about her when we watched the sunset in the park? It was all very sudden and tragic. It happened when I was in the West Country. It was in the papers, and on the television, but being away I missed it. Mike told me when I got home – not that he knew my friend, but he'd heard me talk about her. Anyway it was a house fire - down in Brighton. They both died – Rita and her husband – I'd never met him, but they died together. They ran a B&B. Rita must have been a great landlady. She was so generous. Anyway, the whole thing burned down. The news hasn't quite sunk in yet."

Tea was pouring all over the tray and splashing off onto the carpet. Anita hurried into the kitchen to grab a roll of kitchen paper. In her hurry, she failed to notice Martina pinned behind the door through which she had been listening attentively.

"Sorry, I wasn't watching what I was doing." Stella was stabbing at the spillage with copious sheets of paper. "It was your news... it took me by surprise. Do you know exactly how it happened?"

Anita disappeared back into the kitchen with the soggy mess of paper, once again failing to discover their eavesdropper. Calling over her shoulder while gently closing the pedal bin, she said,

"It was just a hideous accident, a chip pan of all things. I make oven chips – I thought everyone did nowadays. Chip fat is so dangerous. Poor Rita - what an awful way to die! I do hope she comes through to me - once she's settled. Sudden death can take a while to sink in, but I would like to know that she forgives me for failing her. Maybe I'll see her next time I watch the sun go down."

The fine hair on Stella's neck was rising. Her hand went up to stop it and she shuddered. Was this some hideous coincidence, or was this yet another path that in some macabre way led to Martina? Stella removed her glasses, wiped them on her hanky and replaced them, vainly hoping that this small gesture might restore some normality: might help her to see things more clearly.

Anita sat back down in the armchair and Martina eased herself from the kitchen to the hall, ready to dart upstairs if necessary. Hearing Anita's mention of her parents' deaths imbued her with a sense of importance. She wanted to burst in and declare her interest - claim her fifteen minutes of fame. Instead she skulked in her new hiding place, her ear pressed against the door.

"You'd have liked Rita. She was such fun when she was a girl - always on a diet – and always the first one to buy a cake or a bag of doughnuts - hopelessly generous – hopelessly optimistic. She always wanted a large family. I wonder if they had children. It didn't mention any in the paper. Do you remember when we were in the park – I told you about my friend and the sunset? That was her. I know I didn't mention it at the time, but the last time I was here I could not get her out of my mind. My guide must have been trying to tell me that she was in danger too, but I didn't listen to him. I failed to disassociate her danger from yours. Somehow I'd got the whole thing - you and Martina and Rita all muddled together. That happens sometimes. I suppose it proves I'm not very good at my job. I don't know. Anyway, I knew she was in danger and didn't help her. I feel so guilty. I really should have tried harder to get in touch with her. I hadn't seen her for years. We lost touch when we left school. That was - oh twenty, twenty-five years ago. But, you see, I didn't have her married name - so I'd probably never have managed to trace her."

Aware that she was dwelling on her own

problems, something she tried hard not to do, Anita stopped talking and smiled to show that her tears were over for now. She patted Stella's arm, then tactfully eased the subject round to Stella.

"This was your mother's chair, wasn't it? She's here now. I think she's often here with you. She's cross – no – not cross - frustrated. Tell me what you want?" The question was not aimed at Stella. Anita, who appeared to have withdrawn into herself, was addressing someone she alone could see. Stella wondered if she saw a world full of spirits floating around on clouds, all clamouring to be heard. The thought of her mother on a cloud made her chuckle. Quickly she clasped a hand over her mouth, not wishing to appear disrespectful. Anita hardly seemed to notice. She carried on speaking, pausing occasionally to listen, smiling at some unseen presence, frowning at times as if unsure what to say, before nodding and carrying on with the message.

"Right, your mother wants you to go back to work. Have you been thinking about this? Well, she thinks it would be the best thing for you. Stop worrying about 'the other thing', everything will be revealed in due course. She is talking about the baby. Soon, she says, soon you will know everything. You already know which path you must take. She says you will understand this. Follow your path. She keeps saying that. 'Follow your path and you will find the truth'. She says she only did what she thought was best, at the time. She never meant to hurt you. It was wrong, she sees that now. She wants you to forgive her. There is a young woman here, she looks very like you, she is handing you a rose."

Suddenly Anita sat up straight and shook her head as if to clear it, "She's gone," was all she said. Then she opened her eyes wide and lifted her eyebrows, as if expecting a comment.

None came. Stella was wondering if Anita could actually hear her mother. Or was it more of a telepathic exchange? As for that message - 'follow the path'- what path? Did she mean the avenue? If so why not say so? Stella wondered why spirits were so hooked on riddles. 'Why not call a spade a spade?' When she was alive her mother was the plainest speaking woman on the planet. Had death transformed her into some sort of enigmatic oracle? Meanwhile Anita was apparently still waiting for a reply.

"Hum, interesting," was all Stella could muster as she scuttled into the kitchen to see if an efficacious pot of tea might help. She pricked up her ears, when she thought she heard the front door closing, but when she looked the hall was empty. The curtains at number 7 were twitching, but Stella couldn't see them, or the leather clad figure striding off up the road.

CHAPTER 22

The friendship between Stella and Anita, now open and free, developed rapidly. They would meet up in M&S for an indulgent coffee, before spending a leisurely morning window shopping or sitting in the park watching the antics of the ducks. For the first time in her life Stella had found a true friend. She was happy. She went about humming with a noticeable spring in her step.

This altered state did not go down well with the other resident at number 9. Hardly a conversation started without Stella announcing, 'Anita said' or 'As I was saying to Anita...' Jealousy wrapped itself around Martina as insidiously and permanently as her coat; eating into her mind leaving holes where hatred and malice entered. Martina had thought to have seen the last of Anita. She saw the woman as an obstacle, an unwelcome complication, a threat, and as such she had to be dealt with - again.

Neither did Stella escape Martina's judicial ruling. In Martina's eyes it was Stella who had jeopardised their relationship. It was Stella who had allowed Anita in, welcomed her and encouraged her to worm her way between them. In Martina's eyes, betrayal was a capital offence. Stella had been caught. Now she too must be tried and convicted. Martina was ready to pronounce sentence.

Martina's mind was fast losing any tenuous grip

she may have had on reality. For her, life had been so much easier when Stella had been 'Just another mark'. What had started as a game had become a hope, and now was fast becoming fact. They were related – of that she had no doubt. Stella was Martina's mother, Martina was Stella's child. With this belief came a legitimate entitlement to Stella's estate. What she had once simply wanted was now her birth-right and no stupid psychic was going to snatch it from her. This charlatan, this Anita, was sucking up to her mother, stealing her affections from under her nose. It was also obvious to Martina that Anita was poisoning Stella against her. She had to be stopped. Permanently this time.

*

Martina resumed her act as the dutiful daughter. Every time Stella and Anita sat down to one of their cosy little chats Martina was there - making tea, plumping cushions, fetching and carrying without so much as a muttered grumble or a hint of a frown. Sweetness and light oozed from her. Where Anita had wormed Martina wormed back, ingratiating herself to the two older women. Meanwhile, beneath this façade her mind was filled with ways to remove Anita from the scene, to eliminate her. Why pussyfoot around using euphemisms? Why not just kill her and be done with it? After all, who else would a grieving parent turn to for comfort and solace, but their loving daughter? Next Saturday was Stella's forty-second birthday - what better, more appropriate chance would she have? She decided to throw a birthday party and invite Anita.

*

A week before her birthday Stella started back full time at the chicken factory. It was not a particularly auspicious occasion. Her coming and going was commented on by the girl whose eyes were too close, but mostly she slipped back unnoticed in her anonymous navy suit and shoes. 'The Tie' said he hoped she felt better then tactfully kept his distance. Stella did notice that his teeth looked extremely white. Her fingers and mind adjusted immediately to the keyboard and screen and her mouse, probably the only one to have really missed her, was soon clicking away as though the two of them had never been apart.

*

When Martina announced she was throwing a party, Stella's immediate reaction was one of horror. She had visions of rampaging drug addicts and unsavoury, unwashed characters littering the front garden with dog ends; offending her home and her ears with inappropriate behaviour and foul language. Once assured that it would be a very exclusive, even civilized do, Stella relaxed. Martina even persuaded her to pop into Marks to buy a new dress, and leave the catering and guest list in her capable hands.

*

There were just three at the party: the Birthday Girl, Anita and Martina. But the balloons, presents and a special cake – also from M&S – crowned with forty-two candles – made it more than just afternoon tea. There was a choice of wine or tea, chocolate biscuits and crisps and the three guests managed to create a party atmosphere, any previous hostility seemingly long forgotten.

Anita's gift, beautifully wrapped in dark-blue paper covered with flying angels, contained a long narrow scarf of burgundy chiffon, just like the ones she herself wore. Stella removed her blue square one and replaced it with the new present. The choice of colour was fortuitous, being the exact colour of the wine Martina accidentally spilled all over it. There was a long pause during which hostilities could easily have broken out, but Anita saved the day by refilling Martina's glass whilst declaring, 'accidents will happen. Let's not cry over spilled wine!'"

Unwilling to let Anita take all the glory, Martina offered her present to Stella.

"I hope you like it. Many Happy Returns, Mum."

That was the first time Anita heard Martina call Stella 'Mum'. She hoped that the girl did not see her flinch, covering herself by enthusiastically urging Stella to open the proffered parcel. Her curiosity as to what it might contain was, however, totally genuine.

It was a thin packet, covered in pink paper more

suitable for a christening than an adult birthday. Anita sensed something was wrong – she stared apprehensively at the gift, as did Stella. Impatiently Martina snatched it away and pulled off the wrapping. There they lay, exposed and vulnerable. Stella just stared, unable to speak, unable to move, barely able to breath. Anita helped her to a chair and brought her a glass of water. No one did anything for what seemed like an age. Until, slowly and deliberately Stella got up, placed her chair back under the table and walked on through the hall and up the stairs. She did not count the steps, nor did she avoid the right facing leaves.

Anita threw a glance at Martina whose face broke out in a grin which spread from ear to ear. Pushing past her Anita hurried after her friend.

She found Stella on the bed crouched in a fetal position, still clutching Martina's present. The tears streamed from her face as she rocked and cradled her treasure. By the time Anita had calmed her down and persuaded her to come back downstairs, Martina had opened some more wine and lit the candles on the cake. The crowded candles gave the room a claustrophobic feel, sucking out the oxygen and filling the air with an eerie unnatural light. Martina's grimace had relaxed into a charming smile, as she proposed a toast to the 'Birthday Girl'.

They got through the party somehow and, as Anita drove away, Martina tried not to stare at the dark patch on the tarmac, exactly where Anita's White Fiat had been parked. She slipped her hand into Stella's giving it a little squeeze and was pleased to feel a reciprocal, if faint, tightening of Stella's fingers around her own. Once they had washed up and settled down on the sofa, Martina took Stella's face in her hands.

"I didn't mean to like upset you. You do know that don't you?" Her voice was softer than usual and she looked Stella straight in the eyes as she spoke.

Stella returned the stare before looking away and wiped an imaginary crumb from her skirt. "They weren't yours to give. You had no right to take them."

"They do look beautiful though, don't they? And it will protect them; they're so fragile."

The present lay on the table, in front of the two women. The tiny hand and foot prints had been mounted on stiff board and set in a simple clip frame. The accompanying hand written card read, "To Mummy, with love, Martina".

Martina laid her head on Stella's shoulder. Feeling the muscle stiffen, she waited for it to relax before she spoke again.

"I do so want them to be mine. I love you so much."

Slowly, but deliberately Stella got up. "You had no right." She was about to leave for bed when Martina grabbed at her.

"I think I do," she said. "I had another dream. Two actually. Please Stella, listen to me. Then if you still feel the same I'll never mention it again. I promise."

Stella tried to listen with her ears, not her heart.

Some internal radar told her to keep a safety net of rationality between them, to offer her a level of protection she suspected she might need. But Stella was no match for Martina. Stella was heading for the rapids without a life-jacket. Martina smiled at Stella and began to describe her latest dreams.

*

"I was standing outside by the rose bush. I think it was night. Anyway, it was very dark. Like the only light was coming from the bush. The roses were lit up like fairy lights on a Christmas tree. It was so pretty. Anyway, there was this woman there. She looked more like me than you, but I got the feeling she was related to both of us. She picked a rose and gave it to me to give to you. That was all. I woke up then, but I could still smell the rose in my bedroom. That was it. Like short and sweet."

Stella said nothing.

"The next one was a like couple of nights ago. I woke up (in my dream) and there was this old Indian standing beside my bed; scared the living daylights out of me. He had all these beads and thing dangling from his chest. In the centre was a wheel made of bones and twigs. He took it off and put it round my neck. It was bloody heavy – can't think why! It was only made of twigs and stuff. I had to hang my head it weighed so much. He lifted it up and stared at me, like he knew me. I mean really knew me."

"His headdress was made of feathers: eagle feathers, don't ask me how I knew that – I just did

- now that must have really weighed like a mega ton. And his eyes... they were all squinty, like he had been looking at the sun for too long. He told me his name, but I can't remember it... something to do with buffalo? He wasn't violent or anything, but I was really scared. I mean he was an Indian - I nearly shit myself – sorry, but I don't like Indians... even at the cinema they terrify me. He kept talking to me, but I haven't a clue what he was saying. Oh, there was like one phrase, 'Little Stella' he kept on calling me 'Little Stella'. Weird or what? Then I like woke up and realised I had only dreamt him. He wasn't like real. Thank God."

*

Stella lay awake that night. The words the young prince had said to her all those years ago kept going round and round in her head. 'Do not trust him. Never trust him. No matter what he tells you, you must not trust him. He will try to fool you, but he would eat you given half the chance.' She was afraid to go to sleep. She did not want to dream; not tonight. The thought of walking down that avenue again, of meeting the tiger or her guide, filled her with dread. 'What could she say to them? Did they know what had happened today? Anita had told her they saw everything, knew everything. Maybe they could see the future. Were they laughing at her feebleness, her stupidity? Would Martina turn out to be just like the tiger?' Fear ate its way into her brain that night, but it was nothing compared to what was to follow the next morning.

Sweet Dreams

*

The news flash on the stand outside the paper shop read, 'Local woman hit by bus'. Stella walked inside and picked up a paper. There on the front page was a grainy photo of Anita. Apparently her car had failed to stop at the traffic lights on the corner of the high street and it had careered into the number 94 bus. She was dead. Stella felt the punch hit her chest as the air left her body in one loud scream. Her new feelings of love, friendship and trust emptied out onto the shop floor as she wrestled with the hideousness of the facts. That it had been her bus made it more unbearable, more personal. It must have happened immediately after Anita had left number 9. Just minutes before, she had been standing on the pavement next to Martina waving her off – to her death. Stella sighed, 'Poor Martina, this will hit her hard too'.

A wave of maternal concern replaced the nausea of shock. Stella had welcomed the signs of warmth developing between Anita and Martina. She gathered her composure, stepped over the pile of vomit, without apologising to the astounded shop keeper, and hurried home to break the news to the poor girl. Her control was fading. Her thoughts merged into an illogical, unmanageable jumble. 'Any other day but a Saturday I'd have been on that bus, coming home from Carlisle Road, making one of the twelve left turns before arriving at my stop. It was my bus, my party; it was my fault.

CHAPTER 23

Martina's feigned horror and sorrow were delivered with such skill that Stella felt truly sorry for the girl. In return Stella received a considerable amount of comfort back. No doubt she would have felt less predisposed to believe in this show of sympathy had she known that the Fiat's brake leads had been cut through with her own bread knife and that the dark stain on the road outside her house was tantamount to a blood stain. However it was in blissful ignorance that she began once more to lean on her surrogate daughter with an unhealthy need. This dependence increased over the coming weeks in direct proportion to her rapidly declining health.

Once again Stella's weight plummeted. Her cheeks hollowed in and the bones of her shoulders, hips and knees stuck out grotesquely. She was forced to leave work yet again and submitted herself to Martina, letting her play the dutiful daughter-cum-nurse lavishly doling out hot drinks and pills. Behind her nurse's mask of benevolence was a wall of malign hate: Stella had betrayed Martina and she was about to pay the price.

Martina's so-called dreams came fast and furious. She had long since lost touch with which were genuine and which invented. It no longer mattered. There was, however, still considerable method in her madness. Her mind was set to destroy Stella, to punish her for such bare-faced treachery.

Sweet Dreams

Each dream placed a greater emphasis on the mother daughter link; each one grew more and more fanciful, yet horribly credible. Stella's mind was greedily receptive to the creative deception she was fed along with each potentially lethal mouthful of drugged food. It took just three weeks to reduce Stella to a state of compliance. Martina recognised when the time had come. Stella's bones were ripe for the picking. She was as helpless as one of those poor chickens in Hell.

Propped up in her bed, the yellow street light cast its jaundiced eye over Stella' gaunt face. Her head pressed against the hollow-fibre of the pillow without sufficient weight to cause a dent. Martina held the cup to the dry, narrow lips. She showed no trace of her repulsion to their scaly, reptilian appearance. Her patient, her victim, tried in vain to swallow. Gulping and spluttering she pushed the drink away.

"God, what am I going to do with you? I've called that useless doctor again. He says like he can't make house calls. So I told him I thought you were dying and he like laughed. The silly sod told me to bring you along to the surgery. I said you're anaemia was back with a vengeance and threatened to call an ambulance. He told me not to be so dramatic! What a wanker! You'd have been proud of me – I like really told him what he could do with his effing surgery. Come on, try again. You must eat something. You're a bag of bones. It's chicken soup – please Mum, try to swallow some."

*

Martina had been calling Stella 'Mum' consistently - ever since the party. Whether Stella noticed or not she made no comment. Martina's wish to be a legitimate member of the Sankey family had ceased to be a matter of choice having been eaten away by jealousy and a profound sense of betrayal. But for practical, mercenary reasons it remained necessary to establish her right to inherit. She had, in fact, called the doctor, that much was not a lie, as she knew she would need to prove how sick Stella was; suffering once more from the same pernicious illness that had hospitalised her and put her life in danger not so long ago.

A willing victim, Stella no longer cared what she was eating or what was eating away at her. Without strength or will it no longer mattered to her. It was like living through one of her worst dreams, only less clear - incomprehensible. Unable to challenge its veracity, she allowed it to flow on to its inevitable end. At some point she would wake up and life would go on; more dreams would follow and eventually she would die. The thought of death no longer filled her with fear. 'Who had said, 'Death is easy?' Was it Martina? Anyway, whoever it was, they were right. If this was dying, whether in reality or in a dream, it was so perfectly easy.'

As she drifted in and out of consciousness phantoms called to her: her mother who chided her, and her father, who coughed in her face. Runs-With-The-Buffalo sang to her and danced around her bed, chanting his rhythmic, repetitive chant. The tiger breathed hot, sour breath on her and his huge rough tongue licked at her forehead as if familiarising itself with her flavour. Anita was the only one who spoke any words to her: her ghostly presence continually warning of imminent danger – prophecies that burned unheeded into Stella's brain, like the fever that consumed her skeletal body.

And always, cutting through this mist was Martina, coaxing, exhorting her to drink, to eat, to sign. 'What was she signing?' Her hand moved across the page guided by the young woman's firm grip: a grip which left marks on the transparent skin. These were not the tiny pink prints of baby sized fingers, but large blue-black impressions bearing evil intent that moved the pen over the Last Will and Testament of Stella Sankey. Exhausted by the effort, Stella let the pen slip from her hand and fell into a deep sleep.

*

Martina pulled her leather coat tightly around her and strode off down the path, pausing to rattle on the window of number 7, then on to the bus stop on the opposite corner of Maple Street. The 94 carried her all the way to the bus depot before she got off. The world was her oyster, but she opted for the unknown wilds of Surrey, on a Green Line bus. A magical mystery tour was just what the doctor ordered: a dose of fresh country air. It was an adventure in honour of her dear, soon to be departed friend. She paid for her ticket and climbed on board her chariot.

*

The driver dropped her off by a triangle of grass with a phone box and a dog-pooh bin. He told her that the last bus back left this exact spot at five thirteen pm. She flirted with him, making sure he would recognise her again. The time – the exact time – featured in their conversation. She might require an alibi. This was a time to attend to detail not lower her guard. The bus pulled away and she waved goodbye before marching across the green to the little general store-cum-post-office. Stuffing a paid-for packet of crisps and a nicked can of Coke in her voluminous pocket she swept out of the shop, pausing to throw two fingers up at the astonished woman behind the counter. Guided purely by instinct now, she turned left, then left again before heading off into the country.

Unused to exercise, Martina took a short break in a convenient lay-by and ate her crisps. Greedily she tipped the remaining crumbs into her hand and snuffled them up. She wiped her greasy hand against her coat leaving a shiny smear, then blew into the empty bag and burst it before tossing it into the hedgerow and continuing her adventure. After cutting through a little copse, she found a footpath. She climbed the stile and strode off along the path. As she marched along she counted her steps. Two hundred and five steps later the path swung to the right. She followed it counting once again from number one. Twenty paces more and she reached a point where the path forked. She took the path to the right. Another forty steps and she stopped. On her left were two large gateposts that supported a pair of heavy iron gates. Pressing her face against the bars she could see a tree lined avenue stretching out before her.

*

The gates were ajar. There was nothing to say they protected private property, or that trespassers should keep out. Not that Martina would have paid any attention - besides the gates were open. She glanced at her watch, annoyed to see it was almost time to start heading back if she was going to catch the last bus. With a shrug she turned around.

"WAIT!"

Martina turned, but all she could see were the tall trees which lined the broad avenue. They ceased calling her, but continued whispering to one another in an incessant rustling chatter. Goose pimples crawled on her arms. She had never been here before and yet she knew this place. 'The trees, the avenue, the gates; this is Stella's avenue. This is the dream that has haunted poor, stupid, soon-to-be-dead Stella. Why is it me standing here - not Stella? Something is wrong. Something is very wrong'. Martina laughed a nervous, false laugh, before pinching herself as hard as she could, in the hope that this was just a dream.

Her arm hurt. She could see the red welt rising up where her fingers had bitten into the flesh.

Their presence convinced her that she was wide awake. Nervous but curious, Martina slid through the gates and began to stride along the avenue towards the house. The gravel scrunched beneath her feet - smaller stones than the beach at Brighton, but they made the same sound as they crushed under her Doc Martin's. She counted twelve trees on either side of the avenue, tall pointed trees with thick trunks, bearing long branches covered in thousands of tiny leaves that wriggled about, making a loud whispering noise as the wind stirred them.

It was a very pleasant, uneventful little journey. It only took fifty paces before she reached the front porch of a large, plain, double-fronted Victorian house. She counted ten steps up to the imposing door and avoided the crack on the fourth. Martina wondered why it needed a number. It was the only house for miles around. Beneath the large brass figure 1 hung an equally impressive door knocker shaped like the leaf of an acorn tree. The yellow metal gleamed in the low October sun. As Martina took hold of the knocker she heard the trees behind her sigh a great sigh of relief.

Martina knocked three times.

*

"You are late!"

The door was opened by a woman, although the gloom of the hallway made it impossible for Martina to see her clearly. She spoke quietly, with the impatience of a person who had been kept waiting far too long.

"We always start at exactly a quarter to five. You've got one minute – you'd better hurry."

The darkness of the interior was exaggerated by the former brilliance of the late sun. Martina stepped over the threshold and the door closed behind her, blocking the last vestige of light.

"In there." The unseen woman moved across the hall towards an open door through which could be seen the faint light of a single candle.

"Mind the rug!" The woman threw the warning at Martina who just managed to avoid the tiger skin spread-eagled on the polished wooden floor. In the meagre light she could make out four figures sitting around a table. They appeared to be drinking tea, although her eyes had still not adjusted to the altered light. She felt their eyes turn on her as she entered and the candle began to dance as one of the other women spoke.

"Sit down, Stella. We've been waiting for you…"

*

Martina did not wait for her to finish. She made for the door, forgetting the tiger. To break her fall she reached out and her hand struck the great beast's head, dislodging one of the yellow incisor teeth which held the jaw open. The tooth clattered to the wooden floorboards and the mouth snapped shut. Martina wrenched her hand loose and scrambled on all fours until she reached the door. Taking the ten steps in one frantic leap, she ran back up the avenue as fast as her quaking legs would carry her. Only when safely out through the gates did she stop to take breath.

Her lungs were on fire and her blood boiled as it pumped in her ears. A steady stream of blood poured from the jagged tear on her hand and her whole arm ached. It was as if the tiger's bite had poisoned her. Her legs were shaking too violently to support her, let alone carry her away from this awful place. Eventually she quietened down. Her breathing returned to normal and the tremors stopped. Instinct told her to walk away quickly, without a backward glance. Some other force compelled her to turn around and look back.

*

The gates were firmly closed. Time had fused them together: time rust and age. Loyalty held the twisted rails together; their hinges hidden beneath ivy and woodbine that wound its way around the pillars, obscuring them with years of shared neglect. These decades of growth pushed and pressed against the iron distorting and bending it. There was no way these gates could open. Access was impossible, barred by such dense jungle. There was no sign of trees; no vestige of any avenue, just a pair of rusty old gates abandoned to the ravages of time and nature.

CHAPTER 24

The tiger was waiting when Stella stepped off the train. The station teemed with women in bright coloured saris, all heading for the seafront, waving their bus passes and jostling for position. Stella smiled at her friend, but he merely inclined his magnificent head, signalling her to follow him away from the crush of the crowd.

At the end of the platform stood twin doors, identical other than for the large hand-written notices pinned on them. One was marked 'Life' and the other 'Death'. The tiger stood back waiting for Stella to take her pick.

"If I tell you which door to pick will you obey me?" He asked the question in a very matter-of-fact way which caught Stella off guard.

"Do I have to?" she asked.

"No. It is of no consequence. I already know which door you have chosen."

"You don't, I haven't made my mind up yet."

"You had decided long before I asked you to choose. Now, turn away."

This was not an order; there was no hint of coercion, no compulsion. Nor was it a suggestion. It was a solution. It was as he said - as though she had already decided. She turned away and he spoke again.

"Remember, Stella, before you trust another you must learn to trust yourself. Do not just go with your heart. That is the easiest way to the soul.

Through the heart the greatest damage can be wrought. Nor should you trust the route dictated by your head alone. Take care. Do not lose your heart or your head, until you are sure you can live without them. Now, turn back."

The doors stood in different places, much closer together, both were wide open and the notices had gone.

Stella walked calmly and confidently through the first of the doors. It was so easy.

*

Stella Sankey died in her sleep at 4.44 am on Thursday 20th October 2011

Her Last Will and Testament was held in trust by her solicitors. She had left her entire estate to STF (Save the Tiger Fund).

*

Marian Smith, aka Martina, is at present being held in a hospital for the criminally insane where she is awaiting trial for the murders of Mr Douglas Smith, Mrs Rita Norma Smith, Mrs Anita Turner and Miss Stella Sankey.

*

The whole of Maple Street was demolished in February 2012 to make way for a new Tesco Super Store. The developers unearthed the skeletal remains of a newborn baby girl in the front garden of number 9. The police are not pursuing any inquiries.

Sweet Dreams

Jennifer Button